THE HARMONY OF

YELLOW

c.coles

Published 2026 by C.Coles
Tasmania, Australia

A catalogue record for this work is available from the National Library of Australia

ISBN 978 0 987 5960 4 8

Cover design and book design: C.Coles © 2026

I acknowledge Palawa/Tasmanian Aboriginal people as the original owners of Lutruwita/Tasmania. Place names in palawa kani have been included in this book and I would like to express my thanks to the Tasmanian Aboriginal Centre.

For the author's acknowledgement of palawa kani names in this work, see Tasmanian Glossary on page 273.

For the author's acknowledgement of sources, see Historical Sources, see page 275.

For the author's notes, see page 276.

For the author's acknowledgement of poems for this work, in order of appearance, see page 282.

For the author's acknowledgements, see page 291.

The Harmony of Yellow is a work of fiction. The characters are entirely fictitious. All other resemblance to persons living or deceased is coincidental. However, the geographical setting of this work is real, as are the referenced historical sources.

This book is dedicated to those
who embrace curiosity

I remember your name

in that moment
in the meeting of eyes
I remember your name

in the halting of time
held deeply
in the dignity of your gaze

I can see
you remember me

Chapter One

The sisters turned heads in every aisle. Never mind that their Dutch braids fell like flaxen ropes past vested waists, nor even their pastel patchwork skirts; it was their billowy sleeves that completed a look reminiscent of milkmaids from another time.

Nearing the registers, the smaller of the two, Indigo Bliss Dreary, strode toward the closest conveyor belt, seemingly oblivious of the stares of onlookers. Meadow Dreary trailed behind her sister, aware that questioning stares followed her every move. Indigo Bliss began to unload supplies of chocolate, toilet paper and dog food.

Meadow watched as the young cashier, with fawn-like eyes and a latte tint in her hair, glanced at Indigo Bliss from under thick false lashes. She understood from experience that getting close to her sister would often leave people feeling oddly awestruck. With her violet eyes and good looks, at thirty her sister was still something of a unicorn.

'I've started a fashion blog,' the cashier said to Indigo Bliss. 'You're just like that model famous for wearing purple contacts. Where'd you get yours?'

'I don't wear contacts,' Indigo Bliss raised one eyebrow.

Her sister might seem born for a fashionable life, but preferred wearing farm clothes whenever possible. Meadow, five years younger, had always fancied the idea of buying clothes from a shop, something not home-made.

As the cashier turned to give her a quick once-over, she knew it would soon be established she was a taller-more-faded version of the other. Meadow adjusted her gingham belt.

'Weirdo,' murmured someone behind her, followed by a giggle. 'Freak,' added another voice. She would not turn around. Meadow ignored them, wishing she could blend in better.

'Wow you sure have a lot of these.' The cashier smiled brightly at Meadow, packing the last tins of dog food into bags. 'Going to make someone happy.'

The cashier's words were friendly, like a buttercup held under a chin.

'They are quite tasty,' Indigo Bliss said, deadpan, focusing on the detractors with a heavy lidded look.

The cashier stopped smiling, horror dawning on her face. 'I didn't mean...' she stammered.

Meadow, used to her sister's rather biting wit, shrugged apologetically at the cashier as the supplies were placed into matching black shopping trolleys. Indigo Bliss wheeled her trolley outside. She followed.

The air was brisk, and her cheeks stung with a refreshing cold sensation. It was the season when apples and pears ripened in the sun, and the air smelled sweet. Apart from their monthly shopping day, her life had been nocturnal of late. Meadow found herself longing for the sun, like a pale, leggy seedling searching for light.

The Dreary sisters made their way along the main street toward Huonville, a town encircled by lush farmland, orchards, and situated on the banks of a river.

Her sister crossed the road before reaching the petrol station. It was an unspoken rule to avoid that section of pavement. She shuddered at the smell of petrol fumes. The memory lingered of her grandmother and sister being assaulted by a red-haired woman in a black dress spouting toxic words, 'I'll ruin you...destroy you'. The woman's long black gloves and slender stockinged legs had reminded Meadow of a venomous redback spider.

'It was her fault Gran went away,' Meadow moved closer to her sister.

'And that blasted lyrebird,' Indigo Bliss said.

It was true that the lyrebird had unwittingly initiated their grandmother's exile. Sometimes Meadow wished she'd never shown it kindness, wished these impersonators had never been introduced to Lutruwita. Gran would say that even pudgy-cheeked sparrows were shipped to Tasmania.

Indigo Bliss gestured in the direction of the library, then clicked her tongue, giving her that look, the one that preceded, 'talking about it won't help'.

She followed in silence, aware her sister didn't let pain on the inside show on the outside very often.

It wasn't long before Meadow entered the library and started her monthly haul. First, she searched for books on colours. Next a book from the suggestion table, where she was careful to choose something suited to her reading palate. She didn't know why her taste ran to bitter and sour stories, or why tales of sadness and sorrow soothed her, but they reminded her of ink blooming in water.

Lastly, she took time unearthing several collections of poetry books. Indigo Bliss enjoyed salty spicy books and was fond of travel magazines. Her sister glanced at the poetry anthology Meadow was holding. 'More grim reading?'

Indigo Bliss was right, there was no better description for the cover of the book. But she knew that within the dust jacket depicting a sinister forest, the poems were familiar companions.

Next, the bus stop, and being mid-afternoon not many passengers were waiting. The few that were had their heads down while swiping their phones. Meadow had a good view of the carpark and watched with curiosity as a middle-aged woman drove into a car space, then climbed out leaving the car running. Striding to the back of the vehicle, the woman spent some time ensuring she'd parked perfectly. The way her large eyes focused so intently on the lines reminded her of a barn owl.

Meadow hadn't been inside anyone else's home, but had read up on the home décor magazines in the library. The women on those pages seemed notably stylish and their homes impossibly tidy. The woman would have a perfectly kept home, and put the kitchen to bed every night, just as Indigo Bliss did, with not one plate out of place. She wondered if the parking was all a show, perhaps the woman's home was as cluttered as her bedroom. As usual, once the sisters boarded, they sat close to the front so as to hold onto their trolleys. Destination: the small township of Grove, before beginning the lengthy walk to Mountain River, a locality nestled under the bosom of the Sleeping Beauty mountain range.

Meadow glanced through the window at Beauty's profile, with her hair splayed out in forest-green mountainous waves. Gran had once said Sleeping Beauty looked like she was ready to be awakened from her slumber by true love's kiss. Indigo Bliss had reminded Gran about the alarming twist in an earlier version of the story. That had impressed Gran, who disliked watered down versions of fairy tales.

The sisters had been taught to never dismiss legends and myths, that fantastical stories were the memory bank of their species. That time and again the dark undertones of motherless waifs and enchanted forests were cautionary tales. That imagination often evoked empathy.

She stared out at the sea of apple trees, mostly picked, an occasional mature apple still hanging like a red ornament on a Christmas tree. She nudged at the memory of Gran, five foot tall with salt and ginger hair down to her waist, managing a bull with finesse, and cradling a lamb that wasn't thriving. Gran was always so proud the Drearys lived on the Apple Isle. That their Huon Valley was an artistic hub. Meadow could hardly recollect a time without her grandmother, and prodded a little further to Gran's departure. Her mind clapped shut. Getting upset would attract unwanted attention on the bus.

She tried to think on something else, settling on how her two pups were managing without her. Hopefully they hadn't chewed her sister's rocking chair like last time. As they neared Grove, the bus driver advised he would lower the access ramp to help them haul their heavily laden trolleys off the bus.

The sisters fell into a companionable silence as they walked past acres of green pastures, orchards, and farms with various livestock. Some paddocks were dotted with cattle and others with sheep. They stopped at a fence confining a herd of white miniature Galloway cattle, many adorned with black muzzles and panda ears.

Meadow observed a young calf steering toward his mother, butting her udder hard and starting to drink, his tail wagging. The cow took on a dreamy faraway look.

'Look how confident he is now,' Indigo Bliss said, as the urgency of his feeding waned and the calf began to dance around his mother's legs. 'Cheeky little mite.'

'Nice when they're not in survival mode anymore.' Meadow remembered those vulnerable first feeds with their own calves, how the licked-off newborn would wobble precariously.

Up ahead, the row of poplar trees bordering the front of

their cottage resembled golden pickets. The trees were snowing leaves over the steeply pitched roof like a gilded cloak.

Their cottage was built with still-strong sandstone bricks front and back, wooden planks along the sides. The two sash windows and centred front door had always looked like a face to her, with two eyes and a thistle-purple mouth.

Gran thought their cottage resembled a gingerbread house, and that the old, twisted vines of wisteria and overgrown climbing roses were quaint and whimsical. Meadow heard local children had named it 'the witch's cottage' because of the pointed witch-hat roof, and Gran's penchant for healing with herbs. Meadow kept this from Gran, already indignant about the historic othering and treatment of wise women and healers.

The sisters turned at the sound of a gravelly voice.

'Been to town girls?' Bert from their neighbouring farm hobbled toward his gate.

Meadow nodded. Indigo Bliss shook Bert's hand.

Wearing his standard uniform of a tan trench coat while sporting a colourful vest and red scarf, Bert always reminded Meadow of Mr Badger. In recent years, Bert had been the only one their grandmother thought they should converse with.

Indigo Bliss brought up the newly built house next door. 'I'm not looking forward to having new neighbours,' she jerked her head toward the other side of their cottage.

'Sure went up quick didn't it,' Bert frowned. 'I think it's called a McMansion. It's two lots Mrs Hill subdivided, isn't it?'

'Yes.' Indigo Bliss frowned too. 'Why did she have to sell off her land? Gran would never sell ours.'

'That she wouldn't,' Bert said. 'You girls look so much

like your Gran. Dress just like her and all.'

An uncomfortable silence ensued. The sisters were forbidden to say what had happened to Gran, and Bert was too polite to ask.

'Come and get milk and eggs soon,' Indigo Bliss said.

He waved them off. Bert was a good neighbour. Though he was nearly ninety, he generously organised extra hay needed for their livestock, and bags of chicken food. Bert's goal was to 'expire' on his farm and he would see neither doctor nor dentist. He often told tales of mates coming around to pull out a tooth when the pain became unbearable.

She couldn't imagine being Bert's age and going through such a thing. Mind you, the Drearys were no better, and had never set foot in a medical centre. Gran believed their garden created the best medicine.

Past the poplars, two enduring old trees dwarfed the front of the cottage, one pear, one cherry, both over thirty years old. Neon-green moss covered their branches like lacy coral. She glanced at the knobbly knitted jumpers buttoned around their trunks. After Bert heard that in the township of Geeveston there were trees wearing knitted jumpers, he had told Indigo Bliss, her sister had knitted a surprise birthday present for Meadow: a rose-red jumper for her cherry tree and a hazelwood-yellow for her sister's pear tree. The trunks were substantial, so it had been a real labour of love.

Throughout the year their leaves resembled tangled manes of hair, with seasonal changes of colour.

Indigo Bliss began to tear at stray, woody lavender stalks poking out from their front split-rail fence. Her sister looked to the right of their property to where a brand-new double storey house stood empty. 'No character at all.'

Meadow wasn't sure about the new house yet. It was square with grey bricks and a roof of silver. All she knew was the building of it had led to their nocturnal existence.

Observing the twenty acres of pasture to the left of their cottage, which flowed to another twenty over the river, Meadow offered, 'At least we've still got our land.'

'We just got rid of all the builders, and now we'll have neighbours to deal with,' Indigo Bliss said, her fingers tapping on their front gate. Her sister pushed it open, rousing the small bell attached to it.

Meadow crunched over poplar leaves, then heard scuffling at the front door. Whispering, 'Move back pups,' she manoeuvred past a pair of damp inquisitive noses and nuzzling jaws, and entered the only home she'd ever known. She followed Timba and Tawny's joyful procession into the hallway, glad to be back home too, with its high ceilings, old dark timber floorboards and decorative fireplaces.

The sisters changed out of their town clothes into grey corduroy pants, woollen cardigans and beanies. As Meadow put the shopping away, Timba jumped excitedly, trying to gently nip at her hands and legs. His honey-gold fur was soft, but his teeth were sharp. Tawny, smaller than her brother, licked her hand. A few months old, their eyes gleamed as their bodies wriggled. 'Did you miss me?'

'Calm and assertive, remember,' Indigo Bliss carried a bundle of kindling toward the loungeroom.

Meadow drew the pups into the hallway and smothered them with kisses. 'Where's Spencer?'

Spencer, who had dutifully waited in the loungeroom for Indigo Bliss, barked once when Meadow said his name.

'He has spoken.' Indigo Bliss brushed ash from her hands as she entered the hallway.

Spencer, an old shih tzu, had only been with them for

a few weeks but wanted to be near her sister as much as possible. Those who thought of her sister as an ice queen were mistaken; Indigo Bliss saved her heart for her dogs.

The kettle sang as Meadow entered the kitchen. The pups shifted under her as blobs of cream plunked into her tea cup, their tongues lolling hopefully for one spilt drop.

'Cream in your tea?' Indigo Bliss blew on her rose-petal tea.

Heavy cream went well with everything in Meadow's opinion.

'Do you want something to eat before bed?'

'I'm still getting used to eating breakfast at midnight,' Meadow said.

Her sister nodded in agreement. 'That blasted lyrebird.'

Chapter Two

Rinsing her cup, Meadow observed the sunset filtering pink beams through the kitchen curtain. In the blush glow, the thick plaits of rosy garlic hooked on either side of the window looked schoolgirlish. 'Well I'm off then.'

'I'm going to read for a bit,' Indigo Bliss sang back from the loungeroom. 'Ni-ght.'

Meadow led the pups to the bathroom. The room consisted of a clawfoot tub, mirror, and an old wooden washstand proudly displaying a white enamel bowl and matching pitcher. She teased her hair loose, then cleaned her teeth with home-made remineralising toothpaste. Their grandmother had a thing about fluoride and the pineal gland.

The pups waited at the door, still nervous of the tub after a muddy night outside. Timba bounced in the doorframe; he was the curious and adventurous type. In contrast, Tawny was an old wise soul, gentle and laid back.

She steered them into her bedroom. Her sanctuary. With sunflower and canary-coloured pillows tossed on her unmade bed and trinkets covering her bedside tables, she was like a bower bird collecting all manner of objects in yellow. When she was a girl, Gran had spent much time trying to make her room look charming, finding textured rugs and circular side tables.

But her favourite embellishment was an enormous Huon-pine wardrobe she'd cherished since a child. Gran had cut a hole in the back, placing a door to the outside. Gran said it was old plywood at the back, and it wouldn't hurt to have a secret way out if ever needed.

Meadow didn't know why she became overly attached to things. Her sister had tried to free her room from clutter, moving many of her belongings to the outside shed. But she hadn't felt free, and had missed them so much they all had to be moved back.

She received no visitors, so saw no reason to keep up appearances. She had often wondered if Gran had put so much effort into her room because she hadn't been permitted friends. Rules were rules and the sisters had learned at home. According to their grandmother, Meadow had been an especially companionable and curious child, unlike Indigo Bliss, who'd been a lone wolf. Gran's voice had suggested concern at her nature but expressed relief that Indigo Bliss was a loner.

The sisters had been encouraged to read widely about the world at large and Gran's eyes would shine when teaching them history. Always with the unspoken proviso that the Drearys couldn't travel so encounters with such realms would only ever be within the pages of books.

Meadow called the pups to her window and stared out at her cherry tree, at the wind trying to tear off its remaining garnet leaves. She climbed into her single bed, still in her clothes. Timba and Tawny jumped up, as was their habit.

She patted each pup on the head as they snuggled along the outside of each knee, looking up at her with such interest and trust it reminded her of little children. She remembered the expression on her sister's face last year, after they'd found a baby doll. A doll that could cry. It was in a box of tablecloths and knick knacks Bert had given them from the thrift store. Meadow heard the cry one morning, piercing and repetitive. She'd discovered Indigo Bliss rocking the doll in the kitchen, with a look of such longing or loss, she couldn't figure out which it was. It was the same look Indigo Bliss wore when reading her travel magazines. She'd backed away from the sight of her sister, so laid bare.

The pups closed their eyes. This was followed by little snores. Though it wasn't dark, she was warm and relaxed, and like the pups before her, became drowsy.

It felt like minutes had passed when she awoke to the chime from their old grandfather clock and the noise of rustling in the kitchen.

'I'll have lots of cream,' Meadow called out, lighting her candle and pulling on her overcoat. She stuffed a beanie into her pocket before padding toward the aromatic smell of freshly made bread. The pups followed, eager to have their nightly run outside. Spencer wagged his tail at her; he was getting used to their evening escapades.

The kitchen was their grandmother's pride and joy, with its duck egg blue walls and white trimmings. The story went that their great-grandmother hadn't enjoyed domestic duties, especially in the kitchen. Back then the cottage had been affectionately referred to as the 'house with one fork'. After inheriting the cottage, Gran had painted and hung numerous blue-and-white porcelain plates, leaving not a hand-space free on the wall. In the corner her grandmother's favourite fern-green canisters stood in pride of place. Grandfather Dreary had purchased them, after Gran had said they were the same colour as his eyes.

It was an old house with old things.

'You must've been awake for a while to make bread,' Meadow said as her sister began to cut thick crusted bread into slices.

'I kept wondering…well you know how I am when I can't switch off,' Indigo Bliss handed Meadow a plate with two slices, smeared with generous amounts of butter.

She knew why her sister couldn't sleep.

Not one to dwell on problems during the day, Indigo Bliss couldn't seem to stop her musings in bed.

It reminded Meadow of a poem she'd read about insomnia rising up to haunt and taunt an unsuspecting woman. The woman, musing on bittersweet memories, had tossed and turned on a fevered pillow.

Chapter Three

The sisters lit their lanterns and, with pets in tow, took their steaming mugs of tea and followed the rough stepping stones along their back garden. Past the vegie patch, past the small orchard, past their Jersey cow in the milking shed, past the coop where numerous chickens were roosting, toward the river.

It wasn't long before Meadow could hear the river and feel the mossy ground under her boots. She lifted her lantern toward the river's edge, to see a scattering of purple bladderworts, or as Gran called them, fairy aprons.

The scent from their chimney smoke was sweet and the stars were visible on this moonless night but the cold penetrated her bones. She withdrew the knitted blue beanie from her coat pocket, making sure to keep its oversized pom-pom out of Timba's view. He had a love-hate relationship with pom-poms.

The river was lined with willows, their weeping branches grazing the ground gently as if bending to the will of the river. Nearby stood two stone seats, nestled between several small stone crosses, the old darlings' graves. Gran had started the old darlings mission years before, after hearing about people needing to re-home their furry companions. This had assisted those moving to aged care facilities, and many a senior salt and pepper dog had lived its life out with Gran. Bert had contacts, and would organise delivering the bereft dog. When their grandmother became too busy with other projects, Indigo Bliss had taken on the benevolent role.

At first, her sister wouldn't fuss too much over the old

dog, and would sit in her favourite rocking chair near the fire. Indigo Bliss would pretend to be involved in knitting, while offering the occasional charitable word. It wouldn't take long for the old dog to shuffle away from the fireplace and sit at her sister's feet. At which point Indigo Bliss would subtly fuss and absentmindedly pat.

The sisters shared an affection for animals, and while Meadow tended toward doting, Indigo Bliss was the practical one. Like Gran, her sister could assist birthing a calf entering the world backwards, had raised orphaned lambs and would even remove mice from traps. Indigo Bliss was always left to despatch spare roosters for the pot, especially when it became clear Meadow had not been able to summon the necessary skills.

'We can't keep them all,' Indigo Bliss would state.

It helped knowing her sister and Gran despatched them quickly enough; a gentle cuddle, a lulling of the bird, before the ultimate end. Without Indigo Bliss, she would live on bread topped with butter from Gertie, along with eggs and what she grew.

Indigo Bliss kept Grandfather Dreary's old polaroid camera safe, observing the unspoken rule that the instant photos were for previous dog owners only. Her sister would take a photo of each grey-haired dog doing what it loved best, snuffling fallen apples, outstretched by the fire or chewing on a favourite toy. The photo would be sent to the pining owner if that was what they wished. Most times, a letter penned by the owner would arrive soon after, shakily expressing a grateful kind of poignant relief.

With the approaching arrival of new neighbours, an old dog like Spencer would also form a cover of sorts for any unexplained yapping from the pups. Gran had forbidden the pups to get registered or microchipped; that was final. Gran was suspicious of government bodies and had been convinced the builders and new neighbours would report the Drearys to 'them' for not complying with various building regulations at the cottage.

It hadn't helped when Meadow had observed a shadowy figure staring from the second storey window next door. The woman appeared to be wearing a veil, but upon closer inspection, was standing close to sheer curtains, depicting a greyish silhouette. Meadow hadn't been able to make out the woman's features but sensed an intensity that was disconcerting.

After that her grandmother banned them from going outside during the day, convinced the veiled woman was an inspector. Only midnight to dawn, while keeping a low profile. The sisters had tried to plead their case, that they could quietly take turns in the sun, but to no avail. Gran had told them the Drearys were not made from everyday material. No one went against Gran's wishes without living to regret it, so they'd dutifully complied, with the exception of their monthly shopping day. Not long after Meadow saw the veiled woman, Gran was gone.

While the sisters sat in the discreet and sacred place, Meadow watched the pups at play. Their exaggerated, bouncy movements under the lantern light inevitably ended up with play-growling at each other and Spencer. Timba was high energy and loved to pounce; Tawny preferred to cleverly dodge her brother with agility. The pups called to each other in their puppy language with a bark or growl. Spencer's expression was one of patience; he had acclimated well and had no territorial persuasions.

'Right, time to start,' Indigo Bliss drained her cup and shone her lantern into the willow trees. 'I'll check the Herefords in the top paddock first.'

The pups ran to Meadow and bumped into her legs. 'Come on Spencer.' The old boy followed her through

Gertie's holding yard to the milking shed. Gertie was as gentle as she was beautiful, for with her cream coat and dark eyes she made a handsome cow. The Jersey was in calf so Meadow would milk her for another few weeks, then she'd need to be dried off. She would miss Gertie's gifts of milk, cream, and subsequent cheese and butter. It would be tallow on their fried bread again before long. She rubbed beeswax udder balm onto Gertie's teats, and the pleasant aroma of sweetness and lavender oil flooded the air. Timba, Tawny and Spencer sat so nicely she gave them an occasional squirt of warm milk into waiting mouths.

When it came to collecting eggs it was a different story, there was to be no sampling of the merchandise. She tried to be firm when removing eggs from the often overflowing nesting boxes. Cleaning up broken eggs was not easy in the semi-darkness. The chooks hardly stirred a feather at night, nodding on the roost quietly, as if in a trance.

After giving a customary glance toward the second storey next door, Meadow made her way toward the cottage to drop off the eggs and milk before picking some vegetables. She was met by the figure of Indigo Bliss standing like a marble statue at the back door, a finger to her lips and a beanie in hand. Her pale hair was loose and wild as if a fright had snapped her hairclip from its place.

Her sister was rarely alarmed. 'Listen, can you hear that?'

Chapter Four

Meadow heard it. A thumping at the front door. They didn't have visitors. Now someone was at their front door in the middle of the night. She found it hard to breathe in enough air.

'Who is it?' Meadow mimed a knocking motion. This went against their way of life: Don't draw attention to yourselves; never let anyone into the cottage. The sisters eyes locked in a desperate silent exchange of dread. They turned off their lanterns and placed them on the kitchen table. Meadow picked up her unlit candle and matches before following Indigo Bliss into the hallway.

She saw the outline of a man, visible through the wisteria petals in the stained glass window. He was tall and appeared to be wearing a hoodie.

Meadow's legs shook so much she knelt, pulling the pups and Spencer closer to her. For some reason the pups didn't make a sound, but they moved their oval ears, listening, their hearts beating fast under her grip. Spencer watched Indigo Bliss closely as if trying to ascertain her sister's next move.

'Did you see where he came from?' Meadow whispered.

'No…gate bell rang and the gravel crunched, realised someone was out there.' Indigo Bliss sounded breathless.

Long ago, Gran had organised gravel to be laid all around the cottage so as to hear anyone approaching. Roses had also been planted under the windows so no one could peer in without scratching themselves. The defensive hawthorn bushes, their thorns like three inch nails, were planted along the vertical board fence either side of their yard. Gran always said it was her beautiful and natural alarm system.

The man continued thumping. It became obvious that the only thing the sisters could do was to wait it out. He leaned close enough to leave condensation on the glass. Meadow's skin crawled. Her middle turned to ice. He moved away from the door, his footsteps loud on the gravel before the gate bell jangled unnervingly.

Indigo Bliss stormed toward the front door to see which direction he'd taken. Meadow followed, looking for headlights through the cascade of purple flowers in the glass. None in sight. Meadow lit her candle, and noticed how dilated her sister's pupils were. 'Who'd be out here in the middle of the night?'

Indigo Bliss shook her head.

'It can't have been Bert,' Meadow stared at the door.

Bert visited a couple of times a week to collect fresh eggs and milk in exchange for chicken seed, but he always stopped outside the front gate. Anyway, they'd just talked to him yesterday.

'That wasn't Bert,' Indigo Bliss said. 'Bert isn't tall and he wouldn't be caught dead wearing a hoodie.'

Nervous laughter ensued at the thought of Bert discarding his coat and vest for a hoodie. The sisters slid to the floor. Meadow's uncontrollable laughter sounded maniacal, even to her own ears, and persisted for some time. She laughed without pausing for breath, and placed both hands over her mouth to stop her cackling.

It was in some way a sweet form of release.

Finally she carried her candle toward the loungeroom, her hands shaking so much that subdued light wobbled within the room. 'I can't go out and harvest vegies now.'

For the next hour the sisters tried to distract themselves with reading. Every time Meadow peered over her book, ready to ask a question about the man, Indigo Bliss would hold up one hand: 'I can't talk about it anymore.'

Her sister might not like to dwell, but before tonight Meadow had always felt secure in the loungeroom with its old comfortable dusty-rose furniture, creamy floral wallpaper, and the echoing chime of the grandfather clock. Of course there was Grandfather's old chair which Gran said still had the shape of his large bones imprinted on it. No one ever sat in his chair because it seemed disrespectful somehow.

Eventually she needed to go outside, to the outhouse, and relit her lantern.

'I'll come with you.' Indigo Bliss was in patrol mode.

As her sister stood guard in front of the outhouse near the magnolia tree, Meadow could hear the pups whimpering at the back door. She hushed them as she washed her hands in the terracotta pot nearby.

Indigo Bliss held up a willow-wicker basket. 'You go back in. I'll harvest some vegies quick.'

'I should come with you.'

'It's nearly light. You need to stay with the pups and Spencer.'

'Should we tell Bert?' Meadow was sick to her stomach.

'He's an old man it'll only worry him. Remember the last incident.'

The incident had taken place recently involving Bert, a runaway bull and a gun. It had not ended well for the gun, powerfully crushed under heavy hooves.

There was no one else to call. The sisters had been raised to never seek out the police, to stay off-the-grid and off the radar as much as possible.

Gran had always taught them that.

When Indigo Bliss returned with a basket full of cabbages and round radishes, the sisters tried to busy themselves in the kitchen for the rest of the day. They fermented the crunchy flesh of the radishes and cabbages with ears attuned to the front door.

'Is it something to do with that woman? Or Gran?' Meadow said.

'Not at all.'

But she didn't think Indigo Bliss was so sure.

These days, their routine entailed being in bed by five in the afternoon and awake at midnight. They then worked until twilight. Gran had instructed them to come back inside before dawn, even if there was more work to be done.

Indigo Bliss was kind enough to sleep in Meadow's room that afternoon, on a fold out bed in the corner. This disrupted the pups and Spencer. The old dog kept standing on two legs and nosing Indigo Bliss with glee at the unexpected sleepover.

It might have annoyed her sister but it reassured Meadow.

She pulled her blanket up to her chin. In the quietness she heard the familiar sound of an apple thud to the ground. Normally she appreciated this sign of seasonal change.

Trepidation grew inside her.

She listened for the crunch of gravel.

Chapter Five

After the best part of the week passed and no night visitor reappeared, the sisters hoped it was a one-off occurrence. A case of mistaken identity.

They didn't leave milk and eggs near the gate as usual for Bert. Instead, Indigo Bliss decided to take the produce out to him. Meadow had suggested her sister ask Bert, in that easy way of hers, if he had any family visiting. Late that afternoon, after Bert's tractor came rattling along the road toward their front gate, he turned it off to talk to Indigo Bliss. Meadow could hear Bert saying his children still lived on the mainland, and one day they would come to their senses, and move back to Tassie.

It was his usual reply.

'The hooded man wasn't one of them,' Indigo Bliss said, frowning as she entered the front door. 'We never thought it could be one of Bert's boys anyway.'

Gran always said Bert's sons were good lads.

'Exactly, no way they would...'

There was tapping at the back door. Meadow knew that sound. She opened the back door to see her oldest hen, Clover, a fluffily-footed silkie chicken, peering up at her, head to one side. Clover's legs always reminded Meadow of white Victorian pantaloons. She gathered a container and sprinkled seed onto the mat outside.

Before their nocturnal existence, it had been Clover's pre-bedtime routine to be given extra food. Clover once reigned as queen of the pecking order in the silkie coop, but of late the old hen's eyes were going and her tottering gait had slowed. A bossy hen had taken Clover's place, and not being afraid to show her eminence, would peck if Clover ventured too close.

'We're out of whack, aren't we old girl, we never get to do this anymore,' Meadow said, waiting until the last seed was snatched up.

'Taking Clover to the coop,' Meadow called out to her sister, not bothering with a lantern as it was not quite dark. She was breaking the rules but decided to look in on Gertie in the milking shed too.

Someone was standing in the corner. Someone wearing dark clothes.

A gut wrenching scream rang through the milking shed.

Moments later Indigo Bliss found Meadow pointing toward an old grey blanket hooked on a rake in the corner.

'I thought it was the hooded man,' Meadow's voice sounded husky.

'I hung that last night to dry,' Indigo Bliss pulled down the blanket and folded it.

Meadow patted Gertie, 'Sorry, I must've given you a fright.'

Gertie stared calmly at Meadow, seemingly unruffled as she continued to chew slowly.

'Look, it's nearly dark, let's go for a walk up the road to clear our heads.'

'I couldn't sleep anyway,' Meadow agreed.

Indigo Bliss pursed her lips. 'That blasted man has thrown our routine out the window.'

'True.'

'We can check out the lay of the land.' Indigo Bliss was obviously in planning mode. 'Then we'll have a nap before midnight.'

Meadow studied her sister, who was keen to perform a reconnaissance of sorts. Perhaps there'd be an abandoned vehicle?

The sisters didn't take their lanterns as the neighbouring farms would likely see that as odd. It took some time for their eyes to adjust under the slim moon. Meadow observed that every rock, fence and house was the same as they'd always been. Farmsteads, sparsely scattered upon acres and acres of fertile grazing land.

According to Gran, they hadn't been born at the cottage as their mother was living in one of those alternative places, near a location named for swanlings. Her grandmother had once said it was a community filled with hippy skirts and craftspeople connecting with nature.

Meadow wondered if that's where Gran's love of flowing skirts stemmed from. She reflected on their mother, who from all accounts behaved out of character, leaving her daughters one night, never to return. While visiting Gran, Mother had sent Indigo Bliss to the play room to fetch a favourite toy. Upon returning, her sister had found Meadow alone, laying in her baby sling on the floor. Indigo Bliss said Gran had been pacing along the front path, her voice raw from hollering.

A shiver ran through her. Mother, a taboo subject. Her mother had left a trail of violet shadows behind her, like that poem Meadow had read about a beautiful swan.

All she'd gleaned was that Harmony Belle Dreary had Gran's fiery hair and Grandfather's fern-green eyes. Gran, who'd disliked her own first name, Eunice, and subsequently her married name Dreary, named her daughter something she'd thought enchanting.

They'd never heard from the beautiful, carefully named Harmony Belle again. She sometimes wondered if her mother had been forced to leave.

Meadow tried to picture her mother in her mind's eye, but she'd been such a small baby. There were no vague recollections, and not even a portrait or photo to garner familiarity. And what of their father? Gran knew nothing about that subject apparently. Meadow imagined him as a man with a tragic past, like someone from her poems. When asked, Indigo Bliss would say it was not worth thinking about. Had her mother met him in secret? Or perhaps her sister didn't want to remember him. Meadow's suspicion was the thought was too painful for her sister. Most likely there would always be these unknowns unless her mother returned.

Her greatest fear, the one she pushed away the most, was losing both her grandmother and her sister. That was inconceivable. They managed it all. Gran paid everything with cash. Meadow didn't even have a bank account. She recalled Gran complaining about the three bills the Drearys were forced to pay, but Meadow didn't even know what they were.

Each home they passed had a flickering, dim blue glow radiating from a window or two. 'Wonder what it's like to have a television?'

'Just fill your mind with trash,' Indigo Bliss said.

In Meadow's opinion, her sister sounded more like their grandmother every day. She wondered what things a television screened. 'Got to be something interesting. People watch them for hours.'

'Well it doesn't matter anyway because you need electricity to run one,' Indigo Bliss said with a final nod.

Meadow shrugged. At any rate, she wanted to watch one. On the way back to their cottage she sensed her sister stiffening. 'What?'

'Look, there's a removalist van pulling out from behind the new house.' Indigo Bliss led them swiftly toward their new neighbour.

The sisters noticed an unfamiliar man sitting in a rented one tonne truck, giving them a wave.

'What should we do?' Meadow's pace slowed.

'I'm going to see what's going on and if he's the hooded man,' Indigo Bliss reached out to pull Meadow along with her. 'And you're coming with me.'

She looked at her grass-stained grey corduroy pants, her blue cardigan and matching gloves. She remembered once, when walking by the front fence in her work clothes, someone had yelled out of a car window, 'Bag-lady'.

She wished she was wearing her favourite patchwork skirt.

But Indigo Bliss was striding ahead, taking Meadow with her. At the driver's window her sister peered up at the man, seeing if he wore a hoodie. He left the lights on and climbed down.

Meadow stood back. He was tall, but his wide smile did not suggest aggression. He seemed welcoming. The man was wearing denim jeans and a cream puffer jacket, and began stamping his feet as if to warm himself. His collar-length blonde hair angled in a fringe covering half his face.

'Well hello there,' he said. 'You must be my new neighbours.'

'How did you know that?' Indigo Bliss frowned.

'An old guy told me that some ladies lived next to me. I'm Doyle Lawrence.'

'Bert didn't say he'd met you when I spoke to him before,' Indigo Bliss said briskly.

'Met him tonight at the store.' Doyle flicked his head to one side, tossing his fringe.

Meadow wondered if the veiled woman was inside. Perhaps she was Doyle's wife.

'What are your names?' Doyle leaned forward. Meadow guessed he must be in his early forties. 'Hello, I'm Meadow.'

He nodded politely to her and reached out his hand
to shake hers. She hesitated, then peeled off one glove,
still pinned with particles of hay, and extended her hand
to Doyle. He shook her hand in a gentle enough fashion,
although she wasn't too sure because she'd never shaken
anyone's hand before.

Indigo Bliss grudgingly held out her gloved hand, spiky
with hay stalks. She would not take hers off for anyone.
'I'm Indigo Bliss.'

Doyle winced at her sisters grip.

'Good to meet you,' Doyle said. 'I've lived on farms all
my life so if you need help with fencing or repairs…'

'We keep to ourselves,' Indigo Bliss stated, placing her
hands on her hips.

Meadow watched with interest Doyle being pulled into
her sister's magnetism. She once overheard somebody say
Indigo Bliss was achingly beautiful, and her grandmother
had added, 'like getting slapped across the face'.

Doyle swallowed hard and proceeded to smile straight
at Indigo Bliss. 'Not a problem; I can respect that,' he said.
'But the offer is still there.'

They stood in awkward silence.

'I haven't seen anyone about at your house, or any lights
on,' Doyle flicked his head toward their cottage. 'I looked
for a car but it's hard to see past the trees and hedges.'

'We don't drive,' Indigo Bliss followed his gaze.

'Well if you ever need me to bring you anything back
from town give me a call,' he offered. 'I'll give you my
mobile number if you like.'

'We don't have mobiles.' Indigo Bliss rubbed the back
of her neck.

'What about a landline?' he said.

'No phone, no electricity, no car. Anything else you
want to know?'

Her sister was growing annoyed. Indigo Bliss was the sort that would mind her own business, but if Doyle didn't mind his own, her sister might snap. Meadow valued her privacy, but not with the same intensity as her grandmother and Indigo Bliss.

Was Doyle going to chuckle at their antiquated lifestyle?

Indigo Bliss was giving Doyle a direct and wary stare.

Doyle gave them both a wink. 'Well, I'll be back with the rest of my things soon, so might see you then.'

Meadow waved him off. 'That was fortunate. He was friendly enough.'

'Unfortunate more like it. I can tell he's going to be one of those annoying people.' Indigo Bliss shook her head. 'Always butting in where they're not wanted.'

Once inside the cottage, Spencer and the pups sniffed them curiously before following the sisters to sit close to the hearth. They wanted to discuss meeting Doyle before going to bed.

'Well,' Indigo Bliss patted Spencer on the head. 'Do you think it could have been him?'

'No way,' Meadow rubbed Tawny's ear while Timba chewed at her slipper. 'He was far too nice.'

'Hmmm.' Indigo Bliss's frown deepened.

'Surely we can give him the benefit of the doubt,' Meadow said. 'He was trying to be helpful.'

Indigo Bliss looked at her for a moment. 'You might feel empathy for people but I critique them remember.'

Meadow wondered what it would be like to reverse their roles.

'Glad you didn't say anything about that veiled woman.' Indigo Bliss's shoulders relaxed.

'Didn't want him to think I see ghosts,' Meadow said. 'Maybe I should have, in case she was an intruder.'

'Maybe. So what was he? A peacock?' Indigo Bliss leaned back in her rocking chair. 'What colour did the man speakest?'

'He was like a palomino,' Meadow said, 'with white socks and words of gold dust.'

Meadow viewed the world a little differently than most. It was as if she had a different pair of eyes that observed a person's words in shapes and colours. In addition she'd get the impression some of their features were animal-esque. Years earlier, when a small child, she'd called Gran an old Cape Barren goose with silver words. Gran's eyes had widened and she'd said, 'There you are child, so much like your mother's gift. She saw music in colour.'

Gran had smiled wistfully, but as was customary, did not speak of it again. Having lived with this legacy from her unknown, absent mother, Meadow had turned to Indigo Bliss to share her observations. While her grandmother thought it a gift, her sister believed Meadow's impressions were because she had a vivid mind's eye. Meadow agreed, her perceptions weren't reality so surely were creations of her vivid imagination.

'Gold dust.' Indigo Bliss added, 'Are my words still purplish?'

'Shades of plum, mulberry and lilac.' Meadow was always comfortable discussing her colourful impressions with Indigo Bliss. 'You're like an ivory unicorn with a silver horn and words of lavender.'

'Are you saying I have a horse face.'

'As if,' Meadow grinned.

'White horse socks is a new one,' Indigo Bliss tilted her head.

Meadow pictured Doyle stamping his white socked feet. This was new; she predominantly saw facial features in a unique way. She had recently begun studying paint swatches, with palettes of different shades and tints. It was helpful, when observing people, to put a name to the colour they spoke, and she could also use them as bookmarks.

She was curious about where Doyle had moved from.

'Doyle couldn't stop staring at you,' Meadow tried to sound casual.

'I can already tell he's going to be a show pony,' Indigo Bliss rolled her eyes. 'Did you see all that hair-flicking and stomping?'

Chapter Six

The next morning, Timba and Tawny lifted their heads in unison as someone entered the front gate. Indigo Bliss ushered Spencer into Meadow's room mouthing, 'It's Doyle,' before striding toward the front door.

'What on earth are you doing here?' Indigo Bliss blurted. There was an edge to her sister's voice and Meadow pulled aside her bedroom curtain. She saw Doyle, flicking his fringe and giving Indigo Bliss a lopsided grin. He looked dressy-casual in a cream blazer. She swore Doyle stamped his foot a couple of times before asking his next question.

'I wondered if you would be interested in showing me around the valley?'

'No.' Indigo Bliss stepped through the doorway, causing Doyle to take a step back.

Meadow had witnessed this dance many a time in town and it always ended the same way. Indigo Bliss would become ruder and more abrupt until eventually it would dawn on the man that her sister wasn't playing games. Soon Doyle would understand Indigo Bliss was not being flirtatious or coy.

'So…did you say no electricity at all?' He attempted small talk. 'What about a washing machine?'

'We have a wringer washer.'

'What about a fridge?'

'We've got a cold cellar,' Indigo Bliss said with menace to her voice.

'Well you can always use my freezer…' He swallowed deeply as his voice faltered.

Doyle mumbled something else to Indigo Bliss as she backed inside, closing the door in his face without even a goodbye. Meadow saw Doyle's smile shutter down and his shoulders slump as he turned toward the front gate. It was hard to watch.

She recalled the one time a man paid attention to her like that. The sisters were shopping in town and Indigo Bliss went to purchase something over the road. Meadow had waited under a tree quite like a green leafy parasol over a wooden bench seat. She was enjoying her favourite hobby, listening to the conversations around her. People tended to stop talking when Meadow came near so she'd developed good eavesdropping skills, even from a distance.

Occasionally, a friendly woman would walk past with a smile and shrug, seeming to wordlessly convey to Meadow 'we're all in this together aren't we'.

Then a man with stale alcohol on his breath approached her, his face as red as a cooked crab. He picked a nearby flower, a rose, and handed it to her with aplomb. Weaving slightly, the man confessed his love to her. His words were misshapen bubbles of rosé wine. Meadow, having never set eyes on the man before, froze in place. That was, until Indigo Bliss rushed across the street.

She hadn't thought Indigo Bliss could be even more beautiful, but fury made her sister look terrifically fierce. Her eyes flashed an intense violet, her cheeks flushed, her mane of pale hair flowed behind her. Indigo Bliss appeared at once angelic and yet like a formidable unicorn queen. The man, staring at the breathtaking woman before him, was struck at once by her alarming beauty, then with the danger he'd placed himself in. He fled, in what could only be described as an uneven crab dash.

After that, as she preserved cherries with her grandmother, Meadow asked Gran why she didn't have any desire to find love like that? Why didn't she envision herself getting married? Gran looked at her quietly, then reached out with her cherry-stained hands and grasped Meadow's own. Gran told her some people just didn't feel that way, but rather found love and meaning in other things. In Gran's case, she'd chosen to remain a lone goose after Grandfather died. It was a vivid memory because Gran wasn't one to show affection and her cherry-stained hands clasping Meadow's had left a lasting impression.

She closed her curtain, making her way to the front door with her furry entourage in tow. She noted the obvious annoyance on her sister's face.

'Can you believe that man.' Indigo Bliss leaned against the front door for a moment, as if daring Doyle to return. 'He's annoying enough to be our hooded man.'

'It's not the kind of thing one can ask,' Meadow said, but wondered if her sister eventually would.

'He wanted me to show him around the valley.' Indigo Bliss had a resolute glint in her eye. 'We mustn't let him weasel his way into our lives. Especially without Gran here.'

Meadow didn't know what to say.

'I've heard of his type before, he's that fake nice who'll keep steering every conversation back toward himself,' Indigo Bliss said. 'You watch. He's a humble bragger.'

Over the next fortnight, Doyle made numerous attempts to befriend the sisters. In fact, trying to engage them in conversation became his favourite pastime. One tactic was to drive past slowly in his white ute, trying to catch a glimpse.

Alternatively, he would innocently wave to the sisters from his letterbox.

That he did this at midnight annoyed her sister to no end,

as Indigo Bliss was often the one retrieving mail at that time. Her sister thought for sure Doyle would snoop in their letter box next.

This would be regrettable as letters were the one form of communication Gran viewed acceptable.

'Maybe he's a night owl?' Meadow suggested. 'Or lonely?'

Indigo Bliss scowled when Doyle waved to her, a torch in one hand, holding a letter in the other.

Indigo Bliss was convinced it was all pretence and that the envelope was blank. More than once Meadow had to stop her sister from marching over to Doyle's letterbox to catch him out.

'It might be exactly what he wants,' Meadow shrugged her shoulder.

'I think you're right,' Indigo Bliss nodded slowly. 'He's trying to provoke us into talking to him.'

'Or trying to be neighbourly,' Meadow offered. 'Maybe he doesn't realise he's coming across as…'

'Overbearing, presumptuous.' Indigo Bliss narrowed her eyes at Doyle's house.

According to her sister, Doyle was destined to pry further. Indigo Bliss decided to go shopping for supplies alone. Because she could only manage one trolley she would go twice a month. 'I think I'll go tomorrow,' Indigo Bliss said.

That evening Meadow held her lantern high as they led the pups and Spencer over the stepping stones toward the river. The sisters were both in clothes suited for a brisk night. She wore her blue cardigan with a grey vest, and Indigo Bliss had shrugged on her fleece-lined lilac jacket. Both wore scarves, beanies and gloves, and mugs of tea warmed their hands further.

'I heard the young cockerel trying to crow the other day.'

Meadow recalled the juvenile rooster's earlier attempts at crowing. This had resulted in a single braying sound, followed by an occasional two-tone crow.

'He'll be keeping up with Old Goldy in no time.' Indigo Bliss sipped on her tea.

Many times Meadow had enjoyed chook watching with Gran; they'd laughed so hard, watching their rooster wooing his hens. Gran called it 'tidbitting'. That special 'bok, bok, bok' would bring the hens tottering to him, whereby Old Goldy would stand aside in a gentlemanly fashion generously letting them have the prized worm or grub.

She missed those times with Gran, and felt an ache in her heart.

Several hours later, her sister stepped out from the front door and into the sunlight, pulling her black trolley behind her. 'I'll bring back some of those gloomy books you like,' Indigo Bliss said over her shoulder, striding toward the front gate.

Meadow didn't give her sister any suggestions. She was curious to see what Indigo Bliss might choose. 'Thanks. Can you get me more palette patches from the store?'

Indigo Bliss agreed.

'Right, what shall we do?' Meadow said to the pups inside. Being alone with her sister gone was such an unusual occurrence. She was torn between reading or baking and decided to do some of both.

She took them to the kitchen, and flipped through her favourite cook book. The new potato and leek quiche looked delicious. She had all the ingredients with the exception of the leeks.

Surely she could pop out to the garden and harvest a fresh handful? Gran wouldn't be pleased but it would taste so good. She collected the crushed eggshells drying on the shelf and placed them in her willow basket.

'Stay here.' Meadow also took her scissors and some ash for the garden. 'Won't be long.'

The pets lifted their heads for a moment but stayed close to the hearth, where each had a favourite spot for snoozing near the fire.

As her fingers grasped the wicker basket, she remembered Gran showing her how to mellow or take the spite out of the willow. Gran had guided her young, clumsy fingers on how to pick the willow, soak the rods, and use the bodkin.

Once outside, her head tilted toward the sun. Meadow attuned her ears to the magpies, their warbles and carols sounding like onyx pan flutes. She glanced over the hawthorn hedge, and not seeing Doyle, scattered the eggshells and sprinkled some ash before harvesting the leeks. The soil smelled fresh and slightly sweet. She peeled off boots and socks to stand with bare feet in the warm soil.

She wriggled her toes. Gran always said standing barefoot on the earth helped with your grounding energy, recharging your battery.

Meadow was drawn toward the blueberry bushes, to their red leaves, which seemed to declare winter was a whisper away. On the way back to the cottage she stopped at the chicken coop, collecting several still-warm eggs. A treat, as they were usually cold when she collected them at night.

Realising she'd forgotten her boots, she went to retrieve them. Old Clover came waddling toward her, excited at the prospect of an extra feed so early in the day. Sometimes, like now, Meadow wished more than ever to return to her old life, when she could spend her days in the sun, in the garden she loved. She placed her boots on the ground and scratched the back of the hen's neck, feathers silky to the touch. 'You poor girl. Getting bullied by Henrietta again?'

'So you are home.' A voice called from the other side of the six foot fence bordering the hawthorn bushes. This remark was followed by a blonde fringe, then half a pleasant face appeared. 'You didn't go with your sister?'

Meadow was used to having conversations with her animals, as well as herself, but found herself pinked at being observed while doing it. And there was the state of her dirt-covered-feet. She mustered a weak headshake.

'Lovely day for it.' His hazel eyes crinkled as he patted the top of a hawthorn bush.

'Yes, a good gardening day,' Meadow watched as Doyle stood taller, so as to dislodge a woody spindle-sharp thorn from a stem and inspect it.

'What kind of dog do you have?'

'He's an old shih tzu,' she said, wondering how Doyle could know about Spencer.

Meadow focused on her harvest basket, then at her bootless feet on the ground.

'He must be a night owl. I've heard him barking at night out here.' Doyle smiled at her again. 'He makes quite a racket for one dog. Not that I mind of course.'

Though Doyle's gilded words displayed no judgement she couldn't think how to answer his question. Gran would be uneasy about noise scrutiny. His words faded in bewilderment when she didn't reply and his smiling face dropped. She pivoted from Doyle. 'Better go…' She dared not turn around, dared not see Doyle's look of bemusement as she awkwardly made her escape.

'But I wanted you to meet my daughter,' he called out after her.

She turned back to Doyle. 'A daughter. I didn't know,' she swallowed.

'Come over and meet her,' Doyle tapped his hands on

the top of the hawthorn bush again.

If Indigo Bliss were here, her sister would slap Doyle's hand away from the spiky bush and say 'take your blasted hands off our hedge'.

When Meadow didn't answer Doyle said, 'She's been doing online studies and wants to meet people in real life apparently. Why don't I bring her here instead?'

Her sister would prefer she talk to Doyle's daughter over the fence. 'Sure.'

Doyle left for a couple of minutes, returning with a ladder. Someone climbed the rungs and a young woman peered over the hawthorn bushes. She had copper hair and green eyes and was wearing a pale pink puffer jacket.

'Meadow, I want you to meet my daughter, Charlotte.' Doyle's chin lifted slightly.

Charlotte's wavy hair shimmered as red and gold as an autumn leaf in the sun. Meadow was reminded of two girls on the bus discussing how to do mermaid hair. She wondered if Gran had looked like Charlotte as a teenager.

'Hello Charlotte,' Meadow said, 'welcome to the valley.'

Charlotte turned her head to one side, giving her the once-over. Meadow's mind raced as she scanned the young woman's face, which had not one distinguishable animal-esque feature, none at all.

Finally Charlotte gave a nod of acceptance. 'Thanks, but I like to go by Lottie.'

Meadow's head flung back in shock. Lottie's words were colourless. Without even a hint of tone, tint or shape. Nothing. She'd never encountered this before when meeting someone in person. Meadow realised she was staring.

'Lottie it is,' Meadow said.

'I've been telling Char…I mean Lottie about your storybook cottage.' Doyle stood next to his daughter, not needing the ladder to see Meadow. 'Haven't I?'

Gran would have loved that.

Lottie said, 'You must be into that slow food movement.'

She stared at Lottie blankly.

'You know, growing and harvesting your own garden and stuff.'

'That's how I've always lived,' Meadow said. 'How old are you Lottie?'

'Eighteen,' Lottie advised. 'Why don't you come over now?'

'I'd love to,' Meadow clutched her basket, 'but I forgot something on the stove. Maybe another time?'

'Well how about we make a time,' Doyle tapped the hedge again. 'Say for tea on the weekend?'

Meadow felt their stares as she tried to think of an excuse. Her sister would have thought of one in an instant. 'Sounds good. Do you want us to bring anything?'

'Anything you like,' Doyle said.

'Which night would be best?' Meadow said in a hurried tone.

'How about Saturday, say six o'clock, come around the back.' Doyle held up a pricked finger. 'These thorns are sharp.'

'Stop poking at them,' Lottie rolled her eyes before climbing down the ladder. 'See you then.'

Meadow returned to the cottage as hastily as her shaky legs would carry her. She tried not to think about what Indigo Bliss would say.

While baking the quiche and an apple crumble, she whipped Gertie's cream. Her sister was going to be angry about the invite, and of course would wonder why on earth she'd gone outside during the day. But the idea of visiting her neighbours wasn't altogether unpleasant, and she had a flutter of anticipation in her middle.

Indigo Bliss returned around lunchtime, flushed from her travels. Meadow met her at the door gushing about what happened.

'You went outside!'

'I wanted leeks,' Meadow said, going back to the kitchen to finish a side salad. 'He turned up at the fence and kept picking at the thorns.'

'He did what?'

While slicing baby beets and shelling some walnuts, she began to fill her sister in, further explaining about the ladder and Lottie.

'He has a daughter?' Indigo Bliss shook her head, placing Meadow's colour patches on the table. 'But her words had no colour?'

'None.' Meadow frowned.

'What animal was she?'

'She wasn't…anything,' Meadow filled their teacups with boiling water. 'It's like when I look at myself in the mirror. I only see me.'

'We've always wondered why that is, haven't we?' Indigo Bliss said. 'Imagine, Doyle has been hiding her from us all along.'

'Pot.' Meadow caught her sister's eye over the steam, and they both smiled.

'Was her mother there too?' Indigo Bliss said. 'Could his daughter have been the one spying on you from the window?'

'No, Lottie looks similar to Gran in height, and I got the impression it's just the two of them,' Meadow said, tossing the baby beets and walnuts with some greens and cheese. 'Lottie must take after her mother though because she sure doesn't look like Doyle.'

Indigo Bliss rolled her black trolley to the table and

retrieved a couple of library books. 'Didn't have room for many. I got the bleakest covers I could find.'

She stared at the two covers before her. One dust jacket displayed rotting branches like forked velvet antlers; the other showed an aerial view of mermaid-like seaweed floating on a stormy sea. They were amongst her favourites. 'How did you…?'

'I cheated,' Indigo Bliss smirked. 'I asked the librarian to help me out.'

'I nearly forgot,' Meadow blinked rapidly as they sat to eat the quiche and salad. 'We have to go over for dinner on Saturday night.'

'What!' Indigo Bliss barked, causing Spencer to start.

'We have to,' Meadow wanted to see inside someone else's home. 'I couldn't say no.'

Indigo Bliss pulled a face, then closed her eyes, breathing evenly for a moment. 'Gran was right about new neighbours complicating things.'

Her sister made a fuss before agreeing to go, but said yes in the end, realising it would be an opportunity to do some snooping herself. Indigo Bliss rubbed her hands together.

Meadow pictured Doyle's face after her sister had shut the front door on him.

His slumped shoulders.

She hoped Indigo Bliss would play nice this time.

Chapter Seven

After braiding her hair and donning her best town clothes, Meadow adjusted her gingham belt nervously. Indigo Bliss was resolute, they would get the visit over as fast as possible. At six o'clock, it was dark, and the air was brisk as the sisters walked to Doyle's house, but the potato bake was warm in her hands. Indigo Bliss strode ahead carrying a bottle of Gran's home-made apple cider and a plate of radish florets.

As instructed the sisters went to the back of the McMansion, as Bert had put it, which really was an enormous structure of grey brick, concrete and glass.

'We should be sleeping,' Indigo Bliss's tone was slightly accusatory.

'What if they have strange food?' Meadow changed the subject.

'Just nibble a bit and try your best.'

'Don't mention Lottie's mother unless they bring it up,' Meadow suggested, even though personally curious to know where she was.

'Don't worry about me,' Indigo Bliss said, 'I know how to pick up on social cues.'

Meadow was ready to nudge her sister under the table if need be.

They were greeted by Doyle dressed in jeans and a white cable-knit jumper. Lottie wore the athletic wear Meadow had noticed was quite popular in town. The matching pink leggings and top looked comfortable, made from stretchy, shiny material.

Inside, they ventured into an enormous dining area, its

closed arched doors leading elsewhere. Doyle had decorated in grey, white and pale green tones and it was all clean lines and natural light. It certainly belonged in one of the home décor magazines. A glass dining room table stood before them, laden with pizzas, garlic bread and some chicken wings.

As her sister introduced herself to Lottie, Meadow saw surprise and fascination on Lottie's face as she eyed Indigo Bliss up and down.

'You have a beautiful home,' Meadow offered.

'It's designed to be environmentally friendly,' Doyle said.

'I've read about that,' Indigo Bliss frowned. 'Can you imagine being told how to build your home.'

Seeing the expression on Doyle's face, Meadow nudged at her sister.

Indigo Bliss got the message. 'Oh each to their own and all that.'

Lottie led them to the table. 'I hope you like pizza. I got us a vegetarian one too.'

'Looking forward to it,' Meadow put the potato bake on the table.

Both Doyle and Lottie appreciated the contribution from the sisters. After sitting, Doyle poured the apple cider. He flicked his fringe to the side every now and again as he beamed over at Indigo Bliss, who didn't seem to notice Doyle at all.

'What do you like to read?' Lottie asked Meadow.

'Poetry mostly,' Meadow said, 'and old myths and fairy tales.'

'Not many happily-ever-afters in those,' Indigo Bliss said, her face impassive as she glanced at Doyle without a flicker of a smile.

'What about you?' Meadow took a slice of pizza from the

box Lottie held out toward her. It was hot, and topped with cherry tomatoes and capsicum.

'I'm interested in unconventional books mostly,' Lottie said.

'What kind of unconventional books?' Indigo Bliss was instantly curious.

'Mainly about ancient civilisations and obscure texts like the Voynich manuscript,' Lottie said. 'Atlantis might be just a myth to show us the cycle of rise and fall…or it could have been real.'

Indigo Bliss was astonished. 'Real?'

'Especially after reading the *Timaeus* and *Critias* dialogues,' Lottie said. 'Maybe truth is sometimes written as fiction.'

Meadow made a mental note to read those.

'That's why I'm researching about cataclysmic events,' Lottie said. 'I think there's some sort of pattern and we've been lied to about history and time.'

'Lied to?' Indigo Bliss's eyes narrowed. 'How?'

'Changing calendars for one,' Lottie said. 'And that time is not linear.'

Meadow leaned closer.

'Maybe if we become too technologically advanced the lights are turned off and we are thrown into a dark age,' Lottie said. 'Then sometimes there's a cover up followed by famine and plague, like we're in some kind of loop.'

The table fell silent.

'Or we could be in a simulation with a grid of evolving "myths and legends".' Lottie mimed air quotes. 'And it has to periodically update its files for the next reset.'

'A simulation?' Meadow glanced at her sister.

'Existence could be fractal-like for all we know,' Lottie said. 'You should check out the Mandelbrot set with its never-ending patterns of cardioids and bulbs.'

'More doom and gloom,' Doyle broke off a piece of garlic bread wrapped in foil. 'Lottie's a professional conspiracy theorist into pseudohistory and all things woo woo.'

'They're alternate narratives, and I prefer the term conspiracy realist.' Lottie rolled her eyes at Doyle. 'You know the Mandelbrot set is about mathematics, not woo woo. Anyway, I'm curious, not gloomy, 'cause we've got the potential to change so much.'

'Conspiracy theorist?' Meadow asked. 'I mean…realist?'

'Someone whose viewpoint isn't necessarily mainstream,' Doyle winked at Lottie. 'Her theories are pretty fringe; well, they're hypotheses really.'

'If you're going to get all technical,' Lottie said, 'have you looked up the etymology of the word conspire yet?'

'To be in harmony or to breathe together,' Doyle said, 'but you know why most people use it nowadays.'

'Same as why most people say theories instead of hypotheses, sometimes what people mean changes over time,' Lottie said. 'Anyway, whatever it's called, it's better than being deceived by propaganda.'

'That's the problem isn't it, you believe everything is propaganda,' Doyle said, an amused smile crossing his lips as he twisted the foil from the garlic bread into a shape.

Meadow, watching their faces, saw Doyle's dusty, golden words had transformed into sharp, white-gold spikes. Lottie's were still colourless, shapeless.

'But you think propaganda is a benevolent salve for the masses,' Lottie folded her arms. 'Don't you see that's just as bad as brainwashing.'

'Now don't get carried away,' Doyle gulped some apple cider. 'Your theories are more or less fodder for the gullible. I mean giants and dragons, really.'

'If you can believe in dinosaurs why not dragons?' Lottie raised one eyebrow. 'Why do so many ancient civilisations have carvings of dragons?'

This heated back and forth reminded Meadow of when

Gran and Indigo Bliss sometimes butted heads. Uncomfortable but eye-opening. She glanced at her sister who appeared interested in the scene before her yet sceptical of the subject matter.

Doyle put aside a hat he'd fashioned and spread out his hands in surrender. 'Oh well, let's agree to disagree shall we.' He smiled apologetically at the sisters, as if trying to make it less awkward for everyone. 'In the end I do admire Lottie's curiosity.'

Lottie looked about to say more on the matter, but caught sight of his foil creation, squashing it into an angry ball.

Meadow threw a questioning glance at her sister.

Indigo Bliss mouthed, 'I'll tell you later.'

Doyle studied Indigo Bliss. 'So what do you like to read?'

'I'm into travel books,' Indigo Bliss nibbled on a wing.

'Have you travelled?' Doyle picked up a wing too.

'One day.' Indigo Bliss gave an almost dreamy smile.

Doyle seemed to take this smile as some kind of personal reward. 'Where do you want to go?' His golden words sprinkled over the table like glitter.

'Everywhere.'

Doyle began to rattle off the places he'd visited. The list was long.

Meadow recalled her sisters prediction, that Doyle was fake nice, and would keep steering every conversation back toward himself. She cleared her throat.

'Do you want to see my library?' Lottie said.

'Sure.' Meadow noted the look that passed between father and daughter.

As Lottie ushered Meadow to the wide staircase, she could hear her sister naming far-off lands.

Doyle's laughter was easy, 'Now that's a travel plan.'

Lottie had a minimalist approach to her room that included

a bed, a desk and a substantial bookshelf along one wall. These were made of matching dark wood and the bedspread and pillows were all white. No trimmings. The only colour in the room was a row of crystal rocks, pink, purple, yellow and green, lining the desk. There wasn't a photo of Lottie's mother. Not one of Doyle either. Meadow could relate to that; Gran didn't have photos of their family. The instant camera was only used for the old darlings.

Lottie's room was more like her sister's, except Indigo Bliss collected eclectic pottery, replicating styles from other countries. There was that blue and white Ming Dynasty teapot replica, and even an imitation vase from Ancient Greece, clay brown with figures drawn on. Her sister also had two paintings on her wall, one was a watercolour of water lilies and the other of untidily painted sunflowers in a vase.

'Make yourself comfortable.' Lottie stood before the bookshelf, motioning for Meadow to sit on the bed. Lottie chose several books and sat next to her.

Meadow blinked rapidly.

'You smell like a rose garden.' Lottie sniffed.

'I can give you some of the rose petals and herbs we bathe in if you like.' Meadow suggested.

Lottie nodded.

She looked into Lottie's green eyes and realised her neighbour hadn't blinked. Not once.

'You see the moon might not be what it seems,' Lottie explained, pointing to an image on a cover. 'Maybe the moon is a reflector? It could be like a key…or a mirror. Now that's a rabbit hole, there's videos about the moon mirroring continents on earth…only showing more lands.'

'Not what it seems,' Meadow swallowed hard.

'Or there could be an artificial construction on it, or

inside it. Remember when the moon rang like a bell?'

Meadow shook her head.

'Who knows, it might just be our luminous moon, so I'm keeping an open mind. But on the other hand, there's so many soft disclosures in movies these days, aren't there?'

'I've never watched a movie,' Meadow shrugged. 'We don't have a television.'

'We'll have to change that,' Lottie said, as if this was easily fixable. 'You'd have fun learning about esoteric symbolism in movies.'

Meadow glanced toward Lottie's window with its sheer grey curtains, imagining the moon outside as artificial.

Lottie smiled at Meadow. 'Ready for the next one.'

Meadow leaned away, and looking at the cover of the next book, thought she was not ready.

'It's about hollow earth.' Lottie stared into space.

Meadow, still waiting for Lottie to blink, began to feel light-headed.

'Lately, I've been into shows about mirror-esque worlds. And don't even get me started on transhumanism.'

It was becoming obvious Lottie viewed a lot of television. Was this what people watched for all those hours?

Meadow stood up, accidentally knocking the book from Lottie's hand. 'Oh sorry. I wasn't expecting you to say all that.'

It dawned on Meadow perhaps Lottie was teasing her, a teenage taunt aimed at someone presumed less sophisticated. She went to the bookcase hoping to find books she might recognise. Meadow was met with titles that did indeed reference ancient maps, dragons and giants.

'You sure have an interesting collection.'

'Next time you visit,' Lottie said, 'I'll have researched

more about aliens.'

'Aliens…' Meadow veered toward the window. Her skin pricked with goosebumps; this was where she'd observed the veiled woman watching her.

'I haven't worked out if there are aliens,' Lottie clasped a book to her chest. 'Or if they want us to think there are aliens. I suppose it's how you define alien. Either way they will probably play the alien card soon.'

'They?' Meadow stared at their garden through the sheer curtain. Gran was right about their vulnerability once the hawthorn hedges were bare. She would stop trimming the tangled thickets and rewild them.

Maybe it was the mention of aliens. Or maybe it was the thought of something unknown inside the earth, but Meadow's light-headedness began to turn to dizziness. She sat on the bed again. 'That sounds…'

'If I tell you a secret will you tell me one?' Lottie rubbed her hands together.

'I don't know if I can tell you my secrets,' Meadow shifted her weight.

'Your secret can't be bigger than mine.'

Meadow's family secret had started out hopeful like young green wisteria, tender and sweet, but had ended up like their old twisted wisteria vines, beautiful but suffocating all in its path.

'Well.' Lottie held up a manicured hand. 'Sometimes I think I'm a clone.'

The blood drained from Meadow's face. Her world began to spin, then went dark.

Chapter Eight

She awakened to three worried faces peering down at her. Meadow was on the floor and her legs were up on Lottie's bed. Embarrassingly, her gingham belt had also been loosened.

'Are you all right?' her sister's words were the colour of dark wine.

She could tell Indigo Bliss was worried. 'I'm sorry,' Meadow took a shaky breath. 'I must have hyperventilated with all the excitement.'

'Yes, we don't get out much,' Indigo Bliss said dryly. 'I think we'll get you home.'

Doyle protested, 'You sure you can't stay for dessert?' He was disappointed. He glanced across at Lottie who held her hands up in an innocent gesture.

'Thanks for showing me your room,' Meadow tried to give Lottie a conspiratorial smile, to show her secret was safe with her.

Doyle shook his head.

'Sorry Doyle,' Meadow offered weakly. 'I don't think I'm up for dessert.'

'Don't keep saying you're sorry,' Doyle had concern in his eyes.

Downstairs, Indigo Bliss collected their food containers with one hand while not letting go of Meadow with the other.

'Do you need help?' Doyle said. 'I could help you get Meadow inside your cottage.'

'We're fine,' Indigo Bliss led Meadow through the back sliding door.

Had she ruined her chance at another invitation? Meadow gave a feeble wave goodbye.

'Thanks,' Doyle called to their retreating backs.

'What on earth happened?' Indigo Bliss laced her arm through Meadow's own to support her. 'Was it that veiled woman? Did you see her?'

Meadow shook her head, 'I was looking at Lottie's books and...'

'What books? Did something upset you?' Indigo Bliss whipped her protective older-sister gaze toward Meadow.

Meadow pursed her lips. It was all so unsettling. She'd never kept a secret from her sister before, but didn't want to get Lottie in trouble. 'Nothing really, maybe it was the pizza?'

'Well you certainly know how to make an impression. Maybe that will teach them to invite us over,' Indigo Bliss laughed triumphantly. 'Ha! We'll be free from invites now.'

Her sister always knew just what to say to make her smile, even though Meadow wanted this to be the first of many visits. 'I do worry about Lottie.'

'In what way?'

'Maybe she needs her mother?'

'That's nice of you to care,' Indigo Bliss said. 'Doyle didn't mention her mother, not once. Too busy bragging about his world travels.'

Meadow was sure Doyle had only been trying to impress Indigo Bliss. Sounded like he sure chose the wrong way to go about it.

'What was that girl talking about?' Indigo Bliss said. 'Cataclysmic cycles and dragons?'

For once she didn't want to discuss a subject further.

Inside the cottage, the pups and Spencer began a furious, intent bout of sniffing, trying to decipher the new scents from next door.

Meadow could tell by the pups wriggling, and Timba's nuzzling, they wanted to go straight outside.

'You stay here. I'll go out tonight.' Indigo Bliss knelt in front of the loungeroom hearth, and added more logs to the fire. The roar of flames was immediate. 'Getting you some of Gran's best home remedy first.' Indigo Bliss strode toward Gran's remedy cupboard and returned with a spoon and two glass bottles. Both bottles threw a greenish hue in the firelight.

'Just a teaspoon,' Indigo Bliss instructed. 'We've already broken the rules tonight so I'm going out now instead of midnight.'

Within minutes Meadow was more like herself again. 'I'm fine to help out. It was probably nerves or something.'

'If you're sure?' Indigo Bliss said.

Timba and Tawny looked up at her with imploring eyes. Puppy eyes that looked lined by dark kohl eyeliner. 'I'm sure.'

On the way to the milking shed, Meadow told her sister Lottie could virtually see their entire back garden.

'Just as Gran thought,' Indigo Bliss said. 'Blast that new house.'

After she'd milked Gertie and collected eggs from the nesting boxes, Meadow felt better. She left the remaining few apples to fall on the ground for the chickens, and picked some rhubarb. Out here in the refuge of her garden, she eyed the moon, and chuckled about what Lottie had said.

'Can't be good for her to be fixated on such things,' Meadow said to the pups, and they looked up at her with wide toothy grins.

She stood on the stump near the fence, glancing up toward Lottie's room on the second storey. The lights were off.

'How does she sleep with what she reads?'

As Meadow carried her basket into the kitchen, she realised something was wrong with her sister. Indigo Bliss was leaning over the table, and shaking.

'What is it? Are you sick?'

But Indigo Bliss wasn't sick. Meadow saw her sister's lip trembling—followed by a forced smile.

'What happened?' Meadow said. 'Did Doyle do something to you?'

'No,' Indigo Bliss croaked. 'Why wasn't she at the landmark?'

Meadow knew what her sister was going to say.

'I went to the meeting place,' Indigo Bliss said, 'which means Gran must be in trouble.'

The day their grandmother departed, she had instructed them to make contact with her on every full moon. Indigo Bliss, with her wicked sense of humour, had alluded to the notion of werewolves. Even now, with her sister's furrowed brow before her, Meadow fought the urge not to smile at the thought of their five foot tall grandmother being a werewoman.

If Gran were here, she would say that her direction about the full moon was no joking matter. And she'd been crystal clear about the landmark.

Last month, Indigo Bliss had returned alone, tired and disappointed.

'It's going to be time to go again soon,' Indigo Bliss lifted the lantern to look at the hand-drawn map Gran had left for them. 'What if Gran's hurt? I have to find out if something happened to...'

'You can't talk like that,' Meadow put her basket down. 'You sound as if you're going for more than one night?'

'As long as it takes,' Indigo Bliss sniffed. 'Something's obviously wrong.'

'I…don't want to stay here alone,' Meadow said. 'Couldn't we go together?'

'Gran said one of us must stay here, remember.' Indigo Bliss stabbed her finger at the map. 'This is where she was supposed to be, Collins Bonnet.'

On the map Sleeping Beauty was composed of two mountains. Collins Bonnet shaped her enchanting profile, and Trestle Mountain fashioned her ample bosom.

'I'll go,' Meadow grasped her sister's arm, sensing it wasn't the trek Indigo Bliss was concerned about, but what she might find up there.

They were silent for some time.

'No. I should do it. I know the way,' Indigo Bliss finally said. 'It will be a full moon again in a few days. I'll do one last shopping trip, in case I'll be gone…'

Meadow eyed the map. 'What if the hooded man knocks again?'

Indigo Bliss stared at Meadow for a moment with pursed lips, as if holding something back.

'Look, just stay inside. Don't open it for anyone,' Indigo Bliss instructed. 'If worst comes to worst go to Bert, not Doyle.'

Meadow blinked rapidly.

'Don't forget to leave eggs for Bert. We won't get much more milk from Gertie,' Indigo Bliss said. 'You don't have to worry about hay or chook food, we're stocked up.'

'It could snow. You know what it's like up there,' Meadow gestured toward their mountain.

If Gran wasn't there this time they might have to admit to the truth they'd been hiding from.

'I'll be prepared for anything.' Indigo Bliss said.

'As long as you are sure you should go alone.' Meadow tried masking her concern for Indigo Bliss. 'What was the foil about?'

'It was like a Dad joke,' Indigo Bliss said. 'He made the tin-foil hat because of Lottie's conspiracies.'

Chapter Nine

Meadow glanced up at the moon a lot over the next few nights, hoping Gran would return before her sister left. But as the moon grew to fullness and its bright light intensified, her own disposition darkened and hope waned.

'It'll be a quick shop.' Indigo Bliss pulled on her best boots for town.

'What if Doyle tries to visit the cottage again?' Meadow wheeled her sister's shopping trolley into the hallway.

'Don't answer.' Indigo Bliss checked she had change for the bus. The plan was that she would be back before lunch.

'Make food for my pack,' Indigo Bliss said. 'Remember, I want a lot of cheese, boiled eggs and walnuts.'

Her sister was purchasing extra supplies in town to take with the meals Meadow would prepare. She tried so hard to pretend it was a normal day and that Indigo Bliss wasn't going to leave her, to trek on top of their beautiful, yet wild, mountain.

She filled her sister's backpack with water, placing cheese, fruit, biscuits and walnuts to one side. Next, she carefully wedged inside two small bottles of Gran's home remedy, swathed and insulated in a cloth. Potatoes were added, so Indigo Bliss could cook them in their jackets in the fire. Meadow packed beef jerky, oil, and then flour for damper. At the top she positioned a large number of boiled eggs and sourdough bread.

Gran had taught them bush skills early on, and while Meadow's had lapsed, she was relieved her sister's hadn't. Indigo Bliss still knew where the best caves were to shelter from rain, wind or snow.

As an afterthought, she placed half a block of chocolate on top of the eggs. A recent addition to their household, and in some ways forbidden fruit. Gran was a great believer in home-made everything, including sweets. She would remind Indigo Bliss that she'd better eat the evidence before seeing Gran.

When Indigo Bliss returned, the pack was prepared but Meadow wasn't.

'I bought you some torches and put batteries in them already,' Indigo Bliss handed Meadow several slim torches. 'I'm taking a couple myself, but thought they might be easier for you.'

Her sister's words were a flat, bruised purple.

Indigo Bliss made herself a cup of rose tea.

Gran always said rose tea bloomed the lips but this time her sister's mouth was set in a pale, grim line.

After tonight, her grandmother would have been gone for two full moons.

The closer the time came for her sister to depart the quieter Meadow became. Indigo Bliss went to change into thermal underwear, overalls and her lilac fleece-lined jacket with a hood. When Indigo Bliss came back into the kitchen she was like an explorer from times past. A decidedly hourglass-shaped explorer.

Meadow started to say something then stopped; instead she motioned toward the pack for her sister to take.

When she said nothing, Indigo Bliss looked at her deliberately, seeming to understand. As the grandfather clock chimed that it was midday, Indigo Bliss left.

Meadow followed her sister, who was leaning forward under the weight of her pack.

She didn't call out goodbye as her sister neared the river.

Indigo Bliss did not turn back and wave. She felt grateful for this kindness.

It'd been decided Spencer was to sleep on the floor of Meadow's bedroom. Indigo Bliss had been strict about this as she didn't want to return to a spoilt old dog. The first and most important directive though, was that Meadow would follow all of Gran's initial rules.

'We've slipped up so much already,' Indigo Bliss had said, 'and I think it's going to bite us.'

Looking out toward their top paddock, she continued to observe her sister until she was a tiny speck of movement. Meadow made her way back to the cottage, with a quick glance in the direction of her new neighbours.

It was too early to sleep and she was too edgy anyway. She remembered every detail about the hooded man's silhouette, his height, the set of his shoulders, and realised he must have had a torch in his hand. How else could his outline have been illuminated? It had been a moonless night.

It was tempting to go and look out of the front door, or her front window, to check that no one strange was hanging about. She fought the impulse, sensing it could become a harmful habit.

Instead she stoked the fires and topped up Gran's canisters. She watered all the potted herbs straining toward the sun in the kitchen: dandelion, lemon balm and chamomile.

She couldn't blame her sister for leaving, nor her grandmother before that, but she still felt deserted. Not for the first time, Meadow wondered what colour her words would be if she could view them. Perhaps faded, like the deadheaded flowers from that poem she'd read about loneliness, where a single flower nods amongst dull, discarded daisy petals. The image made her crave something colourful and she sat beside her grandmother's favourite window. Gran's camellia window where pink petals kissed the glass. The flowers of blush, coral and rouge were a welcome flush of colour at this time of year.

By three o'clock Spencer started howling. This seemed foreboding as he hadn't howled when her sister went shopping.

'I know, I know, old boy, trust me.' Meadow pointed toward the treat cupboard. Spencer followed her as she opened the door and produced his favourite chewy soft indulgence. She rearranged the rows of dog food. His past owner had made the Drearys promise to continue feeding him the same brand he'd always eaten. Timba begged at her feet and she retrieved two more treats. Tawny, still by the fire, her nose resting in her paws, lifted her head and wandered over.

'It's just me now.' Meadow sat in her sister's rocking chair. 'So that means I'm in charge and no funny business.' Three sets of eyes turned to her in surprise. Had she sounded commanding like Indigo Bliss?

Perhaps she should go to bed after all, as it might settle the old dog. The loungeroom was again tinged with eeriness, far from the familiar space she usually found comforting. 'Shall we just go to bed?' Meadow asked the pups, who looked at her blankly, appearing to have no opinion either way. She led the pets to her room and dressed into her pyjamas before sliding between her daisy-print sheets. As instructed, Spencer slept on his bed on the floor, while the pups leapt up onto hers.

She closed her eyes. It was quiet for this time of the day. There was normally the hum of a tractor, or the buzz of a chainsaw, one of the costs of sleeping while others were busy working. Ordinarily by now she'd be hearing several teenagers returning home after school, ready to help out on the family farm.

Today it was so silent and solemn she tossed for some time before slipping into a dreamless sleep.

When she awoke, Meadow was disorientated. It was cold and dark. Where was her sister at the door offering a cup of tea? Feeling around her side table she located her matches and candle. Lighting it, she blinked away a red dot from the flame. She wandered past the ashy woodstove, to the cold hearth in the loungeroom. The grandfather clock showed it was past midnight, nearly one thirty, in fact. She'd slept for ten hours straight, had slept through so many chimes, it didn't seem possible.

She stacked kindling in both the hearth and the woodstove before trying to fire them up. Indigo Bliss had a flair for lighting fires but Meadow found herself trying several times to get them roaring. Coughing back the thick smoke from her failed attempts, she added extra kindling just as her sister did.

Dusting charcoal and twigs from her hands, she boiled the kettle, making her own cup of tea. This was accompanied by some of the thickly cut bread she'd baked for her sister, topped with walnut-butter. Her sister was right, she would use a torch tonight instead of a lantern.

In the kitchen, she peered out through the window toward the moon. It was indeed full and there was a halo ring around it, a sign of rain or snow.

She roughly pulled on her work clothes over the top of her pyjamas. She'd already taken close to an hour to get the fires roaring and hadn't even made it outside.

Letting out her three charges, Meadow followed them toward the river, to the stone seats. The torch worked well pointing at most things. It was easy to hold, but in her opinion, it didn't give as broad a light as her lantern. Her teeth began chattering so much she pulled her beanie snugly over her ears.

A strange cry rang out from next door. It came from the direction of the old sprawling oak tree, She froze. Was Doyle outside at night? A horrible thought struck her. Was it the hooded man? Should she warn Doyle?

Timba and Tawny stopped in their tracks, their noses sniffing upward toward the night sky. Spencer stood still, seeming to wait for a cue from Meadow. She switched off the torch and bent close to Spencer's grey head, gesturing for him to follow. Timba and Tawny followed the old shih tzu as she quietly navigated the path under moonlight.

She ushered the pets in through the back door, and whispered 'back soon,' before making her way to the chopping block. Meadow climbed up and peered over the hawthorn hedge. She sighed with relief when she saw Doyle. He was standing near the old sprawling oak tree, shaking his head. Doyle manoeuvred his way around a couple of low-lying branches and looked inside the wide tree hollow with a bright torch. He turned to look at his house, before glancing up at Lottie's room.

She ducked her head, trying to quieten her breath. Was there an animal in the tree hollow? The sisters had been able to fit inside the hollow when playing hide and seek as children. Looking over the fence again, she was relieved to see Doyle moving toward his back door. He hadn't spotted her.

Was he having a pest problem? Did Doyle have any poultry? There were presumably no foxes in Tassie, and as yet, she'd never observed a devil on the farm. The carnivorous marsupials that she'd been warned about regarding poultry were quolls. Quolls had been known to bite the heads off chickens, several in one sitting.

She hadn't personally witnessed this vicious ritual, but her grandmother had found many a headless duck or chicken back in her day. Meadow always found it hard to believe such a sweet looking creature could do so much damage. The only attack on their chickens she'd witnessed was an incident with a feral dog. She had chased him off, leaving a gruesome trail of blood and feathers behind him.

As she returned to the cottage, she thought of how the sisters had played in the old oak tree as children. Mrs Hill had encouraged them to play on her land, regaling her captive audience with tales of dancing, small waists and high heels. This had changed as Indigo Bliss grew into a teenager, and Mrs Hill's expression would initially crumble at seeing her sister. A certain narrow-eyed indignation would possess the woman, and she would be hostile toward Indigo Bliss, openly glaring at her. Mrs Hill had reminded her of a kookaburra with keen sight, and thick pencilled-in eyebrows that swept toward her temples.

Uncharacteristically, Indigo Bliss had become self-conscious for a time, wearing only baggy clothes when outside. Gran's face went all tight when she told Indigo Bliss that Mrs Hill was just a silly woman and to take no notice of her. 'She's just a jealous old lady.'

Meadow had hidden her smile from Gran, who was older than Mrs Hill.

When Meadow returned inside, the pups and Spencer were disappointed their play had been cut short, but she couldn't risk them venturing out again. What if Doyle went back to the old oak tree. Instead she guided them into the loungeroom, near the hearth. Timba jumped up, nipping at the pom-pom on her beanie, while Tawny sat beside Spencer near the fireplace.

'Gertie!' Meadow couldn't leave milking her cow, not quite yet. 'Stay.'

Back outside, she stood still for a moment, listening for the strange cry. Just in case, she climbed the wood block once more, noting bright lights flickering from the lower floor. She knew what that was. A television. Doyle must be a night-owl after all.

After milking Gertie and collecting the eggs, it was difficult to hold the torch, milk bucket and egg basket all at once. She slipped the torch into her pocket, giving the ground a soft muted arctic-glow through her blue cardigan.

'I thought I saw someone out here.' A voice called from the direction of the fence, from the ladder.

Not Doyle, Lottie.

'Why are you out here so late?' Lottie shone torch light into Meadow's face. 'It's four o'clock in the morning.'

'I could ask you the same thing.' Meadow blinked, trying to give what she hoped was a concerned smile. 'Does your Dad know you're out here?'

'I don't normally call him Dad, he likes being called Doyle,' Lottie said.

Her new neighbours were particular about their names. Meadow wanted to ask Lottie about the old oak tree, and if Doyle was having trouble with pests. But upon reflection, it might sound like she was the interfering type.

Lottie was still in her pyjamas. 'You'll get a chill. Look at you.'

Shivering, Lottie looked at her PJs. 'Be right back.'

Meadow called after Lottie not to worry, that she had to go inside anyway but her neighbour was already opening the back sliding door of her house. Lottie returned wearing her pink puffer jacket and a novelty animal hat of a kitten. 'I was hoping you'd come over again.'

'Really,' Meadow said, thrilled at another invitation.

'How about today?' Lottie tilted the torch toward her watch, 'after breakfast.'

'Are you sure it's all right with...' Meadow trailed off, not sure if eighteen year olds normally had to check with their parents. In Meadow's case, Gran would never allow a visitor.

'He won't care,' Lottie grasped one side of the ladder. 'But I can go ask him.'

'No,' Meadow said. 'No, that's fine, I'll come and visit. You go inside and get warm.'

'Any time after nine.' Lottie stared at Meadow for a moment. 'Your sister can come too if she wants. Just come around the back door again.'

'I don't think she can.'

Lottie shrugged, as if that was Indigo Bliss's loss, and still shivering, climbed back down the ladder.

What unusual hours her new neighbours kept. Meadow uttered 'I suppose we can't talk' to the ground, forgetting the pups were inside.

Gran's instructions were going to be hard to follow, especially when her overly friendly new neighbours could make a sudden appearance, day or night.

Chapter Ten

Hours later, with an anticipatory fluttering in her belly, Meadow readied herself to visit Lottie. She'd slept fitfully from four thirty that morning, finally waking at eight to a cold and quiet cottage. She was beginning to realise how much her sister did around the place.

Remembering Lottie's athletic gear, she dressed in what she hoped would be considered casual wear. Her best pair of cream corduroy pants, a white polo neck, topped with a knitted yellow cardigan and matching beanie. Meadow placed a jar of rose petals into her basket, the darkest red with black shadings, her personal favourite, so sweet, spicy and skin softening.

After slipping out the front, she plucked several pears, placing their firmly rounded bottoms carefully into her basket. There were several mushrooms at the base of the trees, red with white spots on them, so fairy tale-like, but not for consumption. She'd read Socrates had been poisoned by hemlock. Meadow would warn her neighbours about the poisonous hemlock growing under the pine trees, occasionally mistaken for wild carrot. Meadow tried not to think of what research Lottie had been up to. Not wanting a repeat performance of the last time, she was going to have to tell Lottie the truth. 'I don't want to hear about aliens or an artificial moon,' she practiced.

But saying those words out loud sounded absurd, even to herself.

As she reached the back of the house, Lottie was waiting near the sliding door, still wearing the same clothes as at their early morning encounter.

Lottie clapped her hands together at the pears, and found an enormous lime-coloured plastic bowl to place them in. 'Looks like a display piece doesn't it.'

'I've got a good book on preserving I can lend you.'

'Sure. I want to start doing farmy things.'

Once again Meadow found herself staring at Lottie's mouth. No colour nor shapes. She concentrated hard, trying to envision what type of animal Lottie might look like.

'Have I got something on my face,' Lottie's hand touched her cheek.

'No. Not at all.'

'Do you want to come up to my room and I'll show you more books?'

'I need to tell you something.' Meadow took a deep breath. 'I don't think I have the stomach for your conspiracies…I mean alternate narratives.'

'What about a really tame one?' Lottie suggested, then clicked her fingers. 'Yep, we can start off easy.'

'Well,' Meadow said, 'maybe.'

'You sit here. I'll be back with nothing too fringy.' Lottie turned on her heel and trotted from the kitchen, her kitten ears bobbing.

Meadow noted the arched doors to the loungeroom were now open. The room was white on white and she observed the backs of two white lounge chairs and a leather sofa. A large black painting hung on one wall. A rather unusual piece of artwork.

Meadow sat, swivelling in the dining chair while crooking her ear toward their cottage, listening for Spencer. There was only the familiar sound of a chicken here and there, singing that showy laying-of-an-egg song.

Lottie returned to the dining room empty-handed. 'I've been thinking it might be easier to show you what I'm talking about.'

'Show me?' Meadow shook her head, not comprehending.

'On the telly. C'mon.' Lottie pulled Meadow toward the loungeroom, picked up a remote, and turned on the black artwork.

'So that's the television!' Meadow exclaimed.

'One of them.' Lottie turned and pointed to a puffy white chair. 'Sit in the recliner and make yourself comfy.'

Lottie scrolled and sifted through many titles on the screen.

Meadow sat into the soft, squishy chair. It almost enveloped her entire body.

'Pull the lever on the side and you'll get the footrest up,' Lottie said.

Meadow did as instructed and for a moment wasn't sure where to put her legs, now pushed to either side. In the end she lifted them onto the footrest as graciously as she could, hoping she hadn't transferred any stray particles of hay. She was like some sort of human potpourri vessel when it came to hay, with stems and flowers sticking to all her clothing. 'This one's not even a conspiracy, not in the least bit fringy,' Lottie said. 'I'll get you started while I get us snacks.'

Meadow watched images of a veiled sun, like a faded moon. A man's voice began to narrate smoothly. 'Scientists and historians have debated about which year was the worst in history. Some believe it was the year five hundred and thirty-six, when darkness brought famine and plague. Many think volcanic eruptions set off this global disaster.' As she kept pace with all the images of darkness and stony fields, Meadow was stunned. How did they live without the sun on their face for a year, nor the warmth of the soil under their feet. It sounded much worse than her current nocturnal life.

Lottie re-entered the room carrying a tray with a snack

Meadow hadn't eaten before. 'Got some corn chips and chocolate milkshakes.' Lottie paused the video, then handed Meadow a bowl of orange triangles and a milkshake.

'He said the sun became like the moon for a year,' Meadow said. 'They called it the year of darkness. They couldn't grow food.'

'Bet they were vitamin D deficient.' Lottie sat in an identical chair, the other side of the sofa, pulling out the footrest. 'I wonder how many resets were by design versus natural disasters.' Lottie placed her food on a side table, flipped open a notebook she'd tucked under her arm.

'You think it was by design?' Meadow took a sip of the milkshake. It met with her approval but after crunching on a corn chip she wasn't so sure; they were tangy, and left orange dust all over her fingers.

'Maybe not,' Lottie pressed play. 'But you never know.'

On the screen Meadow saw paintings of people surrounded by ash, and statements that the sky was blended with strange elements.

Out of the corner of her eye, she caught Lottie observing her with a look of interest, or perhaps concern. She remembered the awkwardness of waking to three worried faces, her feet up on Lottie's bed. Meadow steeled herself. No matter what she viewed on the screen she would not repeat that performance.

She was finally watching a television.

'This one's interesting,' Lottie chose another video.

Ancient cathedrals were displayed, some Gothic and gargoyled. A woman appeared on the screen; she had short brown hair and wore red glasses. Behind her, images of bells being taken down slid across the screen.

'There is an alternative history to what you've been

told,' the woman said. 'A hidden past…some of our ancestral culture has been hidden or destroyed. Time, also, has been adjusted, and many centuries are not what they seem. After resets, sometimes fake rulers were inserted, pasted into history.'

Like Lottie, the woman seemed to think those changes had been intentional.

'Bells once rang with golden harmonics,' the woman continued. 'Cathedrals were conductive, built not just for worship but for resonance. The spires drew energy, the bells carried frequency, some say healing frequency.'

Meadow wondered if her mother would have viewed the frequency of the ringing in colour, perhaps like golden harmonics. She vaguely recalled Gran hadn't been impressed about old world bells being melted down.

'If certain ancient relics become visible,' the woman said, 'it might fundamentally destroy what many have believed. Some relics were sewn into tapestries, hidden in music, or encoded in stained glass.'

Meadow noticed that when viewing people on the screen, she could see neither colourful words nor animal-esque features. Just like when she looked at the magazines and paintings in the library.

She tried not to think what that might mean in relation to Lottie, or herself.

Meadow had so many questions. 'But why would they want to hide history?'

'Maybe covering up that people were more advanced than we thought,' Lottie said, pausing the video again. 'Art often held truths that words couldn't.'

She thought of art books in the library, imagining bygone figures painted with haloes of sound.

'I mean, ancient people had advanced technology. The pyramids might have been machines that harnessed power,'

Lottie said. 'And can you believe in the olden days some buildings had blood in the concrete? For durability, or maybe something else.'

Meadow pictured blood dripping into grey mixture, being stirred around like a swirl in a lollipop. It was such an unusual thing to say she glanced over at Lottie. Was this some kind of test to see if she'd faint again?

The look on her neighbour's face was reminiscent of her sister's expression, when considering Meadow's capacity to cope with something unpleasant.

She must have passed because Lottie pressed play and the thought-provoking woman on the screen pointed at images of relics and artefacts smuggled for centuries.

'They should keep artefacts safe,' Meadow said. 'How else will we know where we came from?'

'And maps,' Lottie said, turning off the television. 'Some old maps have dragons, mermaids and sea monsters drawn on them. I mean the legends must've come from somewhere, right?'

Gran sometimes used encyclopedias when teaching them about history, all bound in brown and gold. Meadow had never met anyone who believed there may have been dragons or sea monsters.

'Before the Library of Alexandria was "accidentally" set ablaze,' Lottie mimed airquotes, 'I bet "they" removed a lot of important artefacts.'

They chatted for several minutes before falling into a silence that felt as comfortable as Meadow's chair.

Lottie flipped through her notebook. 'How about that hidden forest at the bottom of a sinkhole in China. It had enormous ancient trees.'

Meadow tried to imagine primitive trees growing out of sight. 'What else could be down there?'

'Exactly. Maybe an undiscovered animal species,' Lottie

snapped her fingers. 'Remind me to give you a couple of books about new discoveries. One day I'll show you a video on maps. Especially after they just discovered seven thousand new islands in Japan.'

'What?'

'Hard to believe but true,' Lottie said. 'Hey, you can visit again tomorrow can't you?'

'Sure,' Meadow nodded. She liked television so far.

'Good,' Lottie said. 'Did you say you have a wardrobe with a door to the outside?'

Meadow was nervous about sharing anything else. She'd already said too much as it was. 'Yes.'

Lottie looked impressed. 'Can I see it soon?'

'Soon.' Meadow tried not to meet Lottie's eye.

A door shut with a thud somewhere in the house. 'That'll be Doyle,' Lottie said, 'coming to get his coffee fix.'

'I'd better go,' Meadow struggled to get out of her chair.

'Do you want me to help out with homesteading stuff?' Lottie said.

'Thanks for the offer.' Meadow gave Lottie her empty glass, and the rest of her chips. 'But maybe another time.'

Rounding the corner Meadow nearly bumped into Doyle. 'Oh don't go on my account,' he steadied himself. 'Stay and have a chat.'

'Sorry,' Meadow took a step back, 'I should go.'

'How about a cuppa first?' Doyle suggested, walking toward the sink and filling the jug.

'I've got a lot to do and Indigo Bliss isn't…' she trailed off.

'Isn't your sister at home?' he asked, at once intrigued.

Meadow tried to give Doyle a vague look, before turning on her heel, and throwing over her shoulder, 'Bye Doyle, thanks Lottie.' She did her best imitation of her sister's stride toward their cottage, not daring to turn around. She wondered if she should start practicing her sister's hands on hips stance next.

Lottie had invited her to visit again. The fainting debacle hadn't ruined her chances of friendship after all. Near the front gate, she narrowly missed stepping on a lifeless fairywren.

The little bird, sometimes with bright blue plumage that dazzled neon-blue in the sun, was instead enfolded in a ring of soft brown feathers. So tiny, and so sad, as if laid out in a feathered wreath tribute.

She willed herself not to think this was some sort of dire warning.

Chapter Eleven

Once she was inside, Spencer and the pups sniffed her curiously. 'Can you smell the corn chips?' She went to the back corner of the cottage, to where the trap door for their cold cellar was.

She descended the old wooden stairs carefully, and was met with rows of neatly labelled jars in her sister's elegant handwriting. She winced. While she'd been watching Lottie's television, her sister was out there alone. As she'd been sitting in a recliner with a milkshake, Indigo Bliss may have been in danger.

She lifted down a mason jar of soup and carried it back to the kitchen, trying to appear upbeat. 'After I've eaten, I'll get you three something from the treat cupboard.'

She rinsed her bowl, then gave the waiting pets a treat before wandering over to the window. Dark clouds had formed across the river, angry and full; heavy showers would certainly follow. Higher up the mountain there were hovering clouds, probably snow clouds. That halo moon had told her as much.

'Either way I don't think we'll be out there for long tonight,' Meadow said.

Forecasted rain wasn't the only problem. She wondered what Gran would say about her over-the-fence encounters and subsequent visits. Ever since her new neighbours had moved in, no matter what time Meadow went outside, their friendliness tendrilled merrily over the fence like honeysuckle.

Indigo Bliss would probably say 'more like blasted Venus fly traps'.

By early evening there was a light tapping on the window and rain pelted so hard it was impossible to sleep. She couldn't seem to read either, and after preparing a large bowl of preserved cherries and cream, was unable to eat them.

For some reason, waiting until midnight to go outside began to bother her terribly, as did the constant chiming of the grandfather clock. The melodic chiming had become grating. She dredged up the recent memory of Lottie saying blood was used in some concrete.

Watching videos with Lottie had been fascinating. But thinking about their content while alone in the cottage was unsettling.

Her breath quickened.

Surely she wasn't unravelling. That thought was even more unpleasant than blood oozing down the walls. She wasn't normally so melodramatic.

She relaxed her clenched jaws, trying to take several deep breaths. This hyped-up feeling was also a different sensation to her default of freezing. Freezing was exactly what she'd done the day Gran and her sister were assaulted. Even under attack Indigo Bliss had pulled that woman off their grandmother with superhuman strength. Meanwhile, Meadow had stood frozen in place, unable to move.

Later Indigo Bliss must have noticed Meadow's regret, as she'd told her fight, flight, freeze or fawn were all perfectly natural reactions. She'd wondered if there was a way to change how one reacted to danger.

She'd never minded her own company, though admittedly it was rare for her to be alone. Her sister said to go to Bert if she needed help but what could she say? That she was concerned someone might knock on her door. She was worried about blood in the walls.

She sought out the pups instead, snoozing by the fire; she needed a distraction. Sitting on the floor next to Spencer, the pups instantly sparked with excitement. Tawny sniffed at her hair, Timba pulled on her beanie, and Spencer licked her hand. The clock chimed again. It was like the forewarning of a bad omen. What had Gran once said, that church bells were sometimes thought to drive out evil. The video Lottie showed her had gargoyles perched atop cathedrals. Weren't they meant to ward off evil too or did the woman say they attracted it?

She placed her head against the pups' furry faces, trying to ground herself in something warm and present. Timba, now bouncing up and down, lifted his head and hit her under the chin. She bit her tongue. Flinching upward she hit the top of her head on the mantel of the fireplace. The pain was blinding. She closed her eyes and staggered away. 'Ouch Timba,' she said through gritted teeth.

When she opened her eyes, she was standing in front of the grandfather clock, shaking it like a wolf with its prey; she leapt back as if she'd touched something hot.

The clock hadn't just stopped chiming. It had stopped altogether.

She was the one who apologised to furniture and expressed regret when pruning the roses. The pain in her head was easing but she couldn't look at what she'd done to the poor old clock. She went to the linen closet, bringing back a single white sheet, and ceremoniously draped it over the silent timekeeper. Mechanically, Meadow retrieved the watch Gran had given her, wound it, changing the time.

Later, as it darkened, the need to escape the cottage returned. She donned a raincoat and took the pets outside. They were drenched within minutes but leaning against her cow felt familiar. She gave several squirts to her awaiting charges, to show there were no hurt feelings. It was a quick milking session. Gertie would dry up soon which was to be expected, and Meadow threw down fresh hay for her well-rounded cow.

She tried her best to stop the pups and Spencer from going to the river. It would be too boggy. Best to get back inside before they faced any more unexpected encounters over the fence.

Gran and Indigo Bliss did not return the following day, nor the one after that.

It rained all week, day and night. Obviously, their grandmother had not been waiting at the landmark, and Indigo Bliss had decided to go further. Sometimes she wished they owned a mobile like Doyle and Lottie, but Gran believed it was far too easy to trace a person on a mobile phone.

Every morning, she went over to watch Lottie's television. Lottie had pressed her to keep visiting, telling Meadow she was new to the area and lonely.

An unexpected windfall.

Doyle was always in his office or the kitchen, so she knew he wouldn't be nosing around their cottage like her sister had feared. Meadow and Lottie spent several mornings sharing stories about Lottie's theories and her farm-life.

The combination of the rain and new neighbours meant that, nowadays, she'd taken to slipping out in the morning without the pets. Gertie was dry, content to grow her calf to full-term.

After collecting eggs and harvesting from her garden, she visited Lottie.

She'd devised an alternative way to take the pets outside, using her wardrobe to take them to another place. A place allowing them to stretch their legs and get fresh air in private. Once through her wardrobe door, there was a secluded, small section of grass between the hedge and her bedroom wall where the pets could play freely. It had gravel and grass and she was able to look over the lavender hedge to observe anyone approaching along the front road. To make the run safe, she'd organised a makeshift fence, keeping them enclosed and secure. She'd constructed a barrier from her corner to the back corner of the cottage. Even though they appreciated being outside, sometimes three sets of eyes would look up at her questioningly, as if asking why she wasn't taking them to the river, to play amongst the old darlings' graves.

Meadow found a firmness forming in her, a resilience that enabled her to look at their hopeful faces and not give in. She reasoned getting out of the cottage was therapeutic, especially after doing away with her nocturnal life. Following the rules didn't seem as important now that she was alone, and her nerve grew each day while interacting with her neighbours. She had substituted her after-dark activities for moments in the sun listening to the magpies and observing the morning fog-line in the valley.

She was, however, beginning to look at the weather differently after watching videos about weather modification. 'It's real you know,' Lottie would say. 'They've admitted it; they use cloud seeding and other things. Some people even want to block out the sun.'

She wasn't quite sure. Without her grandmother and sister's opinion, there was no one to reflect with about Lottie's theories.

Some theories were in what Lottie called her undecided pile. Like the side-by-side photos of famous modern-day people next to someone identical from the eighteen hundreds. Apparently that made them time-travellers but Lottie wasn't sure if it was a distraction; perhaps they'd discovered the fountain of youth, were vampires, or possibly even clones? It was all lost on Meadow anyway because she didn't know who those famous people were. Lottie said if real time travelling existed, it might involve a form of intricate maths, cloning or perhaps there really was technology we didn't know about.

She was the snack person and Lottie made the milkshakes. Her contribution today was some home-made cheese, apple chips and roasted walnuts on a platter. Lottie's favourite so far.

It was almost nine o'clock, and she found the book on preserving pears for Lottie, then collected her favourite hooded cape. It was raspberry-red and fell to her ankles.

When Meadow had discussed with Lottie her fascination with the origins of fairy tales, Lottie had gushed that, 'some myths might be real, for all we know. I mean unicorns and dragons might exist on a different frequency, or are hidden away.'

Meadow had almost told Lottie about the way she saw the world a little differently. Almost.

According to Lottie, people were trained to laugh at conspiracies, and in her opinion, the more people laughed, the more she thought they were probably true.

'Just because we can't see every spectrum of light, like ultra-violet or infra-red doesn't mean they're not there,' Lottie had said. 'And don't get me started on radio waves.'

She wondered what it would be like to view those colours.

Lottie said the Schumann Resonance was the atmospheric heartbeat of the earth, and that changes to its frequency might impact our moods. Or even reflect them.

As Meadow twirled in her cape the pups tried to nip at the hem with each turn. 'Snack time,' she said, swaying as she retrieved some home-made liver treats and dog biscuits.

Collecting the platter she'd prepared, she placed it next to a basket of pears.

Fastening her cape around her throat, she closed the door quietly behind her. Capes were her favourite item of clothing. She would wear one every day if it didn't get in the way while she was milking and gardening.

She stared at the sky, surprised at the blue after so many days of grey. She followed the well-worn track through the new grass to Lottie's sliding door.

Chapter Twelve

'Lot-tie.' Meadow knocked.

Lottie waved her in from the other side of the sliding door.

'Love your cape.' Lottie looked down at her own clothes. 'I'm so boring compared to you.'

Meadow searched Lottie's face to ensure she wasn't teasing. When satisfied Lottie was in fact being complimentary she placed the snack-plate and book onto the table.

'Yum,' Lottie moved alongside Meadow, taking a crunchy apple chip.

Most days now, the scents of lavender, roses or peppermint wafted from Lottie. When Lottie had learned the Drearys didn't have running water at the cottage, she hadn't believed it at first.

Meadow tried to explain. 'I enjoy picking the rose petals, and boiling the water.'

'I get it, like your whole slow living thing,' Lottie said.

Meadow supposed slow living could describe a lot about her life, though when Gran and Indigo Bliss were around, everything felt fast-paced. However, Meadow saw the benefits of modern white goods. The hum of Lottie's refrigerator and the whirring sound of the dishwasher were reassuring. Unlike her own eerily quiet cottage, now without even the ticking of a clock.

'Wait until you see what we are watching.'

'What?'

'Well, 'cause of our Sleeping Beauty mountain I'm showing you retellings of *Little Briar Rose* and even earlier stories.'

'I've read that Brothers Grimm version,' Meadow said. 'But my sister read *Sun, Moon and Talia.* She said something happened to Talia while she was sleeping.'

Lottie raised one eyebrow. 'You just wait.'

Meadow nibbled on an apple chip. Visiting childhood characters was like nibbling on honeycomb, knowing she could expect the same viscosity each time.

Making herself comfortable on her favourite chair she pulled the lever and readied herself for the video as Lottie pressed play.

The narrator of the video showed several clips from various animated movies. In many of them, the young woman was not named Briar-Rose. That name evoked imagery in Meadow's mind of thorny hedges and thickets coiling around a palace, stressing the fate of the beauty sleeping inside. Often-times these versions' portrayals of the offended fairy differed from the thirteenth fairy in the Brothers Grimm.

'Now, let's go back further,' Lottie said, and pointed to the screen.

The colourful animations were replaced by several old exquisite drawings, with a maiden reclining on a bed with a canopy, and opulent gilded furnishings. The maiden was often surrounded by climbing roses.

'So ornate, probably what my sister read.'

'Here we go.' Lottie nodded.

The earlier tale turned dark. Fast.

After Lottie stopped the video she leaned toward Meadow with an appalled, yet knowing look. 'Rape and lies,' Lottie's lips were a straight line. 'The Queen wanted to watch the King eat his own children. Beyond vile.'

'Talia's newborn sucked the flax splinter from her finger?' Meadow's eyes widened, 'she'd been so unaware.'

'One day, I'll show you versions from mythology.' Lottie

nodded toward the cottage. 'Maybe we could check out your place soon?'

She wanted to invite Lottie over to see the animals and the garden but that went against all the rules. And Meadow had a feeling Gran would not make any allowances if she broke the rule about no visitors. Even though Lottie's company in the cottage would be a welcome relief from its oppressive strangeness. 'Hopefully soon.'

'No worries, just let me know,' Lottie said. 'Are you up for another one?'

'I should get back.'

'Go on. I'll make you another milkshake.'

Meadow liked being in demand. 'Sure.'

Lottie searched for various animations based on Hans Christian Andersen's *The Little Mermaid*.

'She never had a name.' Meadow said.

'Exactly.' Lottie pointed to the screen. 'Now keep an eye out for differences.'

Many of these animations had Meadow captivated by the mermaid's hair billowing in the water. It reminded Meadow of a poem she'd read, imagining frolicking mermaids and sea-wind-tangled tresses.

'Look at their hair.'

Lottie paused the video and gave a wry smile. 'You're fascinated with hair aren't you? You're always commenting on it.'

She supposed she was. Twisted braids, dreadlocks, frizzy, tight coils, crimped, wavy, pixie or waterfall-straight tresses had always intrigued her. Was it because of the wildness or its capacity for growth?

It was a new experience for Meadow to be studied, to have someone curious about her habits and quirks. 'I'm not sure why.'

'I get it.' Lottie pressed play again.

Many of these animated versions were familiar, revealing that the un-named little mermaid's heart had been broken, her every step was torment and that she'd been given a knife to kill the prince. That she'd sacrificed herself instead.

Then a voice narrated on the screen while displaying a gorgeously detailed drawing of someone named Undine. 'An earlier story, prior to Andersen, was about a water sprite who marries a knight to gain a soul.' Meadow stared at the next drawing, this time of a blonde woman, her hair blowing in a pale ribbon behind her as she stood beside a river. 'She looks like my sister.'

Lottie paused the video, nodding in agreement.

'Remind me to tell you what I learned about mermaids later.' Lottie pressed play. 'And how they supposedly look.'

Watching this earlier story was well suited to Meadow's palate. The longing of the sprite Undine was reminiscent of inky blooms. She envisaged blooms unveiling underneath Undine in the water, like Queen of the Night tulips. At the end Meadow said, 'Didn't end well for the knight.'

Lottie frowned. 'Imagine believing you had no soul.'

Meadow heard Doyle walk into the kitchen, then water running. 'Love the pears,' he called out. 'I was thinking of going up the road and getting a box of apples.'

Doyle entered the loungeroom tossing his palomino mane. 'Are you watching your fairy tales again?'

'Ignore him.' Lottie turned to Doyle. 'Did you know they bulldozed heaps of apple trees?'

Doyle looked at his daughter. 'Really?'

Lottie glanced at Meadow. 'Tell him.'

Every time she visited, Doyle wanted to hear a story about the valley. To coax her out of her shell? Maybe he thought she needed a little prompting.

'Bulldozed them?' Doyle's eyes widened.

'It was the "tree pull scheme" and farmers were paid to plough acres of apple trees,' Meadow said. 'Gran remembers seeing rows of exposed roots.'

'Different time huh,' Doyle shook his head. 'I suppose there were nearly as many apple trees as people back then.'

'Can we come too?' Lottie pleaded.

'Fine by me,' Doyle said.

But Meadow couldn't go. 'Maybe another time,' she put her cloak back on and fastened it.

'Now that's something you don't see every day,' Doyle grinned. 'You are full of surprises.'

'Give us a twirl,' Lottie said.

When she'd daydreamed about what her future might hold, she'd never dreamed it would include twirling around in front of new neighbours. Doyle and Lottie gave her an encouraging clap.

'Do you think your sister would like to come along? Why doesn't she ever come to watch videos?'

'She's busy at the moment,' Meadow answered Doyle, making her way to the sliding door.

'Same time tomorrow?' Lottie asked.

'Sure.'

Meadow ambled toward her cottage. She was living two lives. One welcoming and interesting and the other filled with loss. The cottage now felt as if it were wallpapered in guilt.

Gran would say guilt was such a wasted emotion, that it filled a person with a certain kind of hopelessness which led to inactivity.

According to her grandmother it was all about intention anyway.

But the cottage wasn't the worst of it.

When she was still going outside at night her garden had turned nightmarish. When at the stone seats glancing across the river to where several old trees stood, they were like hazy, grey mensfolk in the torchlight. The hawthorn bushes also transformed at night, their bare branches becoming claws, the thorns creepy long nails. Not to mention those mournful sounds near the old oak tree which only happened after dark.

The unease seemed to have crawled from the river's mossy embankment, slinking past the purple bladderworts along the rough stepping stones to enter the cottage and lurk in the hallways.

The only way to alleviate the unease was to visit Lottie and then stay in her bedroom. With her fire roaring and door locked it felt manageable. Within the walls of her sanctuary she wasn't reminded of her Gran and sister so acutely.

But the looming shape of the hooded man was always at the back of her mind. And she'd begun to question, as Gran said, the whole ball of wax. Where once the stars and moon were like timeless companions, now a glance up at the night sky caused her to doubt everything she'd ever known about the moon. Caused her to remember those ancient myths about two suns. What else had she been naïve about?

But the thought of not visiting Lottie any more was worse than questioning reality.

Gran said everything looks better in the morning.

She wondered if it was the dark people feared, or what might be lurking in the dark.

Chapter Thirteen

When she arrived the next morning, Doyle was in his kitchen cooking bacon and eggs.

'Thanks, these fresh eggs are the best.' He cracked two eggs into the pan.

'Gran says eggs are a superfood.' Meadow once again admired the light and airy kitchen with its natural tones.

Doyle glanced over at Meadow. 'I haven't caught sight of her yet.'

'I mean, used to say,' Meadow stammered. 'I mean… when she's at the cottage.'

She really was a terrible liar, so tried to focus on Doyle's pan.

'Well she's right,' Doyle flipped the bacon over.

Lottie, preparing their milkshakes added, 'My favourite is devilled eggs.'

Meadow made a mental note of that for a future snack.

Today her contribution was biscuits with golden syrup.

'Tell Doyle about your rooster,' Lottie said.

'Farm stories are the best,' Doyle said. 'I spent a lot of time on farms, remember.'

'Well, this one is about chook watching,' Meadow cleared her throat.

'I'd love some chooks.' Lottie said.

She found both Doyle and Lottie to be a wonderful audience, they nodded encouragingly at the right time and grinned where fitting.

'Well, our Buff Orpington rooster, Old Goldy, does this dance,' Meadow said. 'When he's happy or just feisty; it's his wing dance.'

'His feathers are threaded with spun gold,' Lottie added.

'That's why we call it his golden flamenco dance.' Meadow pictured Old Goldy. 'He starts by shuffling and twirling then stretching out a gilded wing.'

'Meadow's going to show me one day,' Lottie said.

'He sweeps the tip of his wing along the ground,' Meadow reminisced, 'like a hem gracing a polished floor.'

'And his clucking sounds like castanets,' Lottie grinned. 'It sounds like a courtship dance.'

'I'd pay for a front row seat to see that dance,' Doyle said. There was an uncomfortable silence for a moment; she was sure they were waiting for her to do the polite thing and invite them over. She pushed aside the image forming in her mind of Doyle and her sister in a courtship dance. She had an easily readable face and didn't want to betray her thoughts, which at that moment, were of Indigo Bliss shouting 'blasted man' at Doyle's advances.

'Are you sure Lottie isn't boring you to tears yet?' Doyle slid his bacon and eggs onto a plate. 'I mean hanging out with a teenager can get tiresome.'

He grinned at Lottie.

It hadn't occurred to her that their age difference might be considered unusual. She wondered what they had in common, except for books and enjoying videos together. Yet she liked Lottie's company. 'Oh no, she's very knowledgeable.'

'Good,' Doyle retrieved a knife and fork, 'because it's like you've become part of our family.'

She felt familiar warmth rising from her neck to her cheeks, but this time the attention was nice.

'Lottie's lined up something special for you today.' Doyle sprinkled sea salt onto his breakfast.

'Doyle wants to watch it too,' Lottie shrugged. 'Hope

you don't mind. He doesn't watch many shows with me.'

Meadow was nervous at the thought of Doyle joining them.

As Doyle sat with his breakfast at the kitchen table, she moved to her favourite chair in the loungeroom. Flicking the lever, she wriggled her legs until comfortable.

Lottie was close behind with milkshakes and the snacks Meadow had made. 'You ready Doyle?' Lottie called out, nibbling on a biscuit, her hand poised on the remote.

'Yep,' Doyle called back as a chair scraped in the dining room.

'So, I'm going for something a bit more intense this time.' Lottie pushed buttons with finesse. 'It's a movie about clones.'

'Is it scary?' Meadow asked.

'Well the fact it's probably truth told as fiction is quite scary,' Lottie stated, 'but I think you can handle it.'

Something in the way Lottie said that was pleasing. She had redeemed herself from the fainting debacle. So far the only video she'd made Lottie stop was the one about labs using animals to test products for humans.

'No animals?' Meadow checked.

'Definitely not,' Lottie pressed play on her remote.

'Ready.' Doyle entered the loungeroom, and sat on the leather sofa between the two recliners. He had a milkshake too.

Meadow was swept into a world where clones made for the benefit of others were involved in so much action that it made her head spin. The main actress had a startling awakening, while the male lead wore a cheeky grin and was a man on a mission.

There were moments she closed her eyes, and disturbing parts that Lottie warned her were coming up. Alarming parts, that for some reason, she still felt compelled to peek at through her fingers. At one such time, while covering her face with her hands, Meadow turned her head and glanced across sheepishly at Doyle.

'Hey, I close my eyes sometimes too,' Doyle winked.

She almost winked back, then continued watching the movie. The idea people were designed to be used by other people was horrifying. But she made it to the end.

'So?' Lottie said. 'What are your feelings on clones now?'

'I mean they didn't even know to start with,' Meadow said. 'They were doing their best.'

Lottie looked pleased at Meadow's answer.

'What did you think, Doyle?' Lottie said, a slight cautious tone to her question.

'I think it was a good piece of fiction,' Doyle slid forward on the sofa.

Lottie did not look entirely pleased with Doyle's answer.

Doyle, noting his daughter's expression, added, 'But if it's important to you I think the movie was great.'

Meadow pulled the lever, letting down her footstool.

'Better run, that took a bit longer than usual,' Meadow wondered if the pups had started gnawing at the treat cupboard again.

'Better get back to the grind too. Catch you next time,' Doyle stood and left the room with a 'hooroo'.

She had been meaning to ask Lottie more about his work. 'Does Doyle always work from home?'

'He spends so much time on the phone, I hardly see him,' Lottie said. 'Can you come over a bit later tomorrow. Say one o'clock?'

'That'll be fine,' Meadow stood too. 'What are we watching?'

'Tomorrow I'm going to show you about listening to

your gut,' Lottie said, with a lopsided smile. 'Kinda key.'

'My sister's always talking about trusting her gut.' Meadow opened the sliding door.

As Meadow walked across the soft grass, it felt light and springy. She smiled. They liked having her there. She even was optimistic that there hadn't been one incident with the hooded man since her sister left. Had he been someone who was infatuated with Indigo Bliss?

It had always intrigued her the way a group of men behaved when her sister strode by. They would become very quiet or loud and boisterous. Indigo Bliss usually seemed unaware of the attention.

But once her sister had told Meadow that while in town with Gran, a group of men had whistled, becoming quite raucous. Their grandmother had clenched her fists, telling them to grow up. Afterward, Gran had blurted out she didn't want Indigo Bliss to end up like her mother, pregnant at fifteen. Gran of course blamed the men for making her reveal that secret to Indigo Bliss.

It was such an odd thing to say in relation to her sister, who was close to twenty eight at the time, and the opposite of flirtatious. Indigo Bliss didn't have a coquettish bone in her body. For her sister to divulge this information was no trivial thing. It had been a memorable moment, as Indigo Bliss didn't like to dwell on such matters. Meadow added that to her list about her mother.

And what to do about Doyle's infatuation with her sister? Meadow's growing friendship with Doyle was in no way romantic, so when her sister returned, that decision was totally up to Indigo Bliss.

In fact, she was beginning to believe Doyle would have her back if she were in trouble. Sometimes, when listening for a thump at the front door, she'd begun to toy with the idea of telling Doyle about the hooded man.

She took care to bypass the lifeless fairywren again, trying to push it further away from the front gate with a stick. This was both sad and stomach-turning.

Once inside, she shushed the excited whimpers and knelt in the hallway. 'How is everyone going?'

After the obligatory sniffing session, Timba bounced all the way to Meadow's bedroom door. Tawny trotted beside her brother with Spencer following close behind.

They wanted out and were getting used to their new routine.

She pushed through her clothes, smelling of dried lavender. She stretched out her arms, feeling around for the door to outside to the small screened garden.

Later that night, she sat up in bed with a start, finding it hard to breathe. Someone was walking over the gravel near the front door. The pups started at her side; Spencer leapt to his feet. She quickly flashed the torch onto her watch; it was past midnight. Meadow lay back, her heart thumping palpably, almost distracting her from the knocking. Frozen, she made a decision. She wasn't going to run to the window, nor move toward the front door. She wasn't going to look at the figure of that threatening man.

She would stay in her bed, quieten the pets and would not move or make a sound. She would listen for the sound of breaking glass. If that happened, she'd escape through her wardrobe and hide with her pups and Spencer. She'd been lulled into believing this intimidation was over and the disappointment was great. What did this man want with them? Did he know she was alone?

The thumping continued for so long she started humming a tune in her head in rhythm with the violent beats of the thuds, trying to drown them out. Eventually he stopped. She hoped he'd damaged his hands and not the stained glass.

Her throat was dry but she waited as long as she could before moving toward to the kitchen. Feeling around in the darkness, too nervous to take a candle or torch outside of her room, she quietly made her way to the sink. Reaching for a glass she knocked a plate from the sideboard and it shattered on the timber floor. When a second plate smashed to the ground she wasn't so sure it was accidental.

As a third plate smashed to the floor, the sound was cathartic. She felt an unexpected flood of warmth, as if her body was infused with relief. First the clock, now the plates. She was running a risk making so much noise. Was she coming apart, was the stitching of her life being sharply unpicked, like an internal tugging of fabric? She wouldn't tell Lottie about the hooded man because that might frighten her neighbour, but she would tell Doyle. He would know what to do.

As she swept up the plates, it dawned on her she could have harmed the pets. She promised herself that if an irresistible urge struck her again she would smash some eggs instead.

Chapter Fourteen

'So this is a bit more sciency,' Lottie balanced her plate precariously, 'but useful.'

Meadow had made devilled eggs for their snack and Lottie put so many on her plate they'd begun to slide in a perilous way. Meadow had also baked some cheese and onion stuffed bread rolls. Doyle stopped working in his office to see what the spicy aromas were. As Doyle plated himself half a dozen eggs, it didn't seem the time to tell him about the hooded man. Not in front of Lottie.

It was different visiting Lottie in the afternoon, and when Meadow had neared her gate she'd noted with horror that the lifeless fairywren was hanging from the bell on the gate. Turning her head from the pitiful sight, she ignored the gruesome message, hoping Doyle would know what to do.

She followed Lottie into the loungeroom holding her own plate of devilled eggs and a milkshake. She sat in her much-loved reclining chair, placing her cape onto the armrest. Lottie had recently remarked that it was her signature outfit and she supposed it was. Glancing up at the screen, she wondered how Doyle would react when she told him. Would he march over to the cottage to remove the poor fairywren? That might not be advisable. Perhaps instead he would calmly give her some suggestions about the hooded man.

Lottie pressed play and Meadow was presented with an image of something called microbiomes and a central nervous system. The microbiomes were shown in a variety of colours and looked beautiful when magnified.

Words slid across the screen, many she'd never heard of before, but when she saw that the gut-brain signals the central nervous system she hoped Indigo Bliss was using her gut on her travels.

'That's why it's important to trust your gut,' Lottie pointed from her stomach to her head. 'It's like having another brain.'

'Like when your stomach drops or you have butterflies?'

'Exactly,' Lottie stared at the screen as a new video rolled on. A man began explaining different vibrations and how they affect our bodies. 'Why was there a worldwide agreement to standardise tuning musical instruments to four hundred and forty hertz?'

Meadow glanced across at Lottie who nodded.

'That hertz stuff is a rabbit hole.' Lottie pressed stop. 'Especially if you're prone to seeing the sinister side.'

'Like you,' Meadow grinned. 'But why?'

'Well, the four hundred and forty hertz might've been a means of control,' Lottie said. 'Different hertz frequencies can harm or heal. You know, maybe they can program or deprogram.'

That was so surprising, Meadow's head flew back against the headrest. She never knew what to expect from Lottie, even with something as universal as music.

Meadow blinked rapidly, 'actually harm people?'

'I mean we're all a bunch of atoms, vibrating,' Lottie shrugged. 'You know frequency can change how things look. Even how we look. That's why I keep saying maybe there are things we would be able to see if it was the right frequency.'

'Like your dragons?' Meadow half-joked, because in truth, she wondered if she was on a different one with her field of vision.

'Maybe,' Lottie said, glancing at her notebook. 'You know how I'm into Nikola Tesla at the moment, well he said it's all about frequency, vibration and energy. And don't get me started on the fifth element, ether.'

Meadow recognised that look. A rant was about to ensue about Nikola Tesla. Meadow knew them off by heart, he invented most of the technology we use today, he was inventing limitless free energy and 'they' didn't like it, so had tried to erase Nikola Tesla from history. If Lottie started in on various movies about him she thought needed clarification, this could take a while.

'Better go,' Meadow climbed out of her recliner and fastened her cape. Now, in the afternoon, she'd missed the opportunity to talk to Doyle.

'Say goodbye to him for me.'

'You should go and say it to him. He'd like that,' Lottie pointed toward the kitchen. 'He's past the laundry and the third door to your left.'

Feeling even more like a part of the family, she made her way toward Doyle's office.

Nearing the closest door Meadow saw it was shut. She could hear Doyle talking in his office, with a booming voice on speaker. 'He's on the phone,' she murmured to herself, not sure if she should disturb him after all.

The second door was open and something caught her eye in the semi-darkened room. Bottles and jars full of pale pears lined up on two shelves. Inwardly she thrilled with pride. So Lottie had been preserving the pears.

Doyle said her sister's name.

'She's a fucking looker all right,' Doyle said.

'You should've gone with your head and not your cock,' the other voice projected from Doyle's office.

She cringed at his words as if she'd been slapped.

Her cheeks stung.

'I've learned the other one is easier to fool,' Doyle's voice was rough. 'I'm so close. She comes over every day to watch videos with Lottie.'

A birdlike cry escaped her.

Doyle was silent for a moment and Meadow stopped breathing. Had he heard her?

'I tried another visit last night but it's not working. No worries, I'm working on another angle.'

'Are you behind schedule?' the other voice said.

'Not really, I'm still analysing the specimens.'

At first understanding eluded her, then a wave of dread hit her in the gut. For a long moment she stood frozen, as was her way. She forced herself toward the second room.

Nearing the preserved pears she noted with horror the pears morphing into little bodies with feet and heads. Some jars appeared to contain small marsupial mice, floating in a clear solution. As her vision wobbled their pouches seemed to protract with liquid. Other jars contained larger spotted and striped specimens. She struggled for breath, tearing her eyes away from the jars of half-formed creatures.

Meadow felt a hardening of her heart that turned her belly to stone. She ran. She didn't even say goodbye to Lottie. Her mind raced faster than her legs, as she planned her escape, her cape flowing out behind her. She needed to get away. Doyle was the one who'd been scaring them at night. What would he do next? She had to find Gran and her sister. She didn't have a few hours, she didn't even have a few minutes.

Her chest tightened in panic. Even if he didn't know she'd overheard him, what did he mean that he was working on another angle? She looked at her watch, only a couple of hours of daylight left.

She ignored the fairywren hanging from the gate as if it wasn't even there, and entering the front door, was met by Timba, Tawny and Spencer with their usual welcome. They were so familiar after just experiencing something so horrific. She fell to her knees, hugging Timba and Tawny. 'Doyle's bad. We need to go.'

Her voice sounded broken, even to her own ears. She'd been so gullible. Spencer would never make the journey up the mountain. She rushed to the pantry, and threw in cans of Spencer's food, treats, his blanket and his toys into her shopping trolley. 'C'mon Spencer,' her shrill voice rang. Spencer was somewhat concerned as she collected the binoculars.

'No, no everything is all right.' She patted his head, which was difficult as her hands were shaking so badly. 'I'm going to take you to Bert for a bit, he's our old friend.'

As she opened the front door and ushered Spencer outside, he recovered quickly, happy to be out and about in the fresh air. 'This way old boy.'

She ignored the united expression of pleading from the pups lingering inside.

She kept turning to look back at the cottage, not knowing what Doyle might try next. She squinted through the binoculars. No one in sight.

On the way up the road to Bert's house she tried to steady her trembling legs, continuing to pivot and look through the lenses.

'Bert,' Meadow called, and heard some rustling near his front door.

'I'll be down to get the eggs soon,' Bert exited the door, adjusting his red scarf.

'It's not the eggs,' Meadow said. 'I'm sorry to ask this but could you look after one of our old darlings for a bit.'

Bert bent to give Spencer a welcoming pat. 'Remember me.'

Spencer wagged his tail and even held one paw out to Bert. She wondered if Bert was like Spencer's previous owner.

'Girl, you look like you've seen a ghost.' Bert gave her a look of concern, while glancing at her red cape with curiosity. She'd forgotten how safe Bert was, his words were like freshly cut hay, down to earth and full of future sustenance.

'I'm fine, really.' Meadow attempted to steady her voice. 'I know it's a big favour and I wouldn't ask…'

'Say no more.' Bert grabbed the shopping trolley. 'I'm assuming these are his things.'

'Yes.' Meadow didn't want to say any more. It might lead to tears and she didn't want to upset Spencer.

'I'm fine for eggs,' Bert said. 'Just stay safe, girl.'

The kindness in his voice was nearly her undoing.

Bert ruffled old Spencer's fur. 'I reckon it's about time for some tea, old boy.'

Spencer didn't even give her a backward glance. That helped. She turned on her heel, but waited until Bert was inside before peering through her binoculars again. No one near the cottage. No movement.

She felt a rush of adrenaline, sifting through several ideas as she returned to the cottage. She needed to think on her feet, and would lay out enough food and water for the chickens and Gertie to last them a while. The Hereford herd over the river had enough hay to fare them while she was gone, and access to water. She would pack for herself and the pups and trek to find Gran and her sister.

Gran always said not to let fear stop you, to just do it afraid.

She would not be distracted by the disturbing specimens imprinted on her mind.

One of her favourite memories was their grandmother taking them out to candle the chicken eggs. Seeing those little feathered bodies floating inside was like a revered tradition, alive with promise, not suspended in cold glass.

Who was Doyle and what had he done?

Those hours with her new neighbours had been the most enjoyable of her life. How ridiculous she'd been to think Doyle was her friend.

She'd almost told him about the hooded man.

And her other secret.

Chapter Fifteen

The pups were quiet when she entered the cottage. Snuggled together in a mass of tawny fur. 'It's okay.' Meadow tried to sound calmer than she felt.

The pups blinked at her for a moment then leapt up, sensing they were going outside.

'Yes, we are going on an adventure too. No more being stuck inside.'

She tried to remember details about the landmark Gran had talked about. The tree that looked like a woodsman. Her strategy was sound enough, to climb Sleeping Beauty, and search for the landmark on Collins Bonnet.

Except she'd never climbed the mountain before and had no map.

She found one of Gran's old backpacks and filled it with food and supplies. Luckily Gran had left a lot of home-made dried options for the pups. Her trembling had been replaced with a strange and unexpected composure. She turned on a torch and left it in the kitchen to make it seem as though the cottage wasn't empty.

Meadow threw off her cape and clothes before donning her wintery thermal underwear. She packed an extra pair in case she became drenched. Next she put on a shirt, vest, her yellow fleece-lined coat and two pairs of corduroy pants. Lastly, she packed the remaining torches.

Zipping up her last zip, buttoning her last button, she went to the back door. 'All right. Let's go.'

Her newly found composure fled. Her hands were shaking badly again, making it difficult to open the back door. Timba and Tawny ran toward the willow trees.

At the milking shed and the chicken coop she reminded herself to breathe, shooting glances toward Doyle's house. She couldn't see anyone about and suspected Doyle was still on his call. A small part of her wanted to march over to Doyle and ask him why he'd betrayed her, and how he could harm those creatures. Instead she concentrated on the willow trees lining the river. She would soon be hidden under the billowy green refuge of their weeping branches.

She observed Timba and Tawny standing near the stone seats. The scene was typical, her pups roaming amongst the old gravestones. This time though, their stripes were distinct in the afternoon sunlight, as the juvenile Tasmanian tigers turned toward her, looking for Spencer. 'He's fine. Today we go further,' Meadow whispered, showing the pups how to navigate the stones to cross the gushing, running water.

The look of eagerness on their faces was priceless but guilt settled over her. By now Gran would have made sure the young thylacines were going into snow gum woodlands, rainforest gullies, myrtle forests and marshes. The pups were unprepared. It would be hard going and the understorey of the terrains would be thick, the mossy rocks slippery.

She'd spoiled them. She had named them. She'd let them snuggle in her bed. Gran was going to be so mad about that.

She turned, and for a long moment took one last look at the cottage before pushing herself toward the top paddock. If the situation hadn't been so dire, she would have enjoyed the look of utter surprise from the pups, seeing the other side of the river. She ascertained where Rusty the bull was, as the red-coated cattle turned their white faces toward the pups. For a brief moment, she was concerned the pups might try to chase the cattle. Timba lifted an anticipatory paw and Tawny stood tensely.

'Stay, they might bite.' The pups stayed close to her side after that, surveying the cattle with a doubtful expression. Their attention shifted as above their heads a flock of swift parrots swam through the air in the blue cloudless sky. She had a little daylight left but the good weather might not hold for long. She didn't know what would happen next. Trying to unravel the gravity of their family legacy, the mission Gran inherited, was like disentangling a Gordian knot. If she couldn't find her sister or Gran she would go even further, to the other guardians.

Gran had told her about the guardians and that the Snug and Flowerpot Yarn and Weavers Group was a cover for a secret group. That it was formed after the Buckland and Spring Bay Tiger and Eagle Extermination Association was formed. That when Gran's grandparents heard of that Association, they'd decided to organise a group of guardians. The name needed to be ambiguous, something that wouldn't raise eyebrows as to their true mission. As Gran's grandmother had once lived between the townships of Snug and Flowerpot, she'd thought the name would be perfect camouflage.

Cryptic messages about the tigers, as the guardians called them, would be placed in the Saturday paper. No one would be sceptical about communications involving balls of yarn in different colours, and patterns representing different locations.

Meadow hoped these guardians would know what to do. At the very least she could warn them.

If she knew where to find them.

She hastened through the dense woodland, tripping, and pushing branches and twigs out of her way. She was so intent on escaping Doyle that at first she didn't register the branches or the scratches. After several minutes the scratches on her hands stung and she stopped to put on gloves. 'Wait.' She was once again surprised when the pups listened to her. They halted, their noses sniffing.

The pups watched her face, scrutinising her every expression.

The fragrance of peppermint-scented foliage filled the air. Like her fragrant gifts to Lottie. Had Lottie been in on it all along? She turned her face from the pups so they wouldn't see her dismay.

Meadow mainly stayed off the established tracks. Gran had taught them to only use these now and then. She tried to remember where the fire trails were located. Where the boulder fields and heathland were.

Of course Gran always advised against going near any ponds, waterfalls, walking huts or duckboards, as these were drawcards for hikers and tourists. She might get away with walking along a small creek. But she tried not to disturb spiderwebs or break low-lying branches, walking past ferns as tall as herself.

What would Gran think about the specimen jars? Recalling *Frankenstein*, she plainly remembered who the real monster was. Was Doyle the same monster but with a different face? Gran said a lot could be learned from *Frankenstein*.

Every noise, every crack of a stick caused Timba and Tawny to investigate. 'C'mon, we're not there yet.'

But she couldn't stop shaking. Even after the exercise warmed her enough to take off her fleece jacket, her teeth were still chattering. Was she in shock?

Numb, she passed evergreen trees of muted green, displaying their twisted creamy white trunks like gnarled statues.

Lottie had told her that 'mother' trees communicated and

nurtured saplings using fungi like a soil internet. Lottie had heard it was like a wood wide web. Meadow noticed a tree, an ethereal matriarch; its cream and grey branches seemed to umbrella the saplings below in a motherly fashion.

'My kefir,' Meadow frowned, remembering the two jars of the fermenting milk on the bench. She'd been growing kefir grains for Lottie, but they'd starve without a feeding. She supposed none of that mattered anymore.

After a stretch of rock hopping, she stopped at a small hill of boulders, observing the muted orange, green, red and yellow foliage growing among them. The subdued colours were like the watercolour painting Indigo Bliss had in her room, luminous, translucent and dreamlike.

The sky would soon darken, causing a new difficulty to arise. Though Timba and Tawny roamed and played at night they weren't acclimatised to sleeping out in the open in the freezing cold. Especially if it snowed. In the wild, tigers could find their own shelter in ferns, hollow trees or caves. She would have to find a lair for the pups.

She'd never been able to forget what Gran once told her about the last captive thylacine. The poor animal had died at the Beaumaris Zoo in nineteen thirty-six during a cold spell. Some suspected it had been locked out of its enclosure. Gran had learned that the daughter of the previous curator, who'd continued to work at the zoo after her father died, said she'd heard the distress of the animals at night, locked out of their shelter. She'd lived on the grounds but was without keys. When appeals to the new curator for keys fell on deaf ears, she went over his head. The end result: she was informed she wasn't to do nightly inspections, and so there was no need for her to have a set of keys.

Gran thought that the young woman had then been

pressured to leave. Not long after she left the zoo, the last captive thylacine died in the night. Her grandmother insisted that the girl had tried her best for that thylacine, who'd succumbed only a couple of months after they were finally given legal protection.

She drew the pups close.

The light had virtually gone, the sky still a soft vanilla. The trees were swaying black shapes, their branches like fallow deer with antlers losing velvety strips of soft bark. The scene resembled an old black and white photograph.

The bush felt ominous. In the dark, the familiar became unsettling. Was it the isolation? Or was it the fear of being followed that quickened thoughts of shadowy wraiths? She recalled Lottie's recent mention of Tasmanian Gothic, believing the landscape to be beautiful but treacherous, with secrets, unease and events from the past rising up to haunt the present.

Meadow was soon cloaked in a blackness so thick she relented and rummaged around to find her torch. That went against everything Gran had taught her about staying hidden. But she wanted to make progress before settling in for the night.

Once, she thought she heard someone whistling.

No one emerged. Was it the redback lady? The day that woman attacked Gran in town she'd grabbed Gran's arm so tightly that Meadow worried it might break. Had Doyle planned that?

She remembered the woman's frenzied eyes. Shaking Gran like a ragdoll, she'd screeched, 'I'll ruin you,' over and over, with crimson words. When Indigo Bliss fought her off, the woman had screamed that the lyrebird doesn't lie; that she'd destroy the Drearys.

It was all Meadow's fault. Before the attack in town, before the house next door was completed and before the veiled woman, she'd caught sight of that poor lyrebird standing forlornly under a willow tree, looking so dazed, she'd run back to the cottage to get some feed. She'd stepped over stones to the other side of the river and thrown the seed. The lyrebird had pecked it up eagerly. It had reminded her of the way Clover gratefully nibbled her food. After that, it was her evening habit to throw a handful of seed to the other side of the river. The lyrebird sometimes roosted in a willow tree, hopping down to eat the food.

Gran always kept a family of thylacines hidden near their cottage, often beside the river. A safeguard, to ensure the tigers' ongoing legacy if the unthinkable happened to the Drearys' other tigers hidden in the wild. Gran was adamant her thylacines would never attack their chickens or local livestock.

While their parents hunted in the bush, Timba, Tawny and their two siblings often remained close to Meadow, a trusted protector. The pups had been intrigued by the noises the lyrebird made. They would call out their own welcoming, noisy response. At first, it was cute when the bird began to mimic Timba and Tawny's juvenile coughing barks and distinct sounds. Too late, she found out the lyrebird was gone, and that the bird's mimicry might be overheard by someone else. She wondered where the lyrebird had gone with its new repertoire. Surely the mimicry of the lyrebird was what had sparked the assault in town.

Prior to that, Gran often accompanied the sisters on shopping day. But the sighting of the veiled woman had been the final straw. After that, Gran had split the thylacine who lived by the river into two groups. Timba and Tawny were to stay hidden at the cottage, while Gran took their parents and two of their siblings to search for the rest of her tigers. The fear was real that their other thylacines had been found.

Tawny was curled into a damp mass while Timba shivered at his sister's side. Meadow needed to focus. Their trip might take several hours. 'That's if it was daytime,' she said to the pups, 'and I knew where I was going.'

They'd made it over one ridge. If she could make it over one more rise, they would stop for the night.

Chapter Sixteen

Meadow searched for shelter along the untrodden path.

She travelled in a serpentine fashion, zig-zagging over rocks and saplings. The torch highlighted patches of snow, settled deeply between the rocks. Her feet were like ice, and her nose and cheeks were burning. The pups ears and backs were cold to her touch.

She knew the next part of their journey would get even steeper; some sections might be impenetrable. But if she could get them over the next rise that would mean more distance between Doyle and the pups. Soon enough, the terrain was so vertical she was puffing, so unfit next to the pups. She felt a stab of relief when they finally slowed and began to pant themselves.

'Nearly there,' she said, breathlessly. 'You're too big to carry now.'

But she knew they were not nearly there at all. The colder she became, the more she tried to push every thought of Doyle away. She couldn't push away the fact that he must have been planning this for some time.

He'd planned to frighten them, hoping they would run to him for help. He hadn't won over Indigo Bliss but she had almost reached out.

The trio slowed their pace as she searched for a place to rest. Near midnight, she spied a small cave, a warm and dry lair. It was not yet the top of Sleeping Beauty, but they could go no further.

She dropped her pack onto the ground, trying to catch her breath. The earthy smell at the entrance calmed her. Inside, she was once again thankful for the torch, using it to find the flattest section of the rocky sand for her sleeping bag. She dared not light a fire. Instead she ate some of the cheese and onion bread rolls she'd baked for Lottie the day before. She washed them down with cold water. They did not taste the same. They were hard and bitter.

The pups ate home-made dog biscuits, with water in a bowl. Meadow tugged the silver emergency blanket out of her pack for an extra layer. After eating, the pups snuggled either side. She patted each head, thinking she'd almost let Doyle weasel his way into her life. When she looked into their questioning eyes a chill ran through her, as images of the specimen jars filled her mind.

She loosened her hair from its braids, letting warmth flow over her shoulders and arms like a soft blanket. Her teeth still chattered.

Tawny was quiet, but in a cautious way that Meadow hadn't noticed before. Perhaps Tawny sensed their adventure was a dangerous undertaking. Even Timba was withdrawn, staying close to her without his usual peppiness and wriggles. She gave them both extra ear rubs.

Her head tilted toward the entrance of their lair, listening carefully. The only surprise appearance she wanted was from Gran and Indigo Bliss. But in the end all she could do was keep the pups warm and alive and hope Spencer was safe with Bert.

She winced at the memory of Doyle's words. The way he'd spoken callously about her sister, the way he'd sneered about her foolishness, laughing at her gullibility, so full of disdain.

As if sensing her misery, the pups moved closer, and began to lick salt from her cheeks.

She resettled them. Her eyes were heavy but she didn't want to sleep. She might dream of the way Doyle had enjoyed intimidating them at night. She dug her fingernails into her palms, trying to keep herself awake.

As thoughts of Doyle assaulted her she pictured the experiments, like sun-ripened pears that morphed into little bodies with heads and feet. Little bodies lying motionless in their transparent liquid caskets.

The last thing she remembered was warmth from the pups sidled next to her. Then nothing, until the sun shone outside their lair and two nuzzling noses poked at her sleeping bag.

She'd slept in longer than expected. It was already mid-morning and she kicked herself for wasting precious time. It was a quick breakfast for endurance, and she ate some boiled eggs, cheese, walnuts and biscuits. With all the extra exercise the pups were hungrier than usual and she gave them seconds, wishing she had the raw meat her sister normally organised for them.

She rolled up her sleeping bag, tied her fleece-lined jacket around her waist and slung her pack over her shoulder. She moved toward the majestic profile of Sleeping Beauty, thankful at least it wasn't raining.

Her pack dug into her shoulders as she leapt over fallen logs and slid down boulders. They climbed over a rise that took them closer, entering a terrain where everything living was squat and stunted. The bristly heath plants of green and an occasional reddish-brown were mostly up to her knees. The trees were short and sparse, with dead tree trunks peppered throughout.

The three of them were so visible she half expected a hand on her shoulder at any time. And it was becoming difficult for the pups and herself to walk through the boggy terrain.

Her goal was to find the woodsman landmark. She could visualise no further. 'C'mon,' she said, walking away from some large, moss covered rocks where the pups were sniffing coral-like fronds growing upon them. 'Let's go onto the drier boulder field.'

By midday the air was chilling and the day turned bitter cold. She took several deep breaths. The air was so pristine it drew even deeper into her lungs, cleansing them. She didn't stop for lunch, aware snow could be right around the corner.

In the light, in some ways she felt safer up here on the mountain than she'd been in her cottage.

A strange calm came over her.

Although chilled, scratched and dishevelled, she welcomed an unexplained surge of strength. Taking another deep breath she savoured the moment. As the wind picked up she had a shiver of excitement. Her hair danced behind her like wisps of flaxen smoke. She remembered Lottie's observation about her hair fascination.

She wondered at Lottie's belief that frequency can change how we look. Was there a frequency on the mountain that made her more courageous?

Had she become more like her sister?

There was no escaping all of Lottie's theories, even on a mountain.

The temperature dropped and she put her jacket back on, wrapping her blue knitted scarf around her neck.

She heard a noise in the distance. It was either a person or a heavy wallaby. 'Shhh,' Meadow sank to the ground, grateful that Timba and Tawny moved close to her side. She narrowed her eyes, looking through the binoculars, her heart pounding. The rampaging noise stopped.

What if the pups saw a wallaby or pademelon? Gran always said that genetically, the thylacine was the top predator of the food web.

The noise started again and she peered through the binoculars. She could only see vegetation. But the pups were agitated, turning their heads to one side, listening, looking as if they were going to run.

'Please, please, please don't move.' Meadow blinked rapidly.

Their bodies tensed. Within an instant the pups were free from her grasp and racing toward the noise. She dropped her pack and charged after them, picking up a branch for a weapon.

Entering a small clearing, she saw something so unexpected that at first she cried out with relief, 'Oh, it's you.'

Chapter Seventeen

Lottie stood, shivering in her grey gym gear, pink puffer jacket, and novelty kitten hat. Her neighbour had a leather tote bag thrown over one shoulder and her pink nail polish was out of place in the isolated wildness. Observing Lottie's pink lace-ups; it didn't seem the right location for them either.

Lottie was staring at Timba and Tawny with a mixture of wonder and incredulity. The pups looked at Lottie with curiosity. Tawny nuzzled Lottie's hand, as Timba bounced with excitement, wearing a look of disbelief that he'd found another person.

'I can't trust you, get away from us.' Suspicion filtered through Meadow. 'How did you find us?'

Lottie held out her palms upward, imploring Meadow to listen. 'You've got it all wrong.'

Meadow flailed her arms, beginning to wield her stick in what she hoped was a threatening manner. 'I will not let you take them!'

Her voice sounded shrill again, unfamiliar.

'I don't want to take them, or harm them,' Lottie said.

'Is Doyle with you?' Meadow checked the clearing. 'Are you in on this together?'

'No. I'm by myself,' Lottie said. 'That's why I changed times, I wanted you to hear him, to know he was caught up in…'

'What?'

'He's in over his head and is always on the phone with that man in the afternoon.'

'Are you saying I should trust you?' Meadow tilted

her head to the side, trying to rationalize why Lottie had changed her visit to the afternoon.

She began to strategise how to get the pups away from Lottie.

Lottie locked eyes with Meadow imploringly then bent to pat the pups. 'There's so much I wanted to tell you but I was too scared to.'

Meadow held her breath.

'I always hoped…' Lottie observed the pups, 'that our consciousness of yearning would manifest them somehow.'

Meadow lowered her stick and proceeded to call the pups to her side. They came to heel straight away. She sighed with relief, but her body swayed slightly. Her vision started to wobble. She must not hyperventilate, not now.

'You stay there,' Meadow pointed one shaking finger at Lottie. 'I need to think.'

'I'm trapped,' Lottie said. 'Without me it'll be bad for him.'

Meadow felt a twinge of empathy for Lottie she knew she couldn't afford.

'What does he want with my pups?' Meadow's voice cracked.

'It's complicated,' Lottie said. 'He thinks he's competing against those resurrecting the thylacine.'

Meadow wrinkled her nose.

'But unlike the others, he's not doing it the right way.' Lottie nodded toward the pups, 'so he really needs them.'

'But how did he find us?' Meadow knelt between the pups, placing a hand on both Timba and Tawny.

'He heard about your family from an investigator,' Lottie said. 'A rumour about a lyrebird.'

'It was a woman wasn't it?' Meadow was right, it had been her own blunder all along. 'What did she look like?'

'Doyle said she's an attractive redhead,' Lottie bit her lip nervously. 'He thought she was probably onto something.'

'Sounds like redback lady,' Meadow murmured to herself, 'Did she take Gran? My sister?'

'I don't think so,' Lottie said. 'Something changed, she wasn't meant to talk to your Gran.'

'She did more than talk.' Meadow stared at Lottie, 'I was there. I saw her attack my family.'

'I didn't know.' Lottie began wringing her hands. 'All I heard was that she talked to your Gran and now she's gone.'

'Like Gran and my sister,' Meadow barely whispered.

'She'd been pushing Doyle 'cause so much has gone into researching the thylacine already,' Lottie said. 'I was told someone is also trying to bring back the woolly mammoths using Asian elephants,' Lottie looked impressed. 'I think they've engineered woolly mice.'

'Are they close?' Meadow clenched her jaw. 'I mean with the thylacine.'

'Much further ahead than Doyle,' Lottie said, 'but still without a live thylacine.'

Meadow's heart skipped a beat.

'Without them, I think it takes a lot of experimentation.' Lottie shook her head at the pups. 'And patience.'

Meadow pushed away images of little snouts and feet in jars. Doyle must've been cutting corners.

'Doyle's been closely following how modified genomes from grey wolves have evidently recreated Dire wolves,' Lottie said.

That sounded impressive.

'Imagine mammoths roaming the coldest landscapes to help restore them. Kind of phenomenal,' Lottie said. 'I read that the last mammoths were trapped on an island and that helped them live longer. I suppose Tassie could've been like that for the thylacine.'

Their Island, a protection of sorts for so many years.

'The Dire wolves gave Doyle hope,' Lottie said. 'But he doesn't like being left behind.'

'But why did he use such tiny creatures?'

'You'd know better than anyone that thylacine babies can be small like a grain of rice,' Lottie said. 'Makes them easy to transfer to a host species. I wonder if one day they'll use an artificial uterus device.'

That would make her grandmother lose it.

'Then a preserved tiger head was found in a bucket at a museum.' Lottie said. 'I heard they've almost completely sequenced the genome of the thylacine. It's a step closer to ecosystem restoration. But now…'

Meadow stood. 'Gran must never find out about that poor pup's head.'

'It was an adult thylacine,' Lottie shrugged, 'not a pup.'

'Gran made me call them pups,' Meadow said, 'in case anyone overheard in town.' She wouldn't let it slip Gran and the guardians called them tigers, better not to mention the Snug and Flowerpot Yarn and Weavers Group.

Lottie said, 'He was so close to making a move, but wanted to win you over first.'

'How could you do that to us,' Meadow said, 'to me?'

'The valley was meant to be a fresh start,' Lottie stared at the ground, 'and by the time I found out what Doyle was up to, we were friends and I didn't want to lose you.'

She sadly couldn't trust a word Lottie said.

'How did you find us?' Meadow already had the sinking feeling she'd left herself wide open with her torch usage.

'I followed you when you came back from Bert's,' Lottie said, 'into the bush, and when it got dark I tailed your torchlight and slept nearby.'

Lottie shook visibly.

Was she agitated, or just cold.

'I accidentally dropped my hiking tent off a cliff this morning,' Lottie said. 'I didn't sleep much anyway with all the screeching and growling last night. I understand why people get so freaked out.'

A forbidding chill seeped into Meadow's chest and she tucked her blue knitted scarf into her jacket. The pups fur was cold to the touch too. She was torn. On the one hand, her gut told her Lottie was telling the truth. But could she trust her own judgement after being betrayed by Doyle so easily?

Lottie tried to warn her, to let her hear the truth from Doyle's office.

'He keeps attracting bad actors,' Lottie said, wrapping her arms around herself tightly, 'but I already lost my mother. I can't lose him too.'

'You lost your mother?' Meadow said, staring at Lottie, who like Gran, had been reticent in discussing absent mothers.

'Doyle says,' Lottie sighed, 'I'm a clone of her.'

A look of puzzlement crossed Meadow's face. 'You don't believe that surely?'

'He might have the skill set.' Lottie held her hands together as if in silent prayer. 'Can I come with you.'

'Well I can't let you go anyway.' Meadow pursed her lips. 'In case you tell someone.'

'I would never do that to you.' Lottie's eyes widened beseechingly.

Her pleading face reminded Meadow of those times the pups wanted to win her over.

'I'm going to check your bag,' Meadow took Lottie's leather tote bag, 'while you empty out your pockets.'

Lottie ruffled Timba and Tawny's fur while Meadow rummaged through the contents of her bag. Meadow would smash a phone to pieces with a rock if she found one.

All she found was a coil of rope, packets of corn chips, carrot sticks and some fizzy drinks.

Handing back Lottie's bag, Meadow had a sudden thought. 'Why did you bring rope?'

Lottie shrugged, 'I thought it might come in handy for climbing.'

Meadow held the pups close to her side. Lottie half sat, half fell onto the ground. She was pale, and her eyes were downcast.

Meadow wasn't used to seeing the self-assured Lottie like that. 'Sit there while I get you something to eat and drink.'

'I've got snacks.' Lottie's hand trembled as she tried to open her bag.

'Have something more filling.' Meadow reached into her own pack and handed Lottie some biscuits, a couple of boiled eggs and a drink of water.

Lottie ate them ravenously.

'Thanks, I was dizzy,' Lottie said, her eyes brightening.

'Just sit for a minute,' Meadow instructed, while looking for Doyle, or others through her binoculars. She had so many questions. 'Who else knows?'

'Apart from that guy on the phone, there could be others.' Lottie stared at a half-eaten boiled egg.

Meadow turned this over in her mind. 'Who?'

'Umm...' Lottie gave a wan smile. 'I did something to Doyle. I didn't really want to. It's going to make him angry.'

What would that be?

'I gave him sedatives I found in his office,' Lottie said, closing her eyes. 'I couldn't think what else to do. At least it should give us a few hours head start.'

'Will he be all right?' Meadow wasn't thrilled about Doyle's behaviour but didn't want Lottie to get into trouble.

'I followed the instructions,' Lottie nodded slowly. 'Then flushed the rest down the toilet. We've got a septic tank so I thought that'd be okay.'

How had Lottie administered the sedatives. In a milkshake? She rummaged through her pack, retrieving the silver emergency blanket and placed it around her neighbour's shoulders. Lottie shivered into it with relief.

Meadow sat on a nearby rock continuing to keep watch. Timba was exhausted, and lay at her feet like a sphinx with closed eyes. Tawny jumped onto the rock and tucked her head under Meadow's elbow.

She was concerned for Lottie's health, and also that this was a ploy planned by Doyle. But perhaps Lottie did have her best interest at heart. She let Lottie rest.

It took some time before Lottie was strong enough to continue.

'We've got a couple more hours of daylight,' Meadow stood, looking at the sky. 'We'd better go.'

Lottie stood too, the blanket still wrapped around her shoulders.

'Stay in my footsteps,' she instructed, gesturing for Lottie to follow. 'We'll try to keep Doyle from knowing you are with me.'

They walked in silence for some time; the only sound was the squelching of Meadow's boots in the bog. Timba and Tawny, oblivious to any danger, were ecstatic at Lottie's inclusion. They'd never met a new person before and danced around Lottie, sniffing her with curiosity.

'They are so beautiful,' Lottie halted, catching her breath. 'I still can't believe they're real.'

Meadow narrowed her eyes, trying to see if Lottie had hunger in hers. All she saw was wonder and surprise. She opened her mouth, then closed it. She was reluctant to share too much information with Lottie. Not now.

'The pups must come first. I can't tell you anything about them.'

'Understood,' Lottie said. 'I watched a video about people searching for thylacines. 'Cause they haven't been extinct that long. I mean were…'

Meadow stared at Timba and Tawny, at their distinct dark stripes, their thick rigid tails. The pups wolf-like heads and long snouts were so familiar to her. She turned to Lottie. 'I get why.'

'So many people are looking for them and groups have been organised,' Lottie said, 'not to mention sightings by National Park Rangers.'

Meadow remembered Gran's newspaper clippings.

'Nowadays people leave camouflaged wildlife cameras out to try and catch a glimpse.' Lottie scanned the area. 'It's like a hobby, or a mission.'

'You mean there could be cameras watching us,' Meadow said.

'Probably in other areas,' Lottie said. 'I didn't think they would be in the valley.'

Meadow stopped herself from answering where the Drearys' thylacines had originated. She wondered what Lottie would think about Gran's retelling of the legendary 'Ghost of Huon Valley' that had gripped her as a child. After reports that a thylacine phantom had been spotted in Glen Huon and Ranelagh, a flock of sheep had allegedly been driven into the Huon River. Sightings progressed to Mountain River. Gran had heard it may have been a large, brindle dog, its coat pattern resembling tiger-like stripes.

This story would always be followed by Gran's assertion they must protect their tigers at all costs.

Lottie dropped her eyes to the ground. 'I tried to stop him making those poor creatures.'

'The ones in the jars?'

'He put them in the old oak tree,' Lottie grimaced. 'I tried sneaking out a couple of times, but...'

Meadow's stomach flipped, remembering the mournful sounds coming from the old oak tree.

'The rejects he calls them,' Lottie said. 'Doyle said he was doing it for me, for us, so we could stay in one place. He kept trying to get fat-tailed dunnarts...'

Meadow swallowed hard.

'I wanted to tell you...'

She felt queasy, just as she always was when Gran told her stories of how the thylacines were mistreated. But there were admirers who'd been kind to thylacines. She'd never forgotten the story of the young female tiger, living with a bushman who'd nursed her to health. Eventually he set her free and the tiger returned a couple of years later, showing him her pups.

'Apart from Tasmanian tiger they have so many names,' Lottie said. 'Marsupial wolf or striped wolf.'

'Tassie tigers or Van Diemens land tiger.'

'Or Tasmanian wolves,' Lottie added. 'I've heard they were sometimes called zebra opossums or zebra wolves.'

'Native hyaena, hyaena tiger,' Meadow winked at the pups. 'Or Tasmanian panther.'

'Greyhound tiger or bulldog tiger,' Lottie stared at their stripes.

'Tiger wolf, Tasmanian zebra or dingo.' Meadow said. 'Or Opossum-hyaena.'

'How about the dog-headed-pouched-dog,' Lottie said. 'Something like that anyway.'

'Thylacinus cynocephalus,' Meadow added, 'and I think there are even more names.'

Lottie smiled genuinely at Meadow, making full eye contact. Her neighbour was certainly acting as if there hadn't been any betrayal on her part.

'Do most people call them pups?' Lottie said. 'Or joeys?'

'Probably joeys,' Meadow said, 'but I'm so used to calling them pups.'

Chapter Eighteen

At dusk the wind whipped violently through the treetops. Meadow found it hard to hear Lottie, as her words were whipped away. She stopped at a clearing surrounded by large boulders, with a mint-green ground cover.

The clearing hindered the wind but the air was as icy as an arctic breeze. She looked around for a cave or cluster of rocks they could hide in. After a while she found a space big enough for them all underneath an overhanging rock that provided a windbreak.

Lottie was rubbing her eyes, as if she needed sustenance again. Meadow lit a fire at the entrance, hoping they were concealed and far enough away from prying eyes.

With the fire lit, she boiled the billy and heated some soup with dumplings. Lottie continued to be quiet, mesmerised by the fire. Meadow had the unsettling thought that Lottie's appearance might all be a ploy, a way to delay her further. Was it some kind of performance? Lottie's unexpected arrival had slowed them down. She should've been at the landmark by now.

'We need to find that woodsman in the morning,' Meadow said. 'Then I'll know we're on the right path.'

'Woodsman?' Lottie's cheeks glowed by the fire. The warmth from the soup had transferred to Lottie's face.

Meadow tried to recall what she'd been told about the woodsman. It was an old tree with a gnarled face, branch-like arms and appeared to be holding a wooden axe or staff. Meadow fished with her spoon for a soft dumpling, trying to push aside the niggling feeling that Lottie had never been her friend. 'A tree that looks like a man.' Meadow said, not believing that at that very moment, she was planning what she would do if Lottie tried to harm the pups. If need be she would tie Lottie up with the rope from her leather bag.

'You're good at this bushcraft stuff' Lottie gave her a relaxed smile. Lottie cupped her hands around the warm mug, the pups at her feet. Even with the emergency blanket Lottie still occasionally shivered. Meadow reached into her pack and gave Lottie her spare thermal underwear and thick socks. 'This will help.'

'Thanks.'

'They'll be too big but at least they'll warm you up. I'll turn around.' Meadow pivoted, feeling the warmth from the fire on her back. She called the pups to her side, listening for any indication that Lottie might try to run. But there were only rustling, dressing sounds.

'That's better already,' Lottie said, the thermal underwear shirt hanging to her knees.

Meadow looked at Timba and Tawny with their near-closed eyes and wide-mouthed yawning. She stood, putting the fire out and covering it with sand and stones. Further into the rock shelter she laid her sleeping bag on the ground.

Lottie followed her inside. 'I'm exhausted.'

'Yes, time to rest,' Meadow said, noticing white, floating particles outside.

'It's snowing!' Lottie leapt up, the silver blanket flapping around her shoulders as she stuck her hands out, trying to catch the snowflakes. Timba and Tawny joined Lottie, their tongues lolling at the cold and wet sensation.

There'd been nights at the cottage when flakes were floating, and she'd enjoyed watching the cherry and pear trees being sugar coated with snow.

But now was a different story, snow would make their journey harder tomorrow. Outside the cave, the snow continued to gently fall, and as she predicted, began settling on nearby rocks and dusting them with powder.

'Come back inside,' Meadow ordered the three, who with dragging feet complied. Timba and Tawny snuggled next to her on the sleeping bag.

She closed her eyes. The pups jerked their heads. Their ears pricked, their noses rising into the air. Something rustled nearby. She gestured to Lottie, placing a finger to her lips. Meadow waded toward the entrance in her sleeping bag. The pups followed, eyes glittering with excitement. She placed a hand on the back of each pup, gripping stripy fur.

A scrambling, thumping noise became clearer. It was a pademelon or another marsupial. The pups wrenched from her grip, bounding after the by-now startled animal. She turned on her torch and spotlighted their excited, spirited bodies before the pups ran toward something out of sight. 'No, no, no,' Meadow shrieked, turning toward Lottie. 'They're chasing something.'

They were fast. There was no way she could catch them. She continued to flash her torch around, but she couldn't see the pups through the falling whiteness. She stared out into the dark of the night and the white of the snow, both a curtain between her and the young thylacines.

Which direction had they gone?

She called out their names until she was nearly hoarse. Some distance away, she could hear scuffling. Her legs shook so badly she sat back onto the dirt with a thud. If only she'd brought the leads left behind by the old darlings. She knew Gran abhorred the idea of thylacines being led around on a leash, but better that than being captured by Doyle, or lost.

'Fetch me your rope,' Meadow said.

Lottie pulled it from her bag, bringing it to her.

Meadow rummaged in her own backpack for a knife, then started cutting the rope in two, thinking she could tie a harness over each of the pups. It was her fault; she hadn't given the pups raw meat for days.

'Please come back,' Meadow's jaw clenched while she sawed furiously. The rope frayed as she sliced the knife back and forth, and for a moment she imagined sparks.

'Should I go out there?' Meadow turned to Lottie despairingly. 'Or stay so they can find me?'

'I could go and look for them,' Lottie offered. 'Or you go and I'll stay here.'

Meadow shook her head. She didn't want Lottie alone with the pups, no matter how much she wanted to trust her again.

'They've got an amazing sense of smell haven't they?' Lottie said.

'I can't remember.' Meadow blinked, trying to recall, her mind a blank.

'But they should be able to track back to where we are,' Lottie urged.

Lottie was trying to give her some hope, but what if the pups followed the scent all the way back to the cottage. To Doyle.

'You don't understand they might be the last two left,' Meadow said, not looking up from her severing task. 'What if the other groups have…'

'Other groups?' Lottie said.

She held up her hand to signal she couldn't speak on it further. She stood, moving toward Lottie, wishing she could explain about the others. It occurred to Meadow that it was difficult to walk with a knife and not appear menacing. She lowered the knife.

'Are you okay?' Lottie's eyes flashed.

So many thoughts were running through her mind; should she wait, or go?

'How about I take your mind off things?' Lottie offered, her gaze flitting around the shelter.

Meadow shrugged distractedly then sat before returning to her task.

'Antarctica,' Lottie began, with a dramatic flourish. 'There's something weird going on down there. Probably tunnels and entrances going to who knows where.'

Meadow continued cutting the rope.

Lottie put her head to one side and said, 'Continue?'

Meadow absentmindedly nodded.

'And you know I heard scientists have discovered strange radio waves coming from under the ice.'

Meadow stopped sawing the rope and flashed the torch around again. Nothing. She was still torn between following the pups into the night, or staying put so they could find her. She continued cutting.

'I wear my mother around my neck,' Lottie said, touching her throat.

Meadow almost dropped the knife. 'What did you say?'

'Doyle had a memorial diamond of my mother made for me to wear.' Lottie pulled a thin chain from her neck and held up a pink diamond, sparkling in the torchlight.

'Do you remember her?' was all Meadow could muster.

'She died when I was a baby,' Lottie said.

'Lottie,' Meadow said, wondering at the odds of them both losing a mother as an infant, 'that is…'

'They used her ashes for the diamond,' Lottie shrugged. 'We are carbon-based I suppose.'

Meadow studied Lottie for a moment, swallowing hard.

'I keep dyeing my hair this colour.' Lottie held out a

long strand of red-gold hair, 'it's apparently the same as hers. It's hard work because I'm a brunette.'

Lottie's eyes were a sea-green ocean, a storm of pain, eyes lined with dark fronds of seaweed. 'It used to make me feel like I was closer to her. But now...'

Something shifted in Meadow, another hardening, and the curious sensation she wasn't quite herself. Heaviness swept over her in such a way she felt ready to walk off this mountain. Leave all of this chaos behind.

After all she'd done for those pups, and they'd run away without a backward glance, without one thought of how she might be worried about them.

The world was not what she thought, Lottie had showed her that. Could she even trust that Gran knew what was best for them anymore?

'Meadow,' Lottie called, clicking her fingers.

She saw Lottie through a filter of confusion.

'I feel safe with you,' Lottie was saying. 'You make people feel like they can…you know, be themselves.'

She gave Lottie a polite smile.

She knew what Timba and Tawny were doing out there.

She had no right to judge her pups.

She made a decision: she wouldn't run.

What did Gran always say? There is a strength in all of us we've forgotten about until we need it again.

Chapter Nineteen

There was a sound outside. Meadow turned to see two familiar wolfish faces coming toward her. As they neared, the pups seemed vampiric, covered in blood. Gran would seethe at the suggestion that like vampires, the thylacine sucked blood from their victims, allegedly preferring to drink from live prey. It frustrated her grandmother that anyone would buy into the blood-feeding controversy. Gran thought surely they knew carnivores often attack their prey about the neck. Her grandmother would also argue that in her experience the tigers enjoyed organs but weren't necessarily selective eaters.

Meadow had never witnessed the pups hunting so wasn't sure. But viewing their bloodied mouths, she could imagine lore of Tasmanian werewolves. She breathed deeply, then spoke in a calm, reassuring manner.

'Come on my pups,' Meadow said, all fake kindness. 'What have you been up to?'

She knew what they'd been up to.

The pups licked blood from their paws and for the first time Meadow was strangely nervous of her charges. Gran had been furious that in the horse and buggy days, people had reported 'attacks' by thylacines. Gran thought fear was the government's way of controlling the narrative. Othering them. According to her grandmother, any aggression shown was because the poor animal had been caught in a trap or was cornered.

But Meadow had read unease from some bushmen and tiger-men describing encounters with thylacine. Some recounted the tigers tendency to follow people in the bush and their relentless pursuit of marsupial prey. Gran had said they'd stretched the truth, wanting to demonise the tigers further, while boasting of their own bravery. It was always best to concur with her grandmother on thylacines. But now, as Meadow watched the satisfied pleasure the pups took in cleaning the blood off themselves, the hairs on the back of her neck stood up.

Tawny glanced up at her, almost apologetically, her face now clean. Tawny's expression was sweet and familiar again. The same pup Meadow had cuddled after her parents went with Gran. The thought that anyone would trap or harm her Tawny was beyond horrific. She held onto the ropes with a white-knuckled grip.

Timba gazed outside, seeming to want another escapade. There was nothing to do but do what she must. Their satisfaction turned to surprise as she harnessed a rope smartly around each pup.

'Come on, enough excitement, let's get some sleep,' Meadow said.

It was difficult to be tough on them, but she was willing to do anything not to suffer through that again. Timba and Tawny snuggled next to her, one each side as was their way, but this time they shrugged and twisted from the encumbrance placed upon them.

The young thylacines seemed shaky, yet apprised of a certain rite of passage.

'No worse than humans killing for meat,' Lottie stared at Meadow for a moment before closing her eyes.

'Hmmm,' Meadow groaned without further comment. She watched Lottie through sleepy eyelids, expecting a conversation from her neighbour about why Antartica looked so whited-out online.

Lottie, however, fell asleep so soundly that when Meadow

relit the fire before first light, she didn't wake.

It had stopped snowing outside. But it seemed to her the snow never wanted to surrender its icy grip on many Tasmanian mountains.

Once the damper was cooked, Meadow shook Lottie awake. The pups helped, nuzzling Lottie's face with relish. Lottie sat up in surprise, rubbing her eyes and looking around wildly for a moment.

Lottie looked like a ragamuffin kitten with fur the colours of amber and apricot. Lottie's hand rubbed at one marmalade pointed ear, as if grooming herself.

'What? Have I got a spider on me?' Lottie patted herself, looking for the offending pest.

'Don't stop talking,' Meadow urged, staring intently at Lottie. Noting Lottie wasn't wearing her novelty kitten hat.

'O-kay,' Lottie said, 'why are you looking at me so weird?'

Lottie's words were glass-blown bubbles of honey and butterscotch mingled together, full of warmth.

'Am I?' Meadow blinked rapidly. 'Oh it's just... nothing.'

An amused smile touched Lottie's lips.

'I can tell it's something,' Lottie said. 'Come on, spill.'

A transformation had taken place before Meadow's very eyes. 'I can see your words in colour now. Your face is different. Like a ragamuffin kitten.'

Concerned, Lottie's fingers felt her face as if she thought Meadow might be delusional. 'I'm not following you. A kitten?'

Meadow gave her a slow smile. 'It's something I've had since I was young.'

She had a sudden desire to tell Lottie everything. It was such a relief to share her secret, with someone so open to curious and wild theories.

Lottie shook her head in disbelief. Her kitten ears were like radars, conflicted and cautious. 'That's pretty mind-boggling, even for me. I'm not sure...'

Meadow waited, hands clasped tightly.

Lottie stayed silent for some time.

'I thought you of all people would be open to something different,' Meadow frowned, breaking the silence, her chest tightening.

'I am, it's just unexpected, that's all,' Lottie said, looking confused. Then she seemed to shift her thinking. 'So you didn't see me like this until today?'

She nodded.

'Is it like my spirit animal or something?'

'I don't know anything about that.'

'Or maybe it's my aura?' Lottie said, 'my biofield?'

Meadow shrugged, 'I'm not sure why I see things differently.'

'Do people resemble chimeras, or hybrid creatures of mythology, you know like mermaids?' Lottie said, 'Is it disturbing, like that uncanny valley thing?'

Meadow didn't have a clue what Lottie meant by uncanny valley.

The notion others might find what she saw disturbing hadn't occurred to Meadow. 'It's not scary, it's actually mostly beautiful.'

'Well it's beyond fascinating,' Lottie eyes shone. 'I'm going to research this.'

Meadow could only imagine what Lottie might discover.

'When we get home I'll...' Lottie said, her eyes closed tightly shut.

Meadow was pulled back into a grim reality. There would be no more visits to Lottie's, no more sitting in front of the television in her favourite chair.

Another uncomfortable silence ensued.

'Hang on.' Lottie stood, and inclined her head. 'Maybe it was those pills he was giving me.'

'Pills?' Meadow said. 'The sleeping pills?'

'No, pills Doyle said I needed to take, you know, cause of the clone thing.' Lottie's kittenish eyes stared down at Meadow. 'I stopped taking them when I ran away.'

'You can't believe that,' Meadow said.

'Well, he's always talking about cloning,' Lottie shrugged, her head lowering. 'So I thought.'

Cloning was such a familiar word to her now. She kept looking from Lottie to the pups and back, trying to think of what to say. Perhaps the change in Lottie had something to do with the pills, or perhaps it was merely getting away from the charade.

'Enough about all that,' Lottie said, before sitting closer to the fire, pulling the emergency blanket tightly around herself. 'What kind of animal are you? What colour are your words?'

Lottie's yellow words bubbled energetically in the firelight, like one of her fizzy drinks.

'For some reason,' Meadow said, 'I've never been able to see myself that way.'

'Intriguing,' Lottie said.

Meadow gave the pups what she hoped was a reassuring smile. It must've worked because Timba stood on his hind legs for a moment, giving her one paw. Tawny reclined into Meadow and stayed there.

'Well, from now on,' Lottie said in a self-soothing voice, 'I'm going to get Doyle away from those people.'

Meadow wasn't sure about her thoughts on that yet.

Lottie ran her hands through her hair, trying to dislodge twigs and leaves twisted throughout. 'I don't suppose you brought a brush with you?'

'I packed in a rush.'

Lottie stood again, and moving toward Meadow, gave her a hug. Lottie was slight. Meadow patted Lottie's back in what she hoped was a sisterish manner.

'Well, let's eat our damper before it gets cold. This is the last of Gertie's ghee.' Meadow smothered ghee and apricot jam onto the damper. She gave Timba and Tawny some dried meat, but they turned their noses up at it.

As Lottie relaxed in front of the fire, Meadow saw her neighbour in a completely different light. Lottie even blinked more.

She felt a conflicted sense of relief at having Lottie with her. Gran had been right, Meadow was a companionable person.

They ate with the relish of being cold on the outside while warming themselves on the inside.

Chapter Twenty

They left the shelter before first light, with Lottie still apologetic for delaying them. Meadow continued to hope that had not been intentional. The goal was to find the woodsman landmark that morning.

Outside, she stood for a moment observing the stars overhead in the brightening sky. She shone the torch on shivering, snow-dusted trees and crevices filled with white. On the ground Meadow saw bloody pawprints mingled with once-pure snow. A chill ran down her spine as she pointed out the mangle of scarlet slush to Lottie. It showed which direction Timba and Tawny had absconded from.

'At least they came back.' Lottie stared at the miserable sight.

Meadow's shoes crunched into the snow as she leaned over, ensuring the pups' harnesses were snug.

The pups tried to wriggle free and she wished she could make them understand.

'And careful with the melting snow, it'll be slippery on the rocks.' Meadow pointed further ahead. 'We'll try to go on established tracks now and then.'

Timba and Tawny, confident in their newly found hiking skills, tried to race ahead. The makeshift harnesses stopped the pups in their tracks, but her heart still skipped a beat with each lunge. 'You have to stay with me.'

She was watchful for approaching threats as they would be visible. The morning sun made the snow look whiter and brighter still. The pups began to eat it, shaking their heads at the cold. Timba went back for another bite.

'I've been worrying about drones.' Lottie stared up at the sky.

'What's a drone?' Meadow didn't like the sound of that. She clenched the ropes tighter still.

'It flies in the sky and takes aerial images,' Lottie said, her words a concerned and serious shade of mustard.

'Does Doyle have one of those?' Meadow stared upward too. It was obvious how noticeable they would be in this low-set terrain.

'I'm not sure,' Lottie shrugged, her thermal shirt still hanging to her knees.

Of all the things Gran had taught them about not being tracked, Meadow had no idea how to avoid a drone or blood in the snow. Maybe they could travel at night instead. 'Can they film at night?'

'I think so,' Lottie gave an exaggerated sigh.

She had to make a decision. 'If it makes no difference day or night, let's keep going.'

'I'll keep an eye out,' Lottie said, turning to look up at the sky again.

They trekked in silence for several minutes. Lottie said, 'If a drone comes where will we hide?'

She surveyed the open, sparsely vegetated space. The scant trees, growing sideways from blustery weather, would not conceal them. She pointed to a rocky hillock of boulders nearby. 'Maybe behind rocks like those.'

'That's a plan.' Lottie slipped on her novelty kitten hat.

For some time the four continued walking in a line of sorts, the pups pulling ahead, followed by Meadow, then Lottie in her footsteps. They began to climb another rocky knoll, plotting their way over an area like a flat river of rocks.

She continued to scour the terrain, trying to find any message or clue that Gran and Indigo Bliss might have passed by. Sometimes the pups pulled so forcefully and hard Meadow's feet nearly slipped out from under her.

The pups were almost foaming at the mouth to get loose. She didn't think she could cope with another carnage.

'You want me to take one?' Lottie said.

Meadow focused on her stinging wrists and aching arms for a moment. The more time she spent with Lottie, the more she believed Lottie to be trustworthy, but after last night she couldn't risk the pups escaping.

'Not yet,' she answered over her shoulder. 'I'm too nervous they'll run again.'

'It might help if you give me your binoculars,' Lottie said, holding out her hand.

She handed them to Lottie, who at the top of the next rise, scanned the mountain tops above them.

'Can you see the landmark?'

'Not sure,' Lottie said. 'Wow, Sleeping Beauty is sprinkled with snow too.'

She peered at the head and hair of Sleeping Beauty. Beauty's powdered face was a marble sculpture. She was reminded of a travel book her sister had shown her, displaying a similar reclining belle. If Meadow squinted, she imagined Beauty's eyes might open, revealing lashes covered in eye-catching white mascara.

With foreboding she waited for the powdered face to turn, for Beauty's eyes to slide toward her, cold and narrowing. An eerie chill ran down her back. Elementally, did Beauty know Meadow had put the thylacines in danger once more?

'Some people think that mountains are petrified giants,' Lottie said.

Meadow remained alert, remembering that poem about mountains being hunched, brooding beasts asleep.

'I always thought Beauty was beautiful,' Lottie said. 'But this feels quite gothic, like we're being led toward…'

Meadow found herself surprisingly relieved at Lottie's unease.

'Hang on. There's something that might be a tree,' Lottie gushed, 'about the height of a man, I guess. Yes, definitely resembles a man.'

Meadow gave Lottie the two ropes to hold and grasped the binoculars. She peered through them, trying not to look directly at Beauty's powdered face. There was a tree-like form, twisted in a distorted fashion, as if possessing a pair of arms. 'That's not far from here.'

She'd led them to the mountain top, to the landmark.

Once atop Collins Bonnet her foreboding vanished.

Sleeping Beauty was herself once again, a reposed guardian, shielding the valley.

There was a triangle of steel nearby. But that wasn't the landmark she was looking for.

She kept the group moving. As they neared the tree Meadow viewed the gnarled face, and what looked like an axe or staff against a wooden arm. Up close, it was quite the likeness of a person but there were no notes, or any trace of her family. Someone had placed a grey woollen scarf around the woodsman's neck, but when she searched for a message, it was what it was, an abandoned scarf.

She took the ropes from Lottie and tied Timba and Tawny to a nearby rock. Shrugging off her pack, she gave water to the pups. Turning in a full circle, Meadow tried to find anything that could be construed as a sign.

Lottie produced an orange can of fizzy drink, corn chips and carrot sticks from her bag. 'Want some?'

She shook her head at the luncheon of orange. She offered the pups liver treats, but the pups turned away.

'You can see so much of the valley from up here.' Lottie crunched on corn chips. 'There's Huonville and the river too.'

She sat and viewed Mountain River, a sleepy huddle of farms, a patchwork of green and gold squares. She wished she could go back in time, back to her cottage, before the lyrebird, before the redback lady and veiled woman, a time when her family were at least together.

'No one can touch us up here.'

Meadow gave Lottie a strained smile. It was not yet midday and she wondered if Doyle had started searching for Lottie yet.

'Do you want to travel?' Lottie continued to munch. 'Like your sister.'

'I've never really thought about it,' Meadow said with indifference. She had though, she'd thought about it a lot, and the idea of leaving made her middle flutter with uncertainty.

'No surprise where I'd go, if I was allowed.'

'Let's get out of here in one piece first.' Meadow cleared her throat and rummaged in her pack for a snack. 'We have to be careful of tourists up here.'

Timba was straining his neck to get close enough to nibble at the carrot sticks in Lottie's hand. Lottie looked at Meadow questioningly, who nodded, and Lottie let the pups have a stick each.

'We might have to go further, toward Trestle Mountain over there,' Meadow said. 'Gran calls it Beauty's bosom.'

'Bosom,' Lottie smiled, 'that's such an old-fashioned word isn't it.'

She supposed it was.

Their break over, her legs ached as she stood, and her stomach ached too. Perhaps from too much exertion while trying to hold the pups back. She checked Lottie wasn't leaving a trail of corn chips like some kind of feline Gretel.

The air was still crisp as they hiked, the sky now a vibrant blue. Though the sun warmed their heads and shoulders, the wind began to gain force. It grew so fierce it pushed her backward, forcing her to lean into her pack to balance. Even her teeth were cold, so Meadow wrapped her scarf above her chin.

Timba and Tawny were getting annoyed at the ropes again, trying to slip out of their restraints. 'I'm sorry,' she said to them both, 'it's wearing on me too.'

At least they were being restrained by someone who cared. She'd heard so many stories of how thylacines were mistreated. One such time, Gran had disclosed details about the poor female sent overseas in a box so small, she couldn't turn. The tiger's young had been concealed in her pouch. Meadow had thrown up and Gran had been mad, blaming the people who had captured the thylacine all those years ago. Blaming those who'd attacked thylacines for killing livestock. Gran believed dogs had attacked sheep and that their tigers were scapegoats. Her grandmother would go as far as to say thylacines were too weak-jawed to hunt adult sheep.

Indigo Bliss had tried to calm their grandmother, making the point that, historically, people have done horrible things to other people too.

Privately, her sister would say to Meadow that when livestock were important, putting food on the table, people wanted to protect them and of course some may have jumped to conclusions. Unlike Gran, Indigo Bliss thought that possibly there'd been instances where thylacines had been opportunistic predators or had instinctively killed sickly livestock.

Lottie continued surveying the sky through the binoculars.

'Hey Meadow.'

'Yes.'

'Do you see animals with different faces,' Lottie said, 'like people faces or something?'

No one had ever asked her that. 'No,' Meadow said, 'never have.'

'What are you going to do when you find your Gran and Indigo Bliss. I mean about the pups?' Lottie's yellow words became dull and faded, a mingling of an old egg yolk and damp straw. 'And me?'

She hadn't thought that far. She'd presumed Gran would know what to do. 'I'm not sure.'

'I mean it's out now. Maybe your only option will be to go public.'

The idea was so shocking to Meadow she could hardly wrap her mind around the concept.

'You mean, tell people?'

'Yes,' Lottie took off her kitten hat and stuffed it into her bag.

'But, all these years we've hidden them, protected them,' Meadow said. 'Gran will go bush before she'd let that happen.'

'Trust me, once the truth comes out there'll be no stopping it,' Lottie said. 'We are in the information age. And then there's the surveillance capabilities these days.'

She pondered that for a moment. How dangerous would it be to tell the world. Surely people would be on the first plane over to see the truth for themselves.

'You'd have to be smart about it,' Lottie said. 'But I'm sure there'd be a way to mitigate it.'

'Gran will know what to do,' Meadow answered, hoping that like everything else, her grandmother would. But there was a niggling doubt. Gran had never taught them about so many of Lottie's theories, especially regarding time, the moon and that history was skewed.

Surely her grandmother could be counted on as an expert when it came to the thylacine.

It was hard to forget the photo her sister had showed her of a captive thylacine with a chicken in its mouth. Indigo Bliss said that people still speculated if the photo had been staged. Many said the image had been cropped, so people wouldn't notice it was filmed in an enclosure. Surprisingly, a few thought the photo might have been a setup using a taxidermy tiger.

Meadow had stared at the image, not sure if the tiger was alive or taxidermy. She definitely leaned toward alive but, either way it was a puppet. If it was staged, why? How much propaganda had been a form of sabotage? Her sister wondered if back then portrayal of the thylacine had also been driven by competition between states for wealthy settlers.

Indigo Bliss had warned Meadow she'd better not ever mention the dead chicken photo to Gran.

What propaganda could be used on their tigers today? Could the world be trusted to know the truth? As they continued their journey toward Trestle Mountain, shoes and paws making sucking noises in the mud with every footstep, Lottie said under her breath, 'Shhh.'

Chapter Twenty-one

Lottie had the binoculars trained on something in the sky.

'Is it one?' Meadow wished it would snow again, or even that a sudden blizzard could conceal their location.

'I think so,' Lottie's voice trembled. 'But it's off in the distance, heading toward Mount Wellington.'

Meadow glanced toward Kunanyi. Perhaps there was a darkish speck. Lottie handed her the binoculars. She peered through the lenses with difficulty at first as the pups tugged on their ropes. After Lottie offered to hold the ropes, Meadow clearly saw a dot, a small object that seemed unsure about which direction to take. It turned.

'C'mon,' Meadow sludged toward a cluster of boulders, through the boggy mud. 'Let's hide over there.'

But behind the rocks, she witnessed Lottie's face fall.

'He'll just fly over and see us from the other side,' Lottie squeezed her eyes shut.

The blood drained from Meadow's face.

'You stay here,' Lottie walked backwards. 'I'm going to steer him in the wrong direction.'

'You can't do that,' Meadow said, 'I don't think you should go back.'

'I'm worried someone will…that without me he's going to do something he'll regret.' Lottie sped up her backward gait. 'By now, he probably saw the bloodied snow, so I'll tell him I looked for you everywhere but couldn't find you.'

She was speechless. How could she let Lottie go to him? She glanced at the pups for an answer. They stared back. It was a familiar conflict. She'd been raised to believe that the thylacine were as important as people, if not more. Gran would never understand Meadow leading the pups toward danger.

'I'll come get you,' Meadow shouted, 'as soon as the pups are safe.'

'Don't make any more noise,' Lottie called back, the wind whipping at her seafoam words. Lottie turned and ran in the direction of the drone.

Meadow stepped into the shadow of the boulders, retrieving bones from her pack for the pups. She needed to distract them from Lottie's departure, and soon the pups were gnawing quietly, seemingly oblivious. Gripping the rock with her fingers, she had to stop herself from going after Lottie.

Meadow wondered how Doyle would react. Had he realised Lottie had sedated him? After several minutes she squinted through the binoculars again. In her gym gear, Lottie was running a marathon, flitting and bouncing over the boulders.

Finally Lottie stood at the woodland edge, waving her arms, signalling to an object hovering above her. She couldn't see what words Lottie was saying, but through the binoculars she saw the thunder of them. Lottie stood, her hands balled into fists, with utterances that were like a storm of lightning bolts in yellow and rust. The drone dropped from the sky as if struck by one of Lottie's volte-face bolts.

Lottie picked up the drone, walking further away from Meadow's rocky hideout. Sure enough, after some time a tall man, flicking his fringe to one side, left the edge of the woodland.

She sucked in her breath as Doyle stomped toward his daughter. She saw Lottie gesturing in the direction he'd just come, not once glancing back to where she hid. She wondered if Lottie was telling Doyle the story she'd promised, that she'd searched for Meadow but couldn't find her.

She winced when Doyle pointed at Lottie's thermal shirt, still hanging to her knees. Her stomach dropped, she should have told Lottie to tuck that in. Even from a distance, she didn't like the way Doyle's words were heated. It shouldn't have come as a complete shock after what she'd overheard in his office. But she was finding it hard to connect this Doyle with her cheerful and welcoming neighbour.

Lottie ducked her head and changed tack, pointing in another direction, this time toward Meadow.

Doubt struck her so hard she felt winded. Was Lottie leading Doyle straight toward the pups? Had the sedation story been a sham?

Doyle took the drone from his daughter. Lottie folded her arms as Doyle turned his back on her, surveying the terrain. Lottie called to him, pointing again in the direction of the woodland edge, toward Meadow's hiding place but not as close.

Doyle stamped his foot impatiently before surveying the area again. He wasn't sure. He was guessing. After several minutes Lottie continued to redirect her father toward the tree line away from Meadow, nodding her head encouragingly.

Lottie was sending him on a wild goose chase, and it looked as if it was working.

After the thermal shirt debacle, he must have known Lottie had been with her, so Lottie had to play the game. In the end Doyle took the suggested course, and followed his daughter's lead. Relieved, she waited what seemed an age for their return.

They didn't.

'C'mon.' Meadow picked up the gnawed bones and shrugged on her pack. The pups turned to look for their new friend.

'We'll see Lottie later.' The pups had experienced so many losses in such a short time, Gran, their thylacine family, Indigo Bliss, Spencer and now Lottie.

Timba and Tawny followed, falteringly at first, as she hiked toward Trestle Mountain. Her arms and legs were aching, and when she visualised Lottie going back, she grimaced.

Leaving Lottie guilted her.

She kept up a stumbling pace and began to feel dissociated from her legs, as if in a fugue state. They felt like someone else's. Her surroundings resembled her thoughts, bleak and dismal.

It was as if she were just a bunch of atoms, vibrating and blending with the landscape.

Lottie would enjoy that.

The pups eyed Meadow strangely as she journeyed in such a bleary-eyed, clouded state.

No one was in sight but the feeling of being watched was hard to shake.

Timba and Tawny sniffed in the air, their noses scaling upward.

Chapter Twenty-two

'What is it now!' She focused on where Doyle and Lottie had been. 'Are they back?' Meadow rubbed her eyes, which were watering from the cold wind.

A group of people emerged from a cluster of stunted trees, travelling toward her. They were in colourful hiking gear with packs and hiking poles. She couldn't see any of their features as they wore ski-masks or beanies. Some had scarves wrapped around their chins.

There was no doubt in her mind the hikers were going to walk close to where she was. And the pups would want to greet the newcomers.

There were no large boulders to hide behind so she hunched, wondering how to inconspicuously make it to the woodland, further down the ridge and out of sight. It was a fair distance and would mean backtracking later, but was her only option.

She tossed her hair from her face, grabbed the ropes tightly and made a desperate attempt to escape. It was hard going and the mud sucked at her boots in such a way that she was losing one every few steps. She needed to hop on one foot, balance her pack, hold the pups, and retrieve one boot after the other.

After several minutes, one of her boots became so stuck she couldn't dislodge it.

She eventually left it with the pull tab and heel sticking out of the mud, like a submerged brown duck with only its beak showing.

Hobbling with one bare foot through the mud, now up to her ankles, Meadow was sure the hikers would hear the squelching of each step. She turned to glance over her shoulder and saw the trekkers. But it didn't appear they'd noticed her yet.

'Faaark…' She grimaced at the pups, leaning against a tree, with mud caked up to her shins. 'Fuck everything.'

The pups turned their heads to one side, momentarily unsure. Was it the swearing, or that her voice sounded so dejected? She had no memory of swearing before. The old threat of mouths being washed out with soap had worked well in her case. In spite of that, it felt curiously cathartic, the same as throwing a plate, but without the physical shattering she had to clean up.

She held Timba and Tawny close to heel, her hands shaking as she stared through her binoculars. There was a film of mud on the lenses. Were the hikers tourists, or people searching for thylacines? The idea of this group walking past her boot caused her hands to tremble again. All she could do was move further into the woodland and wait them out. With one bare foot that was difficult. The undergrowth was a tangled mess of branches and spiky rocks.

She almost entertained the thought of dashing back out to retrieve her boot, but she'd be too visible. She'd never manage it without unmasking the pups. Definitely not with an excitable pup attached by a rope to each arm. And if she tied the pups to a tree they might escape or start making a racket.

It didn't take long for the hikers, trekking over the well-travelled path, to be adjacent to her. Her teeth were chattering as she heard their playful banter. Their laughter stung, where once she would have smiled. Their words filtered through ski-masks and scarves as multi-coloured slivers, a vivid prism. As she peered closer their words were like a bright and beautiful mosaic of adventure.

Her bootless foot was seriously freezing. She was having difficulty feeling her whole foot, not just her toes. Odd words from the group drifted across, '…over here—a boot—check it out.'

She hid behind a tree, hoping the group would grow bored of her boot. She closed her eyes tightly. Thankfully, when she opened them, the vibrant group looked on the cusp of continuing on.

Until one of them gestured at pawprints on the ground. Two of the group took a few steps and followed Timba and Tawny's prints. To Meadow their pawprints had always looked distinct, resembling crowns. The sleuth duo stopped momentarily in the ankle deep mud, surveying with interest.

She'd done it again. First the lyrebird, then the torch and now the pups were about to be exposed for all the world to see.

She knelt next to the pups, eyeballing them both, begging them in a silent mime not to make a sound. She was ready to make a run for it, boot or no boot.

She stared through her binoculars again, concentrating on the two closest hikers. One wore a novelty ski mask of a fox, and the other a cow hat similar to Lottie's kitten one. These two, a man and a woman, stared closely at the prints. The cow hat had a pair of horns with little cowbells attached. In other circumstances Meadow would have thought it quite amusing.

She heard clapping, and turned toward the sound, as did the group. The hikers followed the direction their heads were now facing, and moved toward the loud noise. Like our cattle, she thought, and her lips twitched. Gran always said to watch the direction of a cow's head, especially with a calf. If the head was pointed straight at you and went down, back away slowly. Meadow snorted at the image of the horns and little cowbells. A terrible, horrifying thought crossed her mind. What if she started to laugh hysterically and couldn't stop herself.

It had happened before.

She tried to think on anything sad and unpleasant, anything that would stop her from laughing. She concentrated on the loss of those she'd never known, like her mother, father and grandfather. She thought about how she had damaged the grandfather clock, and the plates. She thought of the specimen jars. Of Lottie's diamond.

It worked.

She waited until the hiking group were well out of sight before gingerly leading the pups toward her stuck boot. Timba bounced, playing jump rope with his harness. Tawny appeared more like Meadow, uncomfortable, uneasy, and spattered with mud.

She'd only taken a few paces when there was another noise up ahead, out of sight, from the direction of the clapping. A different sound, followed by laughter. Was it the group coming back?

She froze. The sheer disappointment was almost too much. She needed her boot but first peered through the binoculars. She couldn't see clearly over the slight rise, but it sounded as if more hikers were coming back her way.

'We are never going to get out of this,' she frowned, staring through the muddy lenses again. Two people were moving toward her. They were waving goodbye to someone over the rise. She assumed they were waving at the recently retreating group of hikers.

One small, the other an hourglass in lilac.

Then all became clear: she observed a petite woman, her waist-length salt and ginger hair blowing in the bitter wind. She spotted Gran's grey cloche hat.

Beside her, a posture of strength and home. Indigo Bliss.

Chapter Twenty-three

Timba and Tawny were beside themselves, pulling forward and squealing as she squelched her way toward her family. Where had they been? Gran was wearing Grandfather's olive green jacket, the one that hung past her knees, almost reaching her sturdy hiking shoes. And Indigo Bliss, she was the same as the day she'd left the cottage, except she was now holding Meadow's muddy boot.

The pups were ecstatic. She could hold them back no longer. They broke free, bounding toward Gran and Indigo Bliss.

Gran gasped at the ropes. 'I said to your sister they were tied up.'

'I had to, Gran,' Meadow wrapped her arms around her grandmother's neck. She was comforted by Gran's mountain pepper scent. 'If they escaped one more time I might have lost them forever.'

'You did it afraid.' Gran's hatted head came up to her shoulder, and she patted Meadow's back with vigour. 'You brave girl.'

'Where are the others?' Meadow said, surprised Gran was clinging onto her so tightly.

'Our tigers are safe,' Indigo Bliss tugged at the rope harnesses.

'Yes, their parents and young ones are in a secure place,' Gran said. 'Your sister tells me you've named these two Timba and Tawny.'

Meadow glanced past Gran's shotgun, slung on one shoulder, toward her sister.

Indigo Bliss said, 'I thought it would be better if she was prepared.'

Good, her sister had already taken the sting out of it.

'We've been watching you since Charlotte went with Doyle,' Gran said. Hugging now over, she stepped back and gave the pups an affectionate pat. 'It was their parents that alerted us. They knew.'

'They started making such a fuss,' Indigo Bliss shook her head. 'After a while we realised what that meant.'

'We've been circling and waiting to pounce, especially after we saw those hikers heading toward you,' Gran said. 'We didn't want the young pups to see us, not with others about.'

She watched her grandmother's anchor-silver words, carrying the strength she admired so much, keeping the world from going adrift.

'Doyle has been awful to Lottie,' Meadow blurted. 'He told her she was a clone of her mother.'

'He did, did he? Well he better look out because I'm going to bring that man down a peg or two,' Gran had a ferocious glint in her eye.

'A clone?' Indigo Bliss raised one elegant eyebrow. 'I told Gran what he was like but that's even worse than I'd thought.'

Meadow stared at her sister's violet words, like wild heather in a field, so wise and yet hardy.

'Did your gut tell you that there was something wrong with him?' Meadow asked her sister.

'But you must have felt it too,' Indigo Bliss said. 'That's why you're here.'

Her sister was giving her a look of respect; to her it had been perfectly obvious who Doyle was. Meadow had needed a full-blown revelation to kick her intuition into gear.

'We've been doing some digging with the other guardians,' Gran said. 'I thought you'd be safe at home.'

'I wanted to come back for you,' Indigo Bliss said. 'We've got a hidden shack close to here. And Gran knows shortcuts.'

'Your sister was livid when the guardians voted against her going back to the cottage,' Gran frowned. 'We've never had a breach like this before.'

'I get that the guardians are panicked,' Indigo Bliss said, pursing her lips to stop herself from saying more.

That news didn't come as a complete shock to Meadow. It was their family creed. She wondered, not for the first time, what her mother had thought of the creed. Indigo Bliss had once quietly joked that if they had a coat of arms, it would display impressive thylacines, but no one outside the family would be allowed to see it.

'I've been so busy getting them all together and organising our path ahead.' Gran supported Meadow as she slipped her muddy boot back on.

'I promised I would help Lottie,' Meadow wiped her muddy hands on her thighs.

Gran glanced around in a watchful manner. 'That we will.'

'He had jars of…I thought they were preserved pears, but I think they were hybrids with spots and stripes,' Meadow blinked. 'Others were like marsupial mice.'

Gran sucked in her breath, 'I didn't think he could be more vile.'

'I told you he was revolting, Gran,' Indigo Bliss said.

Exactly the response she would expect from her family.

Indigo Bliss looked at Gran. 'What's the plan?'

'You take the young ones back to the others, and fill in for me at the meeting,' Gran turned to Meadow. 'We are going to get that girl.'

Indigo Bliss moved toward Meadow, giving her a gentle side hug. 'Well done you.'

Her sister's words were a cloud of thistle puffs and she wanted to absorb the unexpected softness as she returned the hug. 'What was the clapping about?'

'Gran put on a real show and fainted,' Indigo Bliss gave a lopsided smile. 'So I clapped and called them over to help me.'

'When they arrived, they got me up. We all had a laugh that I was wonky on my feet and carrying a shotgun.'

She wondered if it had been uneasy laughter from the group.

Indigo Bliss gave a wry smile.

'Anyway, I recovered quickly,' Gran said with a wink.

'And when they mentioned the boot and prints…' Indigo Bliss said.

'I told them the boot belonged to a friend who'd phoned us,' Gran said.

'I think Gran's performance made them forget about the prints,' Indigo Bliss said. 'But we were nervous the pups might make a sound or run toward us.'

She understood that nervousness well.

'Give these back to Juke,' Gran handed Indigo Bliss a pair of binoculars. 'I want you to tell the guardians it's worse than we thought and we'll have to discuss Plan B.'

Indigo Bliss nodded, then her voice softened, 'Spencer?'

'He's all right. I took him to Bert,' Meadow said.

'Sensible,' Indigo Bliss relaxed her shoulders.

'After you've filled them in I want you back at the cottage,' Gran said. 'Do you remember the shortcuts?'

Her sister did.

'Right, it's mid-afternoon, so I'll have us at the cottage a bit after dark,' Gran said.

'I don't know how my legs are going to carry me,' Meadow stared at her still-trembling legs. They didn't seem to be responding to her will at all.

Gran ruffled Timba and Tawny's heads before turning to Meadow. 'Make the most of this flat part because we'll be on a steep descent soon. Let's get Charlotte.'

She wondered what Lottie would say if Gran called her Charlotte.

Indigo Bliss left the way she'd arrived, but with Timba and Tawny beside her. Meadow, who a moment before was too exhausted to walk another step, followed her agile grandmother with renewed strength. They made their way along a boulder field as Gran assessed the direction they would take.

'At least without the pups we don't have to worry about being spotted,' Gran said.

'Except by Doyle.' A cold wave of dread washed over Meadow at the thought of him.

'Hopefully your friend Charlotte has persuaded him to continue on that wild goose chase,' Gran said.

'I'm sure she tried.' Meadow, manoeuvring around several large boulders, hoped Lottie was her friend.

'Does he carry a weapon?' Gran adjusted the shotgun sling on her shoulder.

'I have no clue,' Meadow hadn't noticed a gun at his house. 'You wouldn't really shoot him, Gran?'

'I don't make a habit of shooting people, Meadow,' Gran's eyes narrowed. 'But he's in my bad books.'

She saw the fierce protectiveness in the set of Gran's soft cheeks.

'Charlotte took Doyle through there,' Gran pointed toward a woodland tree line further along. 'We won't go that way.'

Her grandmother had the best navigation skills.

'I thought I'd lost Timba and Tawny,' Meadow said, 'but they came back, Gran. I couldn't believe it when they came back.'

'Tell me why you named them.' Gran closed her eyes momentarily. 'Why you kept them in your room.'

'It just kind of happened.' She tried to redirect the conversation. 'Why weren't you there the first full moon?'

'I couldn't get back in time,' Gran said, 'from trying to warn the guardians.'

She'd like to meet these guardians, like her sister had.

'I'd already put all the newspaper ads in the Saturday paper, and it took some time for us to get sorted and meet at the old shack. I didn't want to endanger anyone's tigers.'

Now that she'd climbed Sleeping Beauty, she could picture Indigo Bliss that first time, standing alone beside the woodsman. It must have been bitterly disappointing for her sister to arrive alone, bracing against the hostile wind, only to depart that way also.

'But as you can see I made it for the second full moon,' Gran adjusted her cloche hat.

'What ads?' Meadow said. 'And what's Plan B?'

'You know how our lot are,' Gran gave a knowing smile. 'I put in an ad saying I had four balls of beige yarn, but had misplaced two smaller balls, and needed a pattern for a striped cardigan.'

Although she hadn't followed the nuances of the Snug and Flowerpot Yarn and Weavers Group too much, her sister had said that balls of yarn meant thylacine, and a particular pattern meant a specific shack to meet in.

'Well it took a while, as you'd expect,' Gran said. 'Our guardians are normally like an intelligence community, each one protected from knowing the whole. Not anymore.'

It was surreal to be walking beside Gran again, to be immersed in her grandmother's fortitude.

'So fill me in,' Gran guided Meadow past a ditch. 'We've got a bit of a hike anyway.'

She told Gran about her visits to Lottie's house and the videos they'd watched. She left out the really fringy videos, as Lottie referred to them, and explained to Gran why she'd broken the rules.

Gran stayed silent.

'Lottie is suspicious of the government too,' Meadow pushed aside a bare branch. 'And propaganda.'

'Good traits to have.' Gran steered them toward a tree-lined ridge. 'I must admit I'm intrigued about some of the other things she told you.'

When her grandmother heard Lottie had been so fearless she said, 'I like the sound of her more and more.'

Gran stopped for a moment, dislodging a stone from her boot.

'And the cottage wasn't the same, it was creepy,' Meadow crossed her arms with a shiver.

'No wonder, after the hooded man,' Gran said before continuing. 'Your sister had a feeling, that's why she wanted you to go to Bert if you needed help.'

'I still can't believe it.'

Her grandmother reached across to Meadow. 'If I was there I would've given him a scare that's for sure.'

'I wished you were there,' Meadow said. 'Visiting Lottie helped.'

'Of course,' Gran said, 'you always were such a friendly girl.'

'I nearly told him, Gran. I almost told Doyle about the hooded man.' Meadow could only imagine how deceptively charming Doyle would have been about that. Would he have patted her hand and spoken golden words of comfort?

'We're sure it's him, aren't we,' Gran said. 'That Doyle's

the hooded man.'

'It's him.' Meadow began to feel hot and changed the subject again. 'So what's Plan B?'

'It's not what we wanted to do,' Gran grimaced, ' but it's going to be hard to put the genie back into the bottle.'

Chapter Twenty-four

'It's the drone.' Meadow knew what to look for this time.

Gran frowned. 'Give me the binoculars.'

'It's flown by remote.' Meadow handed the binoculars to her grandmother. 'So Doyle could be anywhere.'

'Well we can't let it go near Indigo Bliss and the pups.' Gran's eyes hardened. 'We must keep it focused on us until I can bring it down.'

Lottie had simply bought them time.

'Must've got it out of that poor girl.' Gran gave back the binoculars and held up her shotgun. 'There's no time to hide. Check no one is around, I'm going to shoot it.'

'I can't see anyone.' Meadow looked through the binoculars in search of people, watching the drone close in on them.

'Flying pest,' Gran murmured. 'Not fighting fair.'

They stood still, waiting. Meadow continued searching for hikers as Gran lined up her shotgun.

'Good,' Gran said, 'closer, that's it, a little closer, you miserable flying spy.'

The drone headed toward them and descended menacingly. Gran took aim and fired. Through the binoculars she was sure something glinted and bounced off the drone. 'I think you winged it, Gran. Keep going.'

She was not concerned about the loud crack, she was used to occasional gunshots ringing out from the various farms in their vicinity. She watched as the drone began to understand its plight and tried to flee.

'You're not going anywhere,' Gran muttered from the side of her mouth as she reloaded.

Her grandmother aimed, fired, and hit the target.

The drone twisted like a cone, spiralling toward the ground. 'Good shot.'

Gran nodded with a smile that conveyed she'd had no doubt whatsoever.

'Should we grab it?' Meadow said.

'Too cumbersome,' Gran said. 'But I'm sure I despatched it.'

'Doyle's nowhere'. Meadow looked through the binoculars. 'He might even be flying it from his place.'

'I haven't a clue how these things work,' Gran said, 'but I wouldn't put it past him.'

'It takes footage so he probably realises we're heading back,' Meadow said, 'to help Lottie.'

Gran slung her shotgun back over her shoulder and trotted at a pace Meadow could hardly keep up with. 'Let me show you my shortcuts.'

Her grandmother went down ravines, past caves, over creeks and shortened the trip by so much that a couple of hours after dusk they'd entered the top paddock of their property. All without using the torch once.

As they neared the willows they saw no trace of Doyle. There were no lights on in their cottage. The torch she'd left on must've gone flat.

They crossed the river further along to bypass their darkened cottage and reach Doyle's brightly lit house.

Meadow checked for Doyle's ute. Nothing. She hoped Doyle wasn't in his house. That he'd miraculously left Lottie behind, that Lottie was sitting in front of the big black-screened television watching videos.

The sliding door was unlocked and Gran carefully entered, putting a finger to her lips as she scoped out the kitchen and loungeroom. Meadow pointed upstairs to show Gran where Lottie's room was located. They crept softly up the stairs before opening Lottie's door.

No one. After a swoop of the other upstairs rooms they found them empty too.

Having never glimpsed the veiled woman a second time, Meadow sometimes wondered if her eyes had been playing tricks on her all along.

'Gran,' she whispered. 'Maybe he's in that room with those poor creatures.'

She led the way down the stairs, turning toward the back of the house. Gran gestured for Meadow to stop while she checked the first room.

She peeked over her grandmother's shoulder. It was a science lab of sorts, complete with lab coats, microscopes and various machines she didn't recognise.

She could tell Gran wanted to investigate further, but instead Gran moved toward the second door. Before entering she turned to give Meadow a troubled, questioning look.

Meadow shook her head. She knew what was in there; she couldn't look at those little bodies.

Gran trudged toward the shelves, turning to look back at Meadow again. The horror in her eyes mirrored Meadow's own that day of revelation not so long ago. Gran took a step closer, looking like she wanted to scoop up the vulnerable spotted-and-striped creatures.

She closed her eyes until Gran exited the room.

'First things first,' Gran murmured to Meadow, and pointed to the last door. 'Is that his…?'

She nodded.

Gran opened the door to Doyle's office. It was empty, except for a couple of boxes stuffed with files and paperwork. The computer was gone. The room must have been designed as a bedroom as it had an en suite. Gran checked the bathroom too.

'If he's bolted, why wouldn't he have taken his specimens?' Meadow wondered, looking at paper strewn all over the floor.

'Must've realised he couldn't get them out of the state,' Gran's mouth twisted in disgust.

'Maybe he's at the cottage?' Meadow backed out of the office.

'That's a strong possibility,' Gran said. 'And perhaps he has Charlotte with him.'

Meadow wondered if he'd been in her bedroom. Had he laughed at her clutter of yellow?

'I'm coming back for those little ones,' Gran said heatedly. 'They will have a place to rest with the old darlings. C'mon.'

They retraced their steps, and exited Doyle's sliding door.

It was dark with only a sliver of the moon to guide them. She handed her grandmother a torch as they moved toward their cottage. Gran relented, shining the torch along the fence to see a ladder leaning against the side.

Gran gave Meadow a puzzled look.

'Was already there,' Meadow said. 'It's a long story.'

They stood silently near the front gate, staring at the lifeless fairywren hanging from the gate. Gran glanced fiercely at the gate, removing the tiny skeleton. 'He did this, didn't he?'

'Yes.' Meadow watched the shock in her grandmother's words, now like disbelieving splinters of ice.

'That monster has left his vile mark everywhere,' Gran growled, then quietened herself, cocking her head to one side. 'Can't hear anyone, can you?'

'I don't think so,' Meadow offered. 'We could go through my wardrobe door.'

'Brilliant idea.' Gran opened the gate quietly, then

passed the red-jumpered cherry tree to Meadow's side of the cottage. Gran's hands ran along the bare wisteria vines encircling the front of the cottage. 'I've missed you, old treasure.'

Gran saw the makeshift fence enclosing the run for the pups; her eyes widened.

'It's a long story.' Meadow handed her grandmother the outdoor key to her wardrobe.

'Stay close, and keep an eye out behind you.' Gran unlocked the door.

Once inside Meadow's wardrobe, they felt around the clothes until they reached the front. 'Slowly, remember.' Gran left the wardrobe, signalling for Meadow to follow.

They were careful to shine the torch in one room at a time. This search was easier, as each room was so familiar. That was until they reached the loungeroom where the sheet still hung over the grandfather clock.

'I know,' Gran whispered, 'it's a long story.'

Meadow nodded. Her grandmother discovered that her normally locked door was hanging off its hinges.

Inside, everything was upturned and topsy turvy. Gran's furniture and favourite knick knacks were in disarray. All her colourful home-made clothes, cardigans, scarves and beanies.

'When all's said and done, it's just fluff,' Gran lifted her chin proudly. 'Stupid man. I would never keep anything of importance in here.'

She was surprised at this. 'Where then?'

Gran pointed to her chest. 'In my vest of course. I took any important paperwork with me when I left.'

Gran opened Grandfather's old green jacket and withdrew a small leather document pouch from her vest. Gran stared at Meadow for a moment, who could see the wheels turning in her grandmother's head, so delighted she'd outwitted Doyle.

'No point fretting about this mess,' Gran said, 'let's see if Charlotte's in our garden.'

But before going outside, they did a quick detour to check Grandfather's old study. Gran was concerned Doyle might have vandalized it as well. Fortunately it was untouched, still memorialised in leather and Huon pine, with his old pipe and tobacco.

Standing in pride of place, a guitar leaned against a bookshelf.

Gran stared at the instrument with a longing Meadow hadn't noticed before.

Outside, following the familiar path over the rough stepping stones, they cut through the darkness with their torches. She checked on Gertie, who blinked in the torch light but continued to munch on hay. No calf, but Gertie was even bigger than last time. The chickens were silent and still, any pecking-order shenanigans over with.

Gran surveyed the willowed area near the river, at the gravestones. 'I'm laying them to rest here, those poor pets in jars. You can count on it.'

Meadow agreed. It was a sanctuary of remembrance, amongst creatures that mattered.

She heard a strange sound, a warbled cry. 'Gran.' Remembering what Lottie told her, she clutched her grandmother's arm. 'I think it's those poor half-formed things in the tree.'

Gran strode toward Doyle's garden. Meadow didn't want to see inside the hollow, but trailed behind Gran as a bitter chill crept along her spine. Another cry.

Meadow let out a gasp.

'Shh,' Gran said, nearing the old oak tree whose branches sprawled to the ground like extended arms hiding a mournful secret.

Gran visibly steeled herself while manoeuvring around some low-lying branches. She peered into the large knoll, pointing her torch into the dark space.

There was another muffled, distraught, sound.

'Meadow come here,' Gran called, 'I need you.'

'I don't think I can,' Meadow peered through her fingers. She couldn't stop imagining some small spotted or striped rat-like creatures clawing their way to the top. Or perhaps something cute like a possum baby, but with a long jawbone attached to its body.

But something in Gran's voice pulled her closer. Nearing the tree in trepidation, Meadows eyes darted everywhere but the knoll. Something in her grandmother's eyes registered disbelief. Meadow peered inside too.

A pair of green eyes looked up from a kittenish face. A face that had a gag on it, connected to a body whose hands and feet were cabled-tied at the front.

Chapter Twenty-five

'Lottie,' Meadow's face lit up with surprise, followed by relief. 'We found you.'

Lottie's kitten ears were flat against her head as if she were preparing to fight. They pulled her out of the hollow, claustrophobic space. As Lottie emerged, Meadow made sure not to look at what might be under her.

'They're not in here,' Gran said. 'Doyle must've worried about the noises they made and put the poor little mites in jars too.'

Meadow's stomach turned to ice.

Gran pulled a pocket knife out of her pocket, cutting the cable ties while murmuring words about how brave Lottie had been. 'Stay sitting for a minute until you get your strength back.'

As Lottie sat on the soft grass, Meadow sat next to her while Gran retrieved a flask of water and a walnut and honey bar from her coat pockets. 'Here, this will help.'

'Your Gran is just like you,' Lottie said. 'Always ready to help.'

No one had ever said she was like Gran. She glanced at her mud-caked boots, her stained pants and grubby hands. An engine roared nearby. It was a white ute. Doyle's ute. The vehicle fishtailed along the road, its headlights dazzling until out of sight.

'Fuck, fuck, fuck.' Meadow's head bobbed vigorously with each cuss.

Gran's expression seemed as shocked by that utterance as by what she'd just witnessed in the jars. Her grandmother's eyes widened. 'What did you just say?'

Meadow was silent for a moment. Something had happened to her filter all right, but she wasn't quite sure what she thought about swearing yet.

'Oh girl, what has that man done to you.' Gran immediately placed blame elsewhere for her granddaughter's perceived imprudence. Gran sat with a dismayed thud.

Lottie gave Meadow a look that seemed to say, 'There's more to you than meets the eye.'

It was the same look her sister had given Meadow earlier.

'Are you okay?' Meadow retrieved a torch from her pocket and turned it on.

Lottie's nod was almost imperceptible.

'We checked for his vehicle,' Gran shook her head in disbelief. 'But he must have been hiding somewhere along the road.'

'He must've realised we'd found Lottie,' Meadow said, wondering if he was going to come back anytime soon.

All three were now sitting on the grass. There was a soft glow in the shadows of the oak tree, with the crescent moon hiding momentarily behind the clouds. In the shadows it felt like the kind of space where she could say anything.

'I know this sounds dramatic,' Meadow said, 'but I don't think my legs will stand up again.'

'I'm a bit shaky myself,' Gran assented. 'I have to tell you girls, I've been surprised more than once today.'

'You came for me,' Lottie said, eyes unblinking as she glanced in Meadow's direction, 'like you promised.'

Meadow felt a rush of protectiveness and fought the urge to swear again. She didn't think Gran could take it.

'Who put you in the tree?' Gran asked.

'Doyle locked me in my room until he decided to fly the drone again from your paddock.' Lottie's hands shook and she dropped the flask.

'We thought he'd flown the drone from here. Didn't we, Gran.' Meadow shook her head in disbelief.

Gran's tightly clenched fists rested wearily on her lap. 'Doyle's lucky he didn't get gored by Rusty.'

'I think his benefactor thought I'd run away again.' Lottie wiped her eyes with the back of her hand. 'It was clear I should stay put.'

'The man on the phone?' Meadow said. 'Was he here?'

Lottie stared at her house. 'Not sure. It was dark when…' her lip quivered.

Gran handed Lottie one of Grandfather's prized old handkerchiefs. It was red and blue tartan and neatly folded.

'Thank you.' Lottie dabbed her face before twisting the handkerchief tightly.

'Well thank you, young lady, for what you did for my family.' Gran patted Lottie's hand.

Lottie looked shyly across at Gran. 'You have a great family.'

'I wouldn't argue with you there.' Gran looked in the direction of Meadow's legs. 'My girl, what a sight you are, did you leave any mud back up there on that mountain?'

Lottie asked. 'Are the pups okay?'

'Fine,' Gran and Meadow said in unison.

'Do you know where Doyle went?' Meadow wondered if he were getting reinforcements.

'He told me we were going to the airport to fly out,' Lottie sniffed. 'But he wanted to try one last time to find the real thylacines.'

Gran sucked in her breath.

'He was coming back for me.' Lottie rubbed at her hands and wrists.

Gran locked eyes with Meadow for a brief moment. It occurred to Meadow, not for the first time, that she pitied the person who ended up on the wrong side of her grandmother.

'I didn't say anything.' Lottie pointed toward her thermal underwear shirt, hanging to her knees. 'This gave me away. So I had to make up where I saw you.'

'I knew you had our backs,' Meadow said. 'Gran shot down the drone.'

'Wish I saw that,' Lottie said.

'We wondered why he didn't take his specimens,' Meadow tried not to think how close they were to the knoll of the oak tree.

'Probably because he couldn't get them through customs,' Lottie said.

Just as Gran thought.

'He was halfway through packing up. Said it was too hot to be here right now,' Lottie said. 'Then his financial supporter said he must find you. No more trying to win you over. Force was now needed.'

'Do you know who this benefactor is?' Gran's words were frosted silver 'Where did you move from?'

'We've moved a lot and last time was from Papua New Guinea,' Lottie said, 'but his backer's not from there, I tried to find out but Doyle wouldn't tell me.'

Meadow imagined that Doyle's rich benefactor would've been angry they'd given Doyle the slip.

'Doyle said he had to try a different angle,' Lottie said. 'That's when he went to your cottage. But he said he didn't find anything useful.'

'Hmmm.' Gran stood, giving Lottie a lift up. 'I think we need to contact the police.'

Meadow was surprised. Gran never went to others for help, with the exception of her guardians or Bert.

'Not yet,' Lottie said. 'Please, it's so complicated.'

All three were silent for some time.

'Right,' Gran winked at Lottie. 'Stay close to me and we'll deal with all that later on.'

Lottie was relieved at that.

Standing side by side, Lottie was just a smidge taller than her grandmother.

Gran glanced at Meadow. 'Let's get Charlotte cleaned up at our cottage; she must be exhausted. Your sister should be back here in a few hours, and depending on what plan they agree on, we'll have a lot of work to do.'

Once inside the cottage, Meadow organised food and PJs for Lottie, still wondering what Plan B was. After the drone incident Gran had kept quiet on their journey in case Doyle was lurking somewhere.

Sitting in the loungeroom her grandmother looked exhausted. Gran had done something quite unexpected, she'd engulfed herself in Grandfather's dusty-rose chair, mumbling that she needed to feel his calmness and comfort. Gran promptly closed her eyes and went to sleep. Lottie collapsed next, tucked up in Meadow's bed.

Meadow wanted to stay awake and wait for her sister while Gran and Lottie rested. She was too twitchy, too worried Doyle might start thumping on the front door at any moment.

Indigo Bliss returned well after midnight. Her sister was bushed, and stood shivering in front of the loungeroom fire, warming her hands.

'Are they…?' Meadow said.

'They are in a safe place, aren't they, Gran,' Indigo Bliss said.

She watched her grandmother's eyes open with a sudden start.

'Yes. Better to keep them away from this mess at the moment. And Spencer too,' Gran yawned then rubbed her eyes. 'So they went with Plan B?'

'Sure did. There was a tug of war between Ava and Juke for a while, but in the end they agreed with what you proposed.'

'What did they agree to?' She glanced at each one.

'I'll tell you all about it,' Gran said. 'Just make a cuppa for me first.'

As Indigo Bliss moved toward the kitchen, she threw over her shoulder to Gran, 'And they want you to take the lead with it.'

Meadow rose to her feet and followed her sister into the kitchen. 'Come and look at this.'

She led Indigo Bliss to her room, to see Lottie, covers tucked under her chin, sleeping peacefully on Meadow's daisy-sheeted bed.

'What a relief,' Indigo Bliss said. 'I've been worrying the whole way back. Are you all right?'

'I think so.' Meadow glanced around the pet-less room.

Indigo Bliss sat in her favourite rocking chair, balancing her teacup. Meadow and Gran couldn't stop staring at her wild hair, full of twigs and knots.

Indigo Bliss, not one to indulge in self-pity, flicked her knotted hair over one shoulder, and said, 'A bath can wait until later. So where's Doyle?'

'Fuck that man. He left Lottie in the oak tree,' Meadow exploded, then put her hand over her mouth.

Indigo Bliss spilt her rose-petal tea.

'It's a new thing apparently,' Gran cleared her throat. 'The honest truth is I'm just too exhausted to care. By the end of all of this, I might be doing it too.'

'Maybe it releases pent-up energy?' Indigo Bliss shook her head. 'Blasted man.'

'Continue,' Gran said.

'The guardians wanted to mitigate this whole mess,' Indigo Bliss caught Meadow up, 'and continue on as we always have.'

'But too many unknowns,' Gran said.

'Exactly,' Indigo Bliss said. 'Who knows what about our tigers? Doyle for one.'

Meadow and Gran nodded.

'They want you to approach the appropriate bodies,' Indigo Bliss said. 'To work out a way to keep the tigers safe.'

'They will help us, believe me, because we are giving them the gift of a lifetime,' Gran said, patting Grandfather's chair as if including him in the conversation. 'Restitution.'

'You should've been there when Lottie first laid eyes on them,' Meadow said. 'People are going to go wild when they find out they're not extinct.'

'That's the issue, isn't it,' Gran leaned forward. 'We don't want to have kept them safe all these years only to have them hunted out of curiosity.'

'Do you mean killed?' Meadow said.

'Perhaps accidentally, or not. But mostly I mean even a photo of them alive would be a prize, wouldn't it.' Gran stood and walked toward the hearth, holding out her hands to the warmth.

'They need to have allocated safe havens,' Indigo Bliss said. 'Gran thinks there should be five protected areas for the five guardians and their families.'

'Like the tigers should've had while they dragged their feet on protection.' Gran said. 'Imagine if the proposed gifted land, De Witt Island or a reserve had happened.'

'I heard in the sixties Maria Island was selected as a sanctuary...in case thylacines were ever found.' Meadow said. 'It's worked for the devil's.'

'True, Meadow.' Gran appeared impressed. 'But our zones would need security, heavy security, twenty-four seven. We would have to have those cameras I hate, watching them at all times.'

'There's a lot of wilderness here in Tassie,' Indigo Bliss

said. 'They'll have the space they need.'

'As long as it's not a zoo,' Gran grimaced.

Meadow and Indigo Bliss exchanged a look of forewarning. Gran's rants about zoos could go on for some time.

'It tortures me to this day that they sometimes wouldn't let those tigers inside their shelters, all so people could watch them. I can hardly believe it but I heard there was a thylacine in the zoo who had a foot amputated, apparently with no anaesthetic.' Gran's chin lifted. 'Just tied down and…'

Meadow's stomach rolled. 'You'll make me sick.'

Gran's head dropped. 'We cannot let history repeat.'

Indigo Bliss opened her mouth, then closed it again. Meadow sensed what her sister was about to say. Privately, Indigo Bliss had confided to her that many zoos had come a long way, then referenced a vet from long ago who'd lanced another thylacine's foot in a zoo, relieving it greatly. After the head keeper continued to kindly nurse him, to all accounts, the tiger appreciated the keeper as a friend.

Things must be desperate for their grandmother to even contemplate seeking out government help.

'Momentum is so important.' Gran said. 'Remember when police stations reported no recent sightings of the thylacine in their vicinities…'

Meadow imagined how grim that report must've been.

'Then of course the government had to go and set up a new protection board. A stalling tactic if you ask me.' Gran said. 'All it did was put our tigers' protection on hold.'

'That was in the nineteen twenties and thirties,' Indigo Bliss pulled at a fern tendril in her hair. 'We have to believe it'll be different now.'

'We mustn't forget what happened,' Gran rallied a little,

'but the guardians don't have much choice. We have to try.'

'Lottie understands all about uploading and streaming videos.' Meadow offered. 'Maybe we could do that to satisfy public curiosity.'

'I like that,' Gran said. 'And the zones will be impenetrable to all.'

'Except for us,' Indigo Bliss said.

Gran echoed, 'Except for us.'

'And we'll make sure the zones aren't near farmland,' Indigo Bliss added.

'Yes, we don't want our farmers or tigers to be affected by even a hint of impropriety,' Gran sighed.

'Gran is going to Hobart tomorrow, to Parliament House,' Indigo Bliss said, 'to see the Minister for Tourism and someone involved with threatened species.'

Going to Nipaluna. That was unexpected. 'What if they try to, you know, trick us?' Meadow said, moving to stand in front of the fire next to Gran.

'If they try to trick us, they're in for a shock.' Gran's words flared up like a just-lit silver sparkler.

'What about Lottie,' Meadow said, 'and tomorrow?'

'Charlotte should come; sounds like she has a couple of good ideas.' Gran yawned again. 'To bed my girls. I can hardly stay standing, I'm so tired.'

Meadow slept in the foldout bed in her room.

Her family were back in the cottage. They'd found Lottie. She tried not to think about the pups looking for her.

Chapter Twenty-six

Meadow sat bolt upright, wondering where she was, for a moment. Lottie was standing near the bed, looking pale in the sunlight.

'I drew your curtains, hope you don't mind,' she said. 'Is this your wardrobe? Can I look inside?'

'Sure.' Meadow watched Lottie closely for any reaction to her cluttered room but Lottie was already venturing into the wardrobe. Meadow rolled to one side. Shifting caused a lot of pain. Too many newly used muscles.

'Can I still try on your cape?' Lottie's voice was muffled from within the wardrobe.

'Of course.'

She came out, twirling with enthusiasm. A distinct floral fragrance wafted toward Meadow. 'Have you already had a bath?'

'I've been up for a while.' Lottie glanced down at her clean gym gear.

Where on earth had Doyle gone? thought Meadow.

As the kettle sang, she said, 'We're going to Hobart today, to Parliament House if you're up to it.'

'Your Gran told me,' Lottie nodded. 'Truth is, I don't want to be alone.'

'Understandable,' Meadow said. 'Let's get breakfast.'

'It's actually lunch,' Lottie clarified, leaving the red cloak on the bed.

Gran had cooked their favourite fare. Roast chicken served with a sweet potato, cheese and basil quiche. Lottie opted out of chicken.

'So Lottie, I hear you're familiar with live-streaming,'

Indigo Bliss cleared away the plates.

'It's my favourite hobby,' said Lottie, her parmesan-and-saffron-coloured words appearing full and satiated.

'Do you think you could explain how that works to these government people?' Gran said. 'How we want the thylacines to be made available to everyone. On screens that is.'

'Sure,' Lottie said. 'I'll do what I can.'

'We've decided to respect your wishes and not say anything about your personal situation yet,' Gran said. 'The main thing is you're safe.'

'As long as you are with us, we'll protect you,' Indigo Bliss offered matter-of-factly.

'But we are going to tell the Minister that Doyle is desperate,' Gran said, 'that he's caught up with people who want the thylacines for money and fame, and who knows what else.'

Money and fame, such a foreign concept to Meadow.

'I want to get there by mid-afternoon,' Gran said, 'so wear your best clothes, girls.'

'That'll brighten up their office,' Lottie said. 'Normally it's black, grey and brown as far as the eye can see.'

'Really?' Gran beamed. 'Let's put on a show.'

Gran wasn't kidding. She walked out of the bathroom wearing her best ankle-length denim skirt topped with a red satin shirt and fuchsia vest. While Meadow and Indigo Bliss wore their usual Dutch braids, Gran had let her hair flow freely in soft salt and ginger waves past her slender goose neck to her waist.

Gran tossed her hair and winked at Lottie. 'I get these the old-fashioned way—by plaiting my hair at night.'

Lottie looked at Meadow and Indigo Bliss, wearing their town-best patchwork skirts and then at her own pink gym gear.

'I look boring compared to you guys.'

'I could take you back next door to get something different,' Meadow suggested.

'I don't want to be the dreary one.' Lottie's eyes widened. 'I didn't mean to say dreary. I meant to say…dull.'

'It's all right,' Meadow said. 'We made up for it with our first names.'

'Well we can't have you feeling dreary, or dull, can we girls?' Gran pointed toward her bedroom. 'I think we are close in size, why don't you go and raid my wardrobe. Don't mind the mess.'

Lottie's face regained some colour in an instant. 'And can I wear the red cape too?'

'Of course.' Meadow grinned.

She collected her cape while Lottie explored Gran's wardrobe, soon returning in a pink patchwork skirt topped with a white blouse with bishop sleeves and large frills on the front and cuff.

They all nodded in mutual admiration as Lottie beamed back.

'Come on girls,' Gran said. 'Take your braids out and be free like Lottie and I.'

Indigo Bliss rolled her eyes, but undid her braids, shaking her head until the ash-blonde ropes were freed. Meadow did the same, her fingers working through her hair until the sisters had kinked waves like their grandmother.

'Wait until they get a load of us on the bus,' Lottie closed her eyes in anticipation.

Meadow was relieved Lottie seemed to be bouncing back so well. She wished she knew more about psychological things so she could help her friend.

They left the cottage in a flurry of pink and white hues, so quiet against the loud shades of rose and rouge fabric squares in their patchwork skirts. Gran's red satin shirt complimented the red cape as Lottie twirled her way along the road.

'We've no time to stop for a chat,' Gran said, as they walked past Bert's house. 'We'll have to update him later.'

Meadow saw Indigo Bliss surveying Bert's property, hoping to catch a glimpse of Spencer.

'His tractor is out of the shed,' Meadow pointed. 'He's probably about to take the old boy out for a joyride.'

'Old Spencer. He'll enjoy that.' Indigo Bliss smiled gently. 'Gran's right, it's better we don't disturb him just yet.'

There were a few children waiting at Grove, near the bus stop, wearing school uniforms.

'They must be in a theatre group,' Meadow heard one girl whisper to her friend. Two bunnies with pigtails, and fluffy words of blush and bubble-gum.

The girls must have finished school for the day and were waiting for a lift. At this time of the afternoon there were only a few passengers going to Hobart. Many were squinting at their mobiles, but upon looking up, stared in surprise at the colourfully dressed women boarding the bus.

Meadow chose the window seat, taking in the scenery as they left Grove and climbed a steep and winding highway. Some farms were lined with pine trees, or fences of shrubbery, their paddocks scattered with sheep, goats, cattle or horses. Several lambs circled an outer fence gleefully, bounding in a collective romp, springing past their grazing mothers.

Then there was a steep decline into Kingston, a town on the outskirts of Hobart close to the water.

'Look how big this place is now,' Gran said in surprise. 'So many shops. Now to Hobart.'

After several minutes, there was another sharp decline as the bus almost nosedived toward their capital city.

'Look at Mount Wellington,' Lottie pointed.

'Beautiful Kunanyi,' Gran nodded.

'Just like Beauty,' Lottie said, 'icing sugar dusted.'

To Meadow, Lottie's words were like green stems of catnip that rose into the air and faded away.

'We're the second oldest capital city after Sydney,' Gran stated proudly across the aisle to Lottie, 'and one of the Antarctic gateway cities.'

Lottie's eyes widened.

Meadow turned to look at Sandy Bay with its university, casino and yachts docked along the sparkling Derwent River. Historic sandstone buildings, churches and cathedrals gave Hobart a distinctly old-world feel. Gran had once told Meadow that high rise buildings were a hotly debated topic in this city.

The bus stopped right in town and the commuters alighted. Gran had them walk to the waterfront first as she wanted to bide some time. A number of people stared as they wandered toward the harbour with its fishing boats, yachts and waterfront restaurants.

Meadow saw what Lottie meant about black and grey clothing. Waiting at a traffic light, she overheard a raven-esque lady with sharp eyes and a black suit suggest their group must be wearing cosplay.

Meadow tried not to focus on the faces in the crowd after that; she was experiencing a colour overload. It was exhausting. She wondered why she hadn't felt that way on the bus. Perhaps it was easier to block out the mayhem of colour around her when people were silently scrolling through their phones.

Trying to push the peripheral blur of colour aside, Meadow concentrated on Parliament House.

It was a magnificent building with historic architecture, manicured lawns, and closeness to the waterfront.

Gran walked straight into the building and made a beeline for the first official. A woman nodded her head toward them; she wore a white shirt with a dark skirt and jacket.

'I have information about the Tasmanian tiger,' Gran said.

'We have a lot of information about thylacines at our museum, not far from here,' the woman replied. Her badge said Sylvia, and her words looked black and white and rectangular in shape. She reminded Meadow of a fairy penguin.

'Look Sylvia, I think you'll find I'm an expert when it comes to the thylacine,' Gran said. 'And need to discuss my findings with the Minister for Tourism.'

'Mrs?' Sylvia studied Gran's face.

'Dreary,' Gran said.

'Mrs Dreary, it's so unfortunate they are extinct,' Sylvia's cheeks blossomed as she scanned the four women carefully, wondering if security needed to be called. 'But surely you can wait for an appointment.'

They were attracting attention and Meadow glanced at Lottie, who appeared to be enjoying every minute of the unfolding spectacle.

Gran held up one hand. 'I do not have time for a run around. I want to see the Minister for Tourism and John Parker. It's a matter of life and death.'

She noted Sylvia narrowing her eyes at Gran.

'I can contact the Minister for Tourism,' Sylvia finally said. 'I'm not sure about the other man though.'

'I've done my homework,' Gran said. 'He's here at the moment.'

Sylvia's lips pursed. She went through a door behind a reception desk, and clicked away on her heels.

'She's just trying to do her job, Gran,' Meadow offered, adjusting her gingham belt, concerned they hadn't made an appointment.

'I'm intentionally causing a disturbance, Meadow,' Gran said. 'We have to portray toughness right now, or they will walk all over us.'

After several minutes a man entered. With sandy streaks in his hair and a light-brown suit he looked like a cat with a thick ruff of fur around his face and neck, thought Meadow. A big cat, a powerful lion, with shaggy hair and beard. He had an air of superiority, and she knew his words would be silver, just like her grandmother's, with strength, clarity and focus.

'Mrs Dreary, everyone.' The man nodded his head, giving them all a full-toothed smile, his streaked mane not moving one inch as he bobbed his head. 'My name is Sebastian Collins. I am the Minister for Tourism. I hear you have some information about thylacines.'

'We do,' Gran said. 'And before you think I'm about to waste your time, you'd better take a look at these.' Gran produced two instant photos from inside her vest.

One photo revealed two juvenile thylacines standing near Gran, her head bent so that only the top of her grey cloche hat showed. It was the day she'd left the cottage, and Gran was getting in a final pat with Timba and Tawny. Taken in that golden hour, the image softly touched the participants in a buttery glow. This was the first time Meadow had looked at the photo. Her heart pounded with pride and longing. The other photo was taken the same day and included Gran turned toward the pups' parents and the four juveniles together.

Sebastian's smile turned into a round surprised, 'Oh.' His amber eyes blinked incredulously. 'These can't be real.'

'They are,' Gran said.

'But, but…' Sebastian said. 'You can't expect me to believe…'

'We don't have much time and I have important things to discuss,' Gran said.

'Right. Can I hold onto these for a moment?' he said. 'Please come with me.'

Gran's chin went up. Meadow recognised that look. Gran knew she had Sebastian right where she wanted him.

Chapter Twenty-seven

Sebastian ushered them into a boardroom overlooking Salamanca Place and the Princes Wharf. He gestured toward the long rectangular table, lined with chairs on either side. 'Please sit.'

The women sat on one side, facing the window, with the exception of Gran, who sat at the head of the table. Meadow glanced out at the established trees bordering the Parliament House gardens.

Sebastian stood, watching them closely for a moment, before clearing his throat.

'Please, there is so much I need to ask you,' Sebastian said. 'But before we begin, can I ask John Parker to join us? He knows a thing or two about threatened species, so your timing is impeccable.'

'Exactly what I had expected. I have little birdies who tell me things,' Gran said.

Sebastian looked as if he didn't want to leave the group alone in case they might vanish. He pulled out his mobile and scrolled through his directory, glancing up at the women before dialling a number. 'Yes John, glad I caught you down here today. Thought you might be on the mainland.'

There was a faint sound of reply, a long-winded reply.

'John,' Sebastian said, cutting him off. 'Something extremely sensitive has happened and I need you here. Immediately.'

Sebastian must have received the answer he was looking for because he hung up.

'John should be here soon.' Sebastian stared at the photos again.

'They can't be traced you see.' Gran pointed to the photos. 'Apparently you can trace digital photos on a mobile.'

Sebastian's eyes widened.

Gran glanced at Lottie. 'Isn't that right, dear?'

Lottie nodded, 'Yes.'

'And there was no way I was going to get film developed,' Gran added. 'Can you imagine?'

Sebastian looked squarely at Gran for a moment and Meadow sensed he was wondering if this were some kind of hoax. He surveyed the room as if searching for a hidden camera. But no one else noticed his expression. She had to say something.

'Sebastian, Gran is telling you the truth. This isn't a hoax,' Meadow offered.

He gave her a curious look, as if questioning how she'd read his mind.

'I'm hoping that's the case,' Sebastian said, and some of the doubt left his face.

There was a knock at the door and John Parker entered, wearing a dark-brown suit. He had thick brown hair. A labrador, with an eager-to-please appearance. Yes, a very boisterous lab.

Meadow watched John survey the women, his eyes resting on her for a few moments longer. Normally people couldn't take their eyes off her sister. But one quick glance at Sebastian clued him in to the seriousness of the meeting. 'Good afternoon all,' John nodded.

Sebastian handed him the photos.

John laughed out loud for a moment, then peered closer. 'Amazing taxidermy,' John said, words of mocha-brown corkscrews springing out of his mouth in astonishment.

'Mrs Dreary is here to tell us they are real,' Sebastian said. 'That they are alive.'

John's face paled, his dark eyebrows drawing together. 'But…that's impossible.' He sat with a thud, missing the seat and teetering on the armrest for a moment. He slid into the chair, leaned forward and put his head down, murmuring to the ground. 'How? How is that possible?'

Sebastian fetched John some bottled water from a nearby bar fridge. 'Would you ladies like a drink?'

'We're fine,' Gran tapped her fingers on the table impatiently. 'Let's get down to business.'

'Assuming that what you have shown us is real.' Sebastian cleared his throat again as he took a seat close to Gran.

'It's real,' Gran said.

'What can we do for you?' Sebastian gave Gran a direct stare.

As far back as she could remember, Gran could out-stare anyone. Meadow watched with interest as Sebastian lowered his eyes first.

'I'll keep it simple,' Gran said, dividing her glances between Sebastian's now level gaze and John's bent head. 'There have been five families in this state keeping the thylacines under our care and protected for decades. Now our secret has been exposed and we believe the only way we can protect our tigers is…'

Gran closed her eyes for a moment, finding it difficult to utter the next words. 'To go public and have them in protected zones.'

John looked up for a moment, and began rubbing his temples.

'Zones?' Sebastian asked, incredulous.

'Yes, five zones. Secure, twenty-four, seven. Keeping our tigers protected in their natural habitat.'

'John,' Sebastian said. 'Feel free to jump in here whenever you want, mate. This is more your area of expertise.'

'I've dreamed something like this could happen,' John said. 'Pinch me, please.'

Gran turned to Sebastian. 'The reason I wanted to talk with you, is that I realise what revealing this will mean. There will be people worldwide trying to get into Tasmania to see our tigers. The tourism will be overwhelming, and… very lucrative.'

Sebastian's eyebrows nearly shot up to his hairline.

'So,' Gran continued. 'We believe a percentage of the monies from tourism should be used on a continuing basis to set up the zones and pay for their security. With other grants to set it all up of course.'

John sat up, his eyes bright. 'She's right, people will come from everywhere and some will try to steal them or even worse, hunt them for trophies, or skins.'

'Exactly, John,' Gran said, looking at both men again. 'There is no way we can let them near our tigers. Even those who wish no harm.'

'Of course,' John said, 'there will be those who believe the thylacine should run free, to stabilise our ecosystem.'

Gran pursed her lips.

Sebastian gestured for her to continue.

Gran pointed to Meadow and Lottie. 'But a couple of clever girls have come up with a solution to that.'

'Solution?' John asked.

'Yes, they can be livestreamed and also have videos,' Gran looked at Lottie, 'put up?'

'Uploaded,' Lottie said.

Gran continued, 'So that people can enjoy them all the time. But never in any lairs.'

'Lottie says some animals are streamed twenty-four hours a day,' Indigo Bliss said. 'And you could have strategic hubs throughout the state, showing the footage, and people could donate or adopt a tiger.'

Gran tapped on the table again. 'I don't want the limelight. Do any of you girls?'

They shook their heads in unison.

'So that means you men can be the public faces, the heroes of our island,' Gran nodded.

A switch flicked at that. Both of the men's backs became like iron rods. Their eyes took on a look suggesting flights of imagination.

'Our group has drawn up maps of where these zones are to be placed,' Gran said. 'Of course the zones will not affect any existing properties.'

John's phone rang and he turned it off, as if it were a mere annoyance.

'Your group?' Sebastian said.

'The Snug and Flowerpot Yarn and Weavers Group,' Gran gave a wry smile. 'Don't let the name fool you, because it's meant to. We refer to ourselves as the guardians.'

Sebastian blinked at this. 'The guardians?'

'Our five families. We are willing for you both to come and view some of our tigers yourselves. Once you have viewed them, everything is to be legally drawn up and quickly implemented. You will have to cut through all the red tape because timing is key.'

Who was their grandmother? Meadow thought. Who could she have been if she hadn't hidden herself away for decades?

'Of course, of course,' Sebastian said.

'And don't try to put one over me,' Gran crossed her arms. 'I'm a sly old lady.'

'When? When can we see them?' John stood, and looked imploringly at Gran.

'You are both to come with me right now,' Gran said. 'No cars, no phones, nothing that allows you to be tracked. If you agree to that, I think we will be able to get this started.'

'And their watches too,' Lottie suggested, the most technologically savvy amongst them.

'For the sake of argument,' Sebastian coughed as he removed his watch, 'what if we are not able to meet your demands?'

'It will be harder for our guardians, but we are willing to give up everything. To live in caves and the bush to keep them safe,' Gran said. 'Somewhere you will never find them.'

Gran's words were like straight grey arrows this time.

They hit their target.

'N-o-o-o,' John groaned. 'We'll work something out, won't we, Sebastian?'

Sebastian stood for a moment then paced before the windows looking over the grounds like a caged lion. 'You know, several years ago, a crowd gathered in Hobart, ready to walk together, to burn an effigy. It was an enormous Tasmanian tiger.'

Meadow gasped, she'd never heard of this before. 'Gran, did you know?' She realised why Sebastian's words had changed from a strong solid silver to a swirling melted charcoal grey.

Gran nodded.

'People were asked to write their deepest fears on paper,' Sebastian glanced outside, 'then place them inside the thylacine before it was incinerated.'

'Yes,' John said, walking to the window to stand beside Sebastian. 'I remember all the drumming as we walked there. My heart was pounding when they flamed the tiger.'

She wondered what each man had written.

'If I recall they made that thylacine effigy look powerful…I was pleased when I heard that.' Gran said.

John tipped his head toward Gran, 'I thought so too.'

'Imagine back in the day, after all those bounties were put on thylacines heads,' Gran frowned, 'they realised how valuable the tigers were for zoos and museums. After some had called our tigers a stupid creature, unattractive and untameable.'

Meadow wished there'd been more admirers, like those who'd thought thylacines were graceful with pretty stripes.

Was Gran going to fire up and yell at Sebastian for what she perceived the government had done? Would Gran thunder about how thylacines were shipped overseas, some dying before reaching their destination, or dying soon after arrival. Gran thought it unfeasible to breed the thylacine in captivity.

If Gran started to rage about the remains of thylacines still in storage worldwide, this meeting might not end well. Meadow glanced at her sister, wondering if she also saw what might be imminent. Indigo Bliss sat forward, tensing as if ready to intervene. Her sister thought that many museums and scientists were simply trying to study and save species, to aid their preservation.

Gran focused her gaze on Sebastian in a way that caused him to leave the window, return to the board table, and bang his fist on it.

John's water bottle tipped over.

Sebastian placed his mobile phone on the table. 'If we can save them from, well, being extinct again, you have my word I will do all I can.'

John moved to the table, placing his phone and watch upon it.

'We need to leave discreetly,' Gran said. 'But first, let people know you will be away on business for a couple of days and won't be contactable.'

'Yes,' John said, 'I'll ring my assistant and tell her I may be in a place with patchy reception, to just take messages.'

'My wife's not expecting me home for a couple of days.' Sebastian said. 'I suppose I can't fill her in?'

'Not on your life,' Gran said.

'Okay, but I need to ring and let her know I'll be out of contact,' Sebastian said.

'Make the calls here if you don't mind,' Gran said, in an unusually soft voice.

Her grandmother didn't want to give them time to overthink this. It reminded Meadow of how she'd used fake kindness to get the pups to heel when they were covered in blood. Gran had clearly chosen the afternoon as the last possible moment to meet with Sebastian and John.

After fulfilling Gran's request, Sebastian led them along an isolated corridor. Outside, Gran steered the men toward the bus stop up on Davey Street. 'Put these on,' Gran said, producing caps and dark glasses for both.

'Disguises,' John grinned, trying to fit the cap over his thick hair.

'Are we going bush?' Sebastian looked at his business suit.

'I have clothes for you that were my husband's,' Gran said. 'You have to understand I needed the element of surprise to keep my family safe.'

'I'm surprised they're going along with this,' Lottie whispered to Meadow. 'I mean we could be serial killers for all they know.'

Meadow supposed their group looked harmless enough in their bishop sleeves and patchwork skirts. She sensed the men had weighed the risk against the importance of discovering non-taxidermy thylacines.

Gran paid cash for all their tickets back to Grove. Then made Sebastian and John sit at an angle least captured by the security cameras.

Chapter Twenty-eight

As the group walked along Mountain River Road, the sky threw coral and crimson above them. Gran stopped outside Bert's gate, as if toying with the idea of going in this time, but instead waved them on. 'Spencer will have to wait. We haven't much daylight left.'

Meadow glanced at her sister.

'See, Bert's not like Doyle,' Indigo Bliss rallied herself when Bert didn't appear. 'He sees the men and knows not to interrupt someone else's business.'

Her sister's words had changed from a light lavender to a resigned mulberry. Indigo Bliss had not let go of her disdain for Doyle's intrusiveness, amongst other things. Meadow had realised too late that Doyle's charm was superficial. His pushiness she'd excused as friendliness. His obsession with her sister she'd pardoned as just being besotted, his palomino stomping was at worst a silly childish habit. But one wake-up call she'd missed entirely was Doyle using Lottie to win her over. Meadow hoped Lottie hadn't discerned that plan, or concurred with it.

Once inside their cottage, Sebastian and John stood sheepishly in the hallway as Gran collected Grandfather's clothes.

Lottie put the kettle on top of the woodstove. 'It's like they think they're getting punked.'

'Punked?' Meadow asked.

'Having a joke played on them.'

'I sensed that in Sebastian before.' Meadow lined up six mugs.

'I still can't believe you don't have running water.'

'When it's all you've ever known.' Meadow picked up the watering can she'd filled from the tank earlier.

'What was your grandfather like?' Lottie said.

'Gone before we were born. He was in a hunting accident,' Meadow said. 'But Gran always thought that wasn't true, that he'd been protecting the tigers.'

'That sucks,' Lottie kneeled to put some more wood into the stove.

She tried to imagine what her grandfather would have looked like. She'd always imagined him to be like a Cape Barren goose but with light green eyes. He would speak the truest, calmest, dependable blue. Gran once said that a goose will stand by the other's side if injured, and not fly off when the flock moves on. Her grandmother had fixed an intense gaze on Meadow: 'If their mate dies they will often mourn in seclusion'.

That had confirmed to Meadow that Gran still mourned her own departed goose.

Gran returned with flannel shirts, corduroy pants and jackets, placing them on a chair in the hall. 'I'll leave these here.'

'When will we head off?' Indigo Bliss reached up for the cast iron pots.

'If we go before midnight we should be there early tomorrow.' Gran lined up the canisters of tea, hot chocolate and sugar. 'It's slower going in the dark.'

Meadow looked for the pups, expecting them to be underfoot trying to get a morsel of something she might spill. She breathed deeply, trying to ignore the ache. Trying to tell herself that Timba and Tawny were safe with their parents and siblings.

She distracted herself by remembering how crafty Gran had been at Parliament House. Her grandmother hadn't shared the shocker she was going to pull by getting the men to leave straight away.

Gran wanted to keep the momentum going with Sebastian and John. 'While the girls cook tea I want to show you something next door.' Gran gave Lottie a small nod, indicating she was safeguarded.

After Indigo Bliss tossed some baby potatoes in a pot, the sisters took Lottie out to the garden. As the light faded, Meadow showed her the chickens and Gertie. They picked snow peas for tea and a fresh bunch for a vase. Though she grew them year-round the plants wouldn't last much longer. She kept expecting to see Timba leap up and nip at the bunch, expected to see Tawny with a small pile of them sitting near her paws.

She offered Lottie some new leaves. 'They taste just like snow peas.'

Indigo Bliss called them over. It was time to go in and cook up some of Gran's canned chicken and apple patties.

'No calf yet,' Meadow said to her sister, placing her harvest basket on the table.

'I hope she has a heifer,' Indigo Bliss said. 'A little clone of Gertie.'

An atmosphere of self-consciousness fell on the kitchen. It felt as uncomfortable as particles of hay going down one's shirt while in the presence of others. For some time they awkwardly heated the patties and chopped chives for the potatoes. Meadow was itching to say something.

Indigo Bliss finally gave Lottie an apologetic shrug. 'Do you want to talk about the clone thing?'

'Maybe later,' Lottie said.

Meadow set the table, pleased with her sister, as the tension evaporated.

'Looks like your Gran is selling these guys on the plan.' Lottie gave each setting a decorated glass tumbler.

The men returned, ashen-faced. The idea that they were being punked appeared to be fading by the minute.

'Sebastian and John have a greater understanding of what we are up against,' Gran said.

The Drearys and Lottie dressed in warm-weather clothing, and Gran sorted Lottie out with some of her hiking gear. Lottie looked so much like their grandmother, with her copper hair poking out from a borrowed pink cloche hat.

The two men donned Grandfather's clothes before tea and ambled into the kitchen rather bashfully. It was strange to have men in the cottage. The table boasted a lot of blue and red in corduroy, checked shirts, beanies and knitted vests.

'Good fit,' Gran said. 'Now eat up.'

Meadow was quiet at first, while Lottie discussed her love of alternate realities with Sebastian and John. As Lottie shared her newest hypotheses about frequencies, portals and why most people can't visit Antarctica, she asked for Meadow's input.

'Well, I'm only new to them,' Meadow noted the men's eyes had grown considerably larger hearing about Antarctica, giants and dragons, 'but they're pretty interesting.'

'If you'd told me yesterday there were actual living Tassie tigers, I'd have thought you needed a tin foil hat,' Sebastian offered.

'Exactly.' Meadow left the table to bring back the dessert of butterscotch pudding. 'Sometimes we don't know what we don't know.'

It pleased her when both Sebastian and John nodded in agreement.

Gran caught Meadow's eye and winked in approval. She seemed interested in this change in her granddaughter.

Meadow had been watching Gran and Indigo Bliss

carefully too, wondering what they thought of Lottie's theories. They were respectfully attentive, and she couldn't wait to ask more later on.

'But prepare yourself for opposition when searching for truth,' Lottie said. 'You know, it's the victors who get to write history—but truth always comes out in the end.'

'And you can't believe every rabbit hole you go down,' Meadow added.

'So true,' Lottie nodded, 'you guys should check out the *Allegory of the Cave*.'

'That's Plato's cave, isn't it?' Sebastian sniffed at the butterscotchy air.

'Yes, and there's heaps of videos on it.' Lottie said.

'Lottie, have you researched the Wallace Line?' John ate a spoonful of pudding.

Lottie shook her head.

'It's like an imaginary boundary line that animals don't cross,' John said.

'Sounds right up Lottie's alley,' Gran nodded at Lottie who grinned back.

Once the dishes were done, Gran gave each person a small pack with supplies in it. 'Saves one person carrying the load,' Gran pointed to her larger backpack, 'but I've got the med kit and extra batteries if we need them.'

Indigo Bliss gave each person a torch.

Meadow wondered how their grandmother was still functioning. She hadn't stopped for months, perhaps years, perhaps decades.

But Gran's mouth was set in that determined way of hers. 'It might be a hard trip for you fellas but it'll be worth it. I promise.'

'Where are we headed, Gran?' Meadow asked, once Sebastian and John had gone outside.

'To the Drearys' shack,' Gran adjusted her shotgun.

Meadow wondered where it was located.

'You weren't far from us when those hikers arrived. That's why your sister and I backtracked, to make sure they didn't see us coming out of that part of the woodland.'

'Imagine if the pups had caught sight of you with those hikers.' Meadow pictured the pups excited faces.

The moon gave minimal light as they made their way past the old darlings' resting place. Once over the river, and into the Herefords' paddock, Gran said, 'We have cattle in the paddock, so stay close to me.'

In the darkness Meadow saw the white faces of their Herefords, like small white moons in the torchlight. Why were some animals despatched, while others had people risking their lives for them? She understood their cattle had a wonderful life, until that one bad day. She knew their chicken hatch rate was generally fifty percent roosters, and that keeping too many roosters with hens would lead to infighting. But it was still hard to accept half of those little fluffballs on matchstick legs wouldn't live as long as the hens.

She glanced at Lottie and wondered what her friend would say. Lottie had understood the pups' rampage on that snowy night. One of Lottie's more interesting theories was that all living food gave us energy in one way or another.

Gran led the group as they entered the woodland, with Indigo Bliss in the rear. The snow gums stood out starkly in the torchlight, pale apparitions like illuminated sculptures, but this time Meadow wasn't fearful as the branches clawed at her. Instead, she enjoyed the fresh scent as she stared up at the slim moon through tall, shadowed myrtle trees and felt only anticipation.

Back at the cottage she'd been watching everyone's words

closely, pondering if the colours had a deeper meaning, something to do with her own intuition.

The problem with this was that she'd viewed Doyle's words as friendly, golden confetti. He should've looked like a snake with slippery serpentine words.

The men didn't talk all that much and she noted John was a good hiker, supposing his job entailed the skill at times.

It was a quiet walk, except for the snapping of twigs underfoot, or the stubbing of a toe on an exposed root. Once again, the trees were like fallow deer antlers, timbered majestic crowns.

Even in the dark her grandmother knew every shortcut, every creek and bend; and with a torch she was unstoppable. They only halted a couple of times to have a snack and a drink. Gran carried a large thermos of hot chocolate which fortified them.

'Best to keep going,' Gran took everyone's old camping mugs, 'so you don't seize up.'

This time they didn't trek up over the ridge toward Sleeping Beauty. They headed in a different direction.

Lottie was quiet.

As the early morning sunlight filtered through the bush, Sebastian and John were tangibly eager.

We have to be careful with this section of the trip,' Gran said.

Meadow wondered what her grandmother meant.

Gran took several more steps, and disappeared.

Chapter Twenty-nine

'Gran,' Meadow instinctively cried out.

'It's all right,' Indigo Bliss said from the back. 'It's a hidden ledge.'

Meadow ran forward to see Gran standing below on a man-made ledge. She called up to the row of faces peering down. 'Be careful. I'm just showing off because muscle knows no age.'

Once they were all on the ledge, and had walked several minutes, they climbed onto higher ground once more. Sebastian and John were blindfolded. They were soon to enter a tunnel and Gran didn't want the whereabouts of the entrance known. Gran and Indigo Bliss led the men.

Passing behind a slab of rock, there was room for a person to comfortably walk through. Meadow smelt the damp earth and rock.

The tunnel was impressive. Supported by wooden beams it was tall enough for them to walk at full height. Within minutes Meadow noted a small circle of light ahead. Gran instructed the men to keep walking, that it wouldn't be long. Once through the other side of the tunnel, they were escorted around an enormous boulder. Gran instructed Indigo Bliss to take their blindfolds off.

They travelled a small path for an hour, until Gran stopped, turned around and said, 'Gentleman, look and learn.' Gran pointed toward some blurry shapes near a number of spiky browned ferns.

The shapes moved slowly, unveiling wolf-like heads, they walked with a tentative gait. A wary gait. Then, behind the spikes of the ferns, stripes appeared, so distinct that Meadow heard a whoop.

It was John, grinning. He playfully pretended to lean on Meadow's arm as if to steady himself. 'They look kind of supernatural.'

As the sunlight filtered through the trees, the stripes were so well-defined that any doubt immediately vanished. The thylacines stared at the group without fear, but with understandable caution.

She scanned for Timba and Tawny but these were not the Drearys' tigers.

'I'm trying to say something profound,' Sebastian said, 'but I'm speechless.' His words were silver bubbles of astonishment.

John took a deep breath, then glanced at Meadow. 'I'm sure you're used to them but it's...' His words stretched out like brown tiger stripes. 'Like nothing I've ever seen before.'

'Even after all this time they're still breathtaking.'

John stared at the Tassie tigers. 'I never want to leave.'

As the thylacines stared at the strangers, Gran moved closer to let them know they were safe. They surrounded Gran, a serene gathering of devotion.

Even the tigers were in awe of her grandmother.

Sebastian was overwhelmed. 'What your family has done...you're all worth your weight in gold.'

Meadow was not used to this kind of admiration. Their family had generally been at the receiving end of rude smears and insults. They'd seemed destined, for evermore, to be considered weirdos, freaks or witches.

Sebastian and John watched the thylacines' every move, reluctant to let the not-extinct creatures out of their sight.

'Where's Timba and Tawny? Meadow asked her sister.

'Probably in there,' Indigo Bliss pointed toward an old

shack hidden by the woodland.

'She's right.' Gran left her circle of thylacines and led the group toward the shack. It was a rude shack, with the tumbledown look of an old hunting cabin. It looked uninhabited with no smoke in the chimney.

Lottie turned to Meadow. 'Who's in there?'

'It must be the guardians,' Meadow said, 'with my pups.'

'Are the others in there too?' John looked at the shack. 'All the tigers I mean.'

'We are not that silly,' Gran said, her shotgun swinging slightly in its shoulder sling. 'They're hidden all over the state.'

Meadow hoped Timba and Tawny weren't frightened in that old shack.

'Wait here while I go and update the guardians,' Gran climbed three steps and opened the door.

'Look,' John pointed, 'I can see some juveniles through the trees.'

'Oh breed, you good things,' Sebastian uttered. 'Breed, breed, breed.'

She could hear the wonder in his voice mingle with a shade of craving. His words of silver changed to a deep, yearning sterling.

Indigo Bliss followed Meadow's gaze. 'So that just happened.'

'It did, didn't it,' Meadow agreed. After all these years, strangers had been let in on their secret. She kept watching the shack door. Waiting.

'They had to keep them in the shack a bit because they're not fully adjusted out here yet,' Indigo Bliss offered.

Would Timba try to cheekily nip at her hands and legs? That would be embarrassing. And of course would be a cardinal sin in front of Gran.

The shack door opened and Timba and Tawny came out, tentatively at first, blinking in the sunlight. When they saw Meadow they bounded excitedly toward her. She held out her arms and embraced the young thylacines.

'I missed you so much.' She kissed their heads and rubbed their ears.

If Sebastian and John had been enamoured before, being within touching distance of living Tasmanian tigers was almost too much. Meadow wondered if John might do an energetic somersault. She caught the glint of an unshed silver tear in Sebastian's eye.

Tawny nudged her in delight, and Meadow was relieved when Timba, distracted by all the attention, didn't nip at her once.

Indigo Bliss knelt, ruffling Timba and Tawny's heads.

Lottie patted them too. 'Remember me?'

Sebastian knelt and clicked his fingers, calling the pups to him. They went to him, fearless. He stroked their non-specimen fur, his eyes fixated on their stripes.

'We will do whatever the guardians want,' Sebastian said. 'I want my wife to see thylacines, and my daughters, and their children's children.'

John joined Sebastian, rubbing their ears like Meadow had. The pups looked up at him with their soft, trusting eyes. John was a natural nurturer, like rich brown soil.

Gran exited the shack and strode toward them. 'It seems they agree to the terms.'

'Yes. Yes to all of it,' Sebastian said.

'Absolutely,' John beamed at Gran.

'Good,' Gran said. 'Let's go and get some breakfast. I think bacon, beans and hash browns are on the menu.'

Gran nodded to Lottie, 'And a vegetarian omelette for you, my girl.'

The pups didn't follow them into the shack, instead

their noses rose into the air, scenting for their siblings. Meadow watched, relieved, as they bounded toward several thylacine approaching the ferns.

'I didn't spoil them too badly,' she shared her relief with her sister. 'They still crave wildness.'

Chapter Thirty

Inside, six people waited around a rough wooden table laden with breakfast fare. The food smelled wonderful. There was no fire in the hearth, only a couple of gas bottles with pans atop.

Gran gestured around the room, her hand sweeping toward three men and three women. Some had well-worn clothes like hers, others wore stylish hiking gear from an upscale shop.

'Everyone, I'm proud to introduce my other granddaughter, Meadow,' Gran said.

Meadow imagined judgemental gazes cutting toward her, as with Sleeping Beauty, dismayed at her gullible choices. That she alone had ruined over a century of guardianship.

'This is Lee.' Gran pointed to a brunette woman with wavy shoulder-length hair and black-trimmed butterscotch hiking gear. She came across as approachable and wore makeup like the women in the magazines at the library.

'She is the brains of the operation,' Gran said with pride.

Lee smiled widely at the newcomers. 'You must be starving, hiking all night like that.'

Her words were a blend of red and pink, in the shape of crystals. Lee was like a southern boobook owl, with round sparkling eyes.

'And Terrence,' Gran said, 'Terry for short. Lee's husband.'

When Terry spoke his words were blue and yellow, each syllable merging into green tendrils. His brown hair was short on the sides while sticking up at the top. His thickly lashed hazel eyes were his most prominent feature, reminding Meadow of an emu. He wore an old pair of grey waders topped with a brown puffer jacket. Meadow tried not to think about the poor Tasmanian emu.

'Well, we're all in a sorry mess, aren't we? At least our tigers are okay,' Terry's now pine-green words rose up toward the rafters. 'And we're going to keep it that way.'

'And Ava.' Gran pointed to a fortyish woman dressed in white with a blonde, highlighted pixie haircut. She was like a posh skier, like the ones Indigo Bliss had showed her from a ski resort in Switzerland. Ava wore a white hiking headband and the darkest fuchsia lipstick Meadow had ever seen.

Ava nodded imperceptibly, her face wary. She wasn't going to welcome anyone.

Meadow watched Ava turn her graceful, ivory swan-like neck toward Gran.

'I know we have to. But this feels dangerous,' Ava said.

The second Ava spoke, Meadow saw white, feather-like words floating toward her grandmother. But this fluffy display didn't fool Meadow. She could tell Ava was not the floaty, fluffy type. She was self-contained. Ava's mission was pure.

It was at that moment Meadow felt hot, overwhelmed by all the new faces and voices. She wanted to go out into the wilderness with her pups.

Gran pointed to a friendly-faced man and a curly-haired woman standing nearest the plate of hash browns. 'Our twins, Phil and Patty.' They were in their late fifties and both wore tan, non-descript hiking gear. But they couldn't have been more different. Phil reminded Meadow of a hedgehog, with spiky brown hair and small round eyes, while Patty was a baby-doll sheep with a cute smile.

'We've been involved for decades,' Patty said.

'Our family are from Buckland.' Phil said. 'And have known about the Buckland and Spring Bay Tiger and Eagle Extermination Association from the late eighteen hundreds.'

Their words had the same woolly, cloudlike consistency, Patty's a pearly cream, Phil's a walnut brown. Meadow sensed their family had been strongly connected to something of substance, aiming to achieve a legacy that would outlast themselves.

'That was before most people realised, you know, the thylacine were in a dangerous predicament,' Phil said. 'Our thylacines were so ill-defined. I think that suggestion they were like vampires, panthers or wild jungle beasts, cynical or not, effected our psyche in Tassie.'

Sebastian ran his hands through his mane of hair. 'It was a different time wasn't it.'

'Our tigers were scapegoats,' Phil nodded. 'Of course there were the government bounties.'

'Buckland is such a lovely town.' Pattie smiled ruefully at the newcomers. 'But back then most people weren't informed about the ratio between predator and prey.'

Gran was clenching her fists. Meadow wondered if she was getting ready to start a quarrel about who the real predators were. Instead, Gran took a deep breath.

'Lastly, this is Juke,' Gran introduced a young man not much older than Lottie. 'He's our youngest guardian.'

Juke's dark hair had distinct stripes shaved from his temples to the back of his head. He wore similar gear to the hikers who'd nearly stumbled upon Meadow. Juke's trendy hiking gear had all the same pockets, zippers and convertible bells and whistles.

Lottie sucked in her breath and Meadow realised that Juke could be considered quite handsome. He reminded her of Timba, with his affable grin and twinkling eyes.

'Well, I reckon you lot weren't expecting to be out here today,' Juke said. 'Sebastian and John, is it?'

The two men nodded.

'I have a lot of ideas about how we can protect our tigers. Hope you're up to the job.' Juke's golden words sparkled like fireworks. 'Has Gran Dreary filled you in on what we've planned? Plan B was the only way.'

He barked them out at such a rate it was hard for Meadow to keep up. She took an involuntary step back as Juke's gilded words glittered like Doyle's had.

'I assure you, we are.' Sebastian shook everyone's hand. 'Thank you for all you've done.'

John moved forward, shaking hands cheerfully with everyone.

'And this is Charlotte,' Gran said, 'she's a brave little thing.'

'Sounds like someone else we know,' Terry said.

Everyone chuckled at that, because Gran was quite brave and quite little herself.

'Eat up,' Gran said.

'So you understand the gravity of the situation,' Juke said, choosing one of the omelettes.

'Yes,' Sebastian and John said in unison.

'I hope so,' Ava said. 'We have a lot to organise.'

These guardians would surely understand her family's lifestyle better than most, thought Meadow, envisioning future get-togethers, perhaps even a celebratory party once the thylacine were safe. She'd never been to a party.

Within an hour, satiated and sipping hot beverages, the table was cleared and paperwork took its place. Lee presented folders, while Gran reached into her vest, producing her contribution of maps, showing various partitioned areas.

The guardians, apart from Gran, were cagey when it came to their own lives and where they lived.

'We're not disclosing anything until it's all ready to be signed,' Phil said, tugging his hedgehog hair.

'Understood,' Sebastian said. 'We are beyond grateful for your sacrifices all these years. 'This isn't just about Tassie, people from all over the world will be affected.'

The Drearys' cover is already blown,' Gran said, shaking her head. 'So ask me if you need personal information.'

Sebastian and John studied the maps, nodding in agreement at how strategically the guardians had used the Tasmanian wilderness.

'This will be a bipartisan effort, I can assure you,' Sebastian said. 'No doubt in my mind. Everyone will be on board.'

John added, 'Mrs Dreary has already explained that the tigers are not to be in contact with humans. Only members of the Snug and Flowerpot Yarn and Weavers Group.'

'We don't want to take any chances that they will be harmed.' Juke focused directly at both the men. 'And we know we can trust ourselves.'

'Only ourselves,' Ava glanced at Lottie, Sebastian and John.

'I told you I can vouch for them,' Gran said. 'Or I wouldn't have brought them here.'

'All these years after your husband…' Terry cleared his throat, 'to have someone attacking you like that, Gran. We have no choice but to move forward.'

'That woman wrecked everything.' Gran questioned Meadow. 'What do you call her?'

'The redback lady,' Meadow said, enjoying the guardians' protectiveness toward her grandmother.

'That blasted woman,' Indigo Bliss stated.

'Yes her, and now Doyle.' Gran made sure to give Lottie a reassuring smile.

Sebastian said, 'I'm sorry, that must have been quite…'

They heard a noise outside. A whirring sound.

Meadow, Indigo Bliss and Lottie left the shack, running outside, trying to look through the treetops, trying to spot a small black object flying close by.

A black object appeared but it wasn't a drone.

It was a helicopter.

Chapter Thirty-one

Returning to the shack Meadow heard Gran roaring at Sebastian and John. 'I vouched for you! Who did you tell? Are you wearing a tracking device?'

'No,' John held up his hands. 'I didn't tell anyone. You were there when I made the call.'

'Same,' Sebastian added. 'And we changed clothes at the cottage.'

Meadow, standing inside the shack door, glanced at the men, who were genuinely surprised. She focused on Lottie, who ducked her head. Meadow had a sinking sensation. Why wouldn't Lottie make eye contact? Was Lottie worried about the chopper? Or was it something else?

She turned to Gran, who signalled with her eyes, 'not here, not now.'

Did Gran think Lottie had leaked where they were?

It was chaos. The guardians crammed paperwork into backpacks, and Gran stuffed hers into the leather pouch from her vest.

'Only the southern tigers are here.' Gran turned to Lee and Terry, who stood at the shack door. 'Take your lot and help Indigo Bliss with ours; the rest of us will try to lead them the wrong way.'

'Oh and take Timba and Tawny as well,' Gran went to Indigo Bliss and whispered something to her. Her grandmother then turned back to the group, 'Phil and Patty, go home to guard your tigers.'

Indigo Bliss flashed violet daggers toward Sebastian and John. 'If you have done this you'll wish you'd never been born.'

Fury once again turned Indigo Bliss into a fierce yet breathtaking creature. When this unicorn tossed her flowing mane, even Meadow flinched. She wondered if John and Sebastian might run like the crab man had.

They didn't.

Indigo Bliss shot one more disdainful glance at the men before calling her tigers and Timba and Tawny to heel.

Meadow followed her sister, hoping to catch one last glimpse of her pups. Timba and Tawny broke away for a moment and galloped toward her for a quick pat before charging back to their siblings. She'd brought them to safety; the rope harnesses had been worth it; the pups were reunited with their family.

'Probably going to land there,' Ava pointed to a nearby clearing of small stunted ferns and short grass.

'Whose helicopter is it?' Lottie frowned at the intimidating chopper.

Ava glared at Lottie for a moment, sizing her up.

Meadow heard Lottie's sharp intake of breath.

She peered through the binoculars, her eyes focused on the rotating blades. 'Wait, there's a blond man inside, looking at us,' Meadow gasped. 'I think he's flicking his fringe.'

'Well, well,' Gran took three steps in one jump, 'that sounds like our old friend Doyle to me.'

'So you didn't betray us.' Gran turned to Sebastian and John. 'We're going to need your help.'

'Gran,' Meadow's voice shook, 'it looks like they are going to land.'

Lottie panicked. 'I've got to get out of here.'

'Stay with us,' Meadow would not jump to any conclusions about Lottie.

'Right,' Gran said, 'Sebastian and John, come with me. Juke, you and Ava go with Meadow and Charlotte. Confuse them. Circle around, leave a trail of broken twigs and footprints, then lose them. Take the shortcuts back to my cottage. You should get there just after dusk.'

Meadow's heart raced.

'No heroics,' Gran looked at Meadow and Lottie with a frown, before leaning close to Meadow. 'I'm going softly, softly but I want you to watch Charlotte.'

It was jarring to have someone she'd trusted a second time appear like a stranger again.

'I will.'

'Everyone clear?' Gran said, pointedly.

Meadow nodded.

'Yes. We are clear,' Ava said.

'We won't let you down,' Juke's words flamed with a rose-gold resolve.

As they split into two groups, Meadow tried to break as many twigs and branches and make her footprints as deep as she could. After circling the shack twice and tracking in the wrong direction from the tunnel, the four gestured to each other. Changing tack, they left no trace as they set out for the cottage.

Meadow hoped everyone would be all right. Gran had her shotgun but who knew what weapons Doyle might have.

Ava led the way and Juke stayed in the rear checking constantly to see if they were being followed. No one dared talk. Lottie was pale again, her cheeks pinched. Meadow handed her a couple of hash browns she'd wrapped and stashed in her pocket. She hoped Lottie was off-colour because Doyle was all of a sudden so close. It was untenable that Lottie might have offered to go into the old oak tree to exploit their kindness. Lottie nibbled on a hash brown, then pulled off Gran's cloche hat and put it in her pocket.

Ava and Juke knew Gran's shortcuts well. Meadow kept listening for gun shots, or for the helicopter to whir past them overhead.

And what of Sebastian and John? Who knew that so soon they would witness the peril of a guardian's life.

'You worrying too?' Lottie said.

'A bit,' Meadow said.

Hours later, she recognised parts of the track. Her arms and legs were in serious trouble, unused to this type of exercise. Thick clouds hid the moon, as if giving them cover.

When they reached the top paddock, she gave a sigh of relief. 'Nearly there.'

Lottie looked tired too. 'Don't forget I live a sedentary lifestyle you know.'

Trekking through ground-level evening fog the Hereford cattle stared at them.

'What do you think has happened back there?' Meadow asked Juke.

'I think they got the tigers away safely. And that we're staying with you,' Juke nodded toward Lottie. 'And Charlotte, until your Gran says otherwise.'

Out of the corner of her eye, she saw Lottie watching Juke.

'Is it Lottie or Charlotte?' Juke inclined his head to one side.

'I like Lottie.'

'Lottie it is,' Juke smiled.

'Your Gran can handle anyone,' Ava said.

That gave Meadow hope because it was true.

'If anyone from the chopper followed us,' Juke turned and walked backwards for a bit, 'we should have a good view from this paddock.'

It was decided Juke and Ava would stay at the stone seats and keep guard, while Meadow and Lottie would fetch supplies. Their torches were dimming and everyone was hungry and thirsty. This way the two guardians could be on alert if anyone turned up.

Lottie kept glancing over the fence toward her brick home, now in total darkness.

'No one's home,' Meadow said. 'No ute either.'

She checked in on Gertie. Still no calf. The chicken eggs were overflowing out of their nesting boxes so Lottie held out Gran's hat like a bowl. 'I think we should boil some eggs for toasted sandwiches.'

She stood up awkwardly, bumping her head on a low-lying beam. Pain exploded in her tongue, the same place as with Timba's earlier collision and the mantelpiece.

'Are you okay?' Lottie looked wide-eyed and innocent.

Through a cloud of pain Meadow had a sudden urge to yell at Lottie and demand the truth from her. She wanted to wipe that innocent expression away. Wanted to ask if she'd pretended to be her friend…was still pretending. Instead, wincing, she catapulted two eggs through the doorway, hitting a tree trunk with forceful cracks and crunches.

Lottie cleared her throat.

As the pain abated, Meadow remembered Gran saying softly, softly.

'I'm fine,' Meadow managed through her teeth, turning her head from the egg-yellow mess sliding down rough bark.

They entered the back door to a quiet cottage. No pups to greet her. No Spencer. After a brief inspection she was reassured it hadn't been disturbed this time. She mechanically lit the woodstove and boiled the kettle and eggs.

The two busied themselves under the lantern light organising warm beverages and making fresh sandwiches.

'Batteries,' Meadow remembered. 'I hope Gran didn't take them all.'

Her grandmother's room was still messier than usual but Meadow found an unopened packet on the dresser. She slipped a couple into her dimming torch, and the rest in her pocket.

Someone knocked on the front door, and Meadow called out. 'Hang on, Juke? Or Ava?'

They'd be checking the perimeter.

'We've got the food ready,' Meadow turned on her torch and headed toward the front door.

It was the hooded man. He thumped hard, nearly shattering the glass petals of wisteria. She dropped the torch and it clanged loudly on the old floorboards. She stooped to pick up the broken plastic case, fumbling for the dropped batteries and reflector.

The man thumped again. 'I know you're in there and if you don't come out he's going to get it.'

Of course it had to be Doyle, or someone he'd hired, and he had Juke. Shaking, she left the torch on the floor, and tiptoed back to the kitchen. She found Lottie, standing stock still with a kitchen knife in her hand.

'Who is it?' Lottie hissed like a kitten in peril.

'I think it's Doyle,' Meadow said, hoping this wasn't an act on Lottie's part.

'I thought Doyle was in the helicopter,' Lottie paled. 'He's lost it…been pushed too far.'

Had Doyle employed a double, or worse? Meadow had no time to think about Doyle's fascination with cloning.

'I'll stall him at the front door,' Meadow strategised, 'if you can go through my wardrobe and see what's happening from the side.'

'Will do,' Lottie said, but she was trembling.

'Do not come around,' Meadow warned Lottie. 'No matter what. Stay away from Doyle.'

It was a test. In some ways it was a test of their friendship too.

As Meadow returned to the front door, Lottie ventured toward the wardrobe.

Meadow shouted, 'Let him go, Doyle.'

'Why would I do that,' the hooded figure retorted.

'Because Gran has her shotgun and she's getting ammo right now.' Where had Doyle been all this time? Did he know they'd found Lottie? Had this been their plan all along.

'Were you impressed with the gift I sent you?' Doyle said. 'My boss is generous organising a chopper and hunters.'

She got a terrible feeling.

'Don't worry, they'll use tranquiliser darts,' Doyle said. 'Well…they're supposed to.'

It sounded like the men were reckless and hungry for thylacines, hungry for money like Doyle.

'We knew you were the hooded man,' Meadow snapped.

'Oh I am so much more,' Doyle said. 'Like the man who planted a tracker in your Gran's pack.'

'That's impossible,' Meadow said, almost to herself.

'I waited until your grandmother brought those suits here, and she took them to my house.'

Meadow tried to think where she was when that happened. In the garden with her sister and Lottie? Doyle must have slipped inside while they were picking snow peas.

What Gran had been wrong about, was that she'd protected them by taking all her precious paperwork. Doyle had waited like a fox, then slipped into the henhouse, planting the tracker in her pack. Trashing Gran's room had only been a ruse.

What Meadow had been wrong about, was that Doyle had been in the helicopter.

Chapter Thirty-two

She flung open the front door. Doyle threw back his hood and pointed a torch and a screwdriver at his hostage.

It wasn't Juke.

It was Bert.

Bert's mouth was gagged, and he had an apologetic yet panicked expression in his eyes. Bright blood was splattered over his scarf and tan overcoat.

'Bert!' Meadow stared in disbelief. 'What has he done to you?'

'You come outside,' Doyle ordered, holding Bert tightly as he backed away several steps.

Doyle's fringe hung dankly over his face; his eyes stared devoid of emotion through greasy strands of hair. Then she saw his eyes flash and his nostrils flare as he snorted brashly. He had become a ghostly-wild-brumby. He stamped his foot, enraged. His mask had slipped and he had nothing to lose.

Meadow did as Doyle asked, a grim premonition of harm flooding her body as she stepped outside.

'Who were you expecting? Jake or Eve was it?'

'No one,' Meadow said, there was no way she would give up Juke or Ava. 'I was just talking to myself…as usual.'

It took all her strength to not glance to the right. To see if Lottie was going to walk up to her father and give him a high five or say something congratulatory.

'We've been catching up, haven't we?' Doyle shone the torch into Bert's face again, making him look like a grotesque marionette. 'Bert here knows very little about you ladies. Pathetic really.'

'Just let him go.' She tried to keep the tremble out of her voice.

'You ruined everything Meadow,' Doyle towered over Bert. With a clenched jaw he picked Bert up like a ragdoll.

Not for the first time, Meadow wondered how Lottie thought Doyle was redeemable.

'Screw you Doyle,' Meadow closed her eyes. When she opened them, the expression on Bert's face made her cold inside.

'Would your Gran let you talk like that?' Doyle's expression changed from surprise to amusement. 'Are you going to come with me or am I going to have to rough this old bloke up a bit more?'

Bert's eyes bulged. He was frozen to the spot.

'If you let him go I'll come with you,' Meadow tried to push aside what Gran always said about never letting someone take you to a secondary place, that you'd have no chance if they took you somewhere secluded.

What else could she do? It was no use hoping Gran would be walking up from the river at that very moment. And it looked like Juke and Ava were oblivious. She needed to move fast, before Bert got hurt.

Meadow went to Bert, and supported one of his elbows, trying to squeeze him reassuringly. 'Go Bert.'

'Don't you try and give me the slip,' Doyle warned, following her closely. The bell jingled as she pushed open the gate the fairywren had dangled from. Meadow sent Bert on his way, still gagged, his hands bound together at his front. She was worried if she took too long with his bindings Doyle might change his mind. She could only hope that Lottie would see the poor man staggering up the road in the dark and go after him when the coast was clear.

'Right,' Meadow tried to exude confidence, but her voice continued to quiver.

'I thought we might take a walk. Over to my place where I have plotted out where your Gran is…'

He stared down his nose at her and added, '…if you make any noise, your Gran gets it.'

His words were now a macabre blood-red, seeping from his lips.

Meadow nodded silently. She thought of the camouflaged wildlife cameras and carefully scrutinised Doyle's property. He certainly enjoyed putting on a grotesque show with brutal arrangements. The creatures in the tree, the fairywren dangling from the front gate and the state of Bert. Her sister was right, Doyle must be one of those psychopaths, so callous and manipulative.

Meadow's stomach dropped.

'I don't need them all. Just a few,' Doyle steered her to the back of his house. 'Even your family's offering will do. Is it male, female and four juveniles?'

She wanted to shout at him they had more tigers than that. Some were in the bush, some were in lairs, and others had gone to the other guardians to stop interbreeding.

'Good trick pretending I was running away,' Doyle opened the sliding door. 'So where's my daughter?'

It took all of her strength to not glance toward the river. Had Lottie gone to help Bert or to warn the others? Were the guardians watching them, their torches turned off, ready to pounce?

'I don't know where she is.'

'No matter,' Doyle said, 'I'll find her, and your Gran and all the other things I want.'

Chapter Thirty-three

Inside Doyle's house, Meadow found it hard to breathe. She glanced at him, wondering how she'd failed to suspect he was so unhinged.

Her only plan was to keep stalling him.

'Right,' Doyle said, 'sit at the table. Here is the first map.'

She sat in front of an open laptop displaying a map of Tassie. Doyle zoomed in to a red spot blinking. The spot wasn't moving.

He pointed at a blue spot. 'That's the helicopter. So they've already got your Gran because she's the red dot.'

She reeled back in shock. The blue dot was right next to the red one.

'We were going to use heat sensors but there's so many marsupials and hikers roaming in the bush, I wanted to go old school with a tracker. Your Gran's a wily one.'

Meadow froze.

'I can contact the helicopter pilot at any moment and tell him we don't need her anymore,' Doyle said. 'Now that I have you.'

The edges of her vision darkened until greyish blooms filled her eyes. She must not faint. It was stress from the redback lady, Gran leaving, Indigo Bliss leaving, the pups, whether Lottie was friend or foe, the half-formed-creatures and Doyle attacking Bert. She closed her eyes and groaned, trying to breathe evenly.

'Huh,' Doyle said, 'what are you moaning about?'

'I don't know as much as Gran,' Meadow's tongue was beginning to hurt again.

'Circle where the thylacines are,' Doyle handed Meadow a pen. 'Go on, it draws on the screen.'

She opened her eyes, feeling the cold pen in her hand. Thankful her vision was clearing. 'I think…umm.'

Meadow fiddled with the pen. Could she stab him in the arm with it? Or neck? Doyle must think she didn't have a propensity for violence to trust her with the small pointy weapon.

'I'll know soon enough if you're lying so don't even bother.'

She stifled a strange laugh. In such a short time she'd gone from anxiety about stepping on a fairywren to plotting a stabbing incident with a pen.

Doyle was not amused. He flicked his dank fringe to one side. Pushed too far, the furious brumby snorted with such force that she felt the hairs on the back of her neck stand on end.

'At a guess I'd say here,' Meadow drew a circle around Richmond. She hadn't been there but hoped Doyle would think it was an option.

'Wrong.' Doyle pressed a button and the circle she'd drawn vanished. 'There's no way you're hiding them in such a popular tourist destination.'

Doyle brought his hand down and smashed the table. Looking at his clenched fist she thought he might hit her. Right at the table where she'd laid all of her home-made treats, made with such care. Where she'd eaten pizza with his daughter. Where her pears had looked like a display piece in a lime-coloured plastic bowl.

The looming Doyle was even scarier than the hooded man thumping on their door. There was no dividing space between them now, she saw the spittle on his lips, the anger in his eyes.

'If you don't do it,' Doyle clenched his jaw, 'I'm going

to send a message to the pilot and tell him to get rid of your Gran. Her blinking red dot will fizzle out, right before your eyes.'

She stared at the screen then at Doyle.

Doyle was wearing an earpiece. Was all his bluster an act? Who was he putting on a show for? Had he been in contact with Lottie all along?

'But if you do what I want no one will get hurt,' Doyle said, his charismatic gold-dust voice reappearing. 'You're such a lovely person. Surely you wouldn't want your Gran to get hurt.'

Did he believe she was still that gullible, to be swayed by his charm?

A red-lipsticked woman pushed through the arched doors, her red hair hanging like a stripe down the back of her black dress.

Redback lady.

'You played the part perfectly,' redback lady said to Doyle, her words weaving a silken red web. 'But I think you've outworn your usefulness, don't you?'

'No,' Doyle said. 'Don't you touch her.'

Was Doyle defending her?

'Get the information I want…or else.' Redback lady didn't even acknowledge Meadow. 'You know I will find her and that will be the last time you see her.'

'Sienna, you will not lay a finger on Lottie,' Doyle said, 'or I swear I'll…'

'You'll what?'

Did Lottie know who Sienna was? Know she hadn't gone?

Meadow stared at Sienna, convinced by her intensity that the redback lady and veiled woman must be one and the same.

Either way Sienna obviously despised the Drearys.

'Make this one tell us.' Sienna grasped the table, her knuckles turning white. 'That's why I kept you around.'

What power did Sienna have over Doyle? Lottie had said that Doyle had bad actors around him. Had Sienna been hired by Doyle's benefactor too?

Meadow saw a flicker of movement at the back door, and turned her head away from the woman as if in disgust. The evening fog parted, allowing a silhouette to be apparent, a quietly moving shape. She saw the figure survey the kitchen scene with a calculating gaze. A cat sizing up its prey, before giving Meadow an almost imperceptible nod.

A calmness came over Meadow, but she decided to portray the opposite.

She dropped her head onto the laptop, pretending to cry.

'Stop that!' Doyle ordered. 'You'll make the laptop wet.'

'I can't help it,' Meadow sobbed loudly, tearlessly. 'You're mean and I thought you were my friend.'

Sienna roared with laughter. 'She really is pathetic, isn't she. Restrain her.'

Doyle bent and grasped Meadow's Dutch braids, pulling her head up. 'You will not hurt Lottie,' he growled at Sienna, as Meadow's head whipped up.

As pain coursed through her head and neck she shrieked. Her scream gave strength to her limbs and she elbowed Doyle as hard as she could. Doyle let go of her braids, and stumbling forward, smashed his head on the table.

She heard the sound of something connecting with Sienna.

'Lottie!' Meadow turned to see the arched back of a kitten before her. This feline was hissing and growling at Sienna with pink painted nails out, like talons.

Lottie had thrashed Sienna with an outdoor bean bag, and small white beans were strewn across the dining room table. Sienna crumbled to the floor, murmuring murderous words. Crimson tendrils coiled around Lottie.

Doyle stood, holding his side, rubbing his head, but appearing only slightly dazed.

Lottie dashed to one of the kitchen drawers and pulled out some large cable ties.

'Quick, help me get her tied up before she starts moving again.'

In the end, Meadow and Lottie might have overdone it with the cable ties. And the masking tape. And the kitchen twine, but Sienna wasn't going anywhere. They couldn't bring themselves to put a gag on her at first, but she wouldn't stop screeching, furious with disbelief.

'You did something I should have a long time ago,' Doyle said. 'We need to get out of here Lottie.'

'Stay,' Lottie said. 'Sienna will finally get what she deserves. Especially with the Drearys around.'

'She'll say that I was behind it all,' Doyle glared at Sienna. Sienna shook her head vigorously.

'I'll vouch for you,' Lottie said. 'She made you do all those things.'

'I can't risk it,' Doyle said. 'Let's go.'

'I'm not running anymore,' Lottie glanced over at Meadow.

'I can't leave you here,' Doyle's words disintegrated into white embers, seeming to voice his regret.

'Yes you can.' Meadow moved to Lottie's side. 'She can stay with us.'

Lottie turned her face away from Doyle.

His face contorted. Meadow wasn't sure if he might drag Lottie to his ute.

Lottie linked her arm with hers.

Giving Meadow a rueful smile, Doyle shrugged in a wordless apology.

She heard voices outside, then the front door slamming shut. Doyle had gone.

Juke and Ava rushed through the back sliding door, nearly slipping on the white beads all over the floor.

'What? Who?' Juke studied Sienna.

'Now she knows how it feels to be tied up,' Lottie said. 'At least she hasn't been thrown into a tree trunk.'

'Sienna did that to you?' Meadow shivered at the thought of Sienna watching her from the second storey. 'Why didn't you say?'

'Something bad would have happened to Doyle.'

Lottie stared at the front door.

'But why does she hate us so much?' Meadow glared at Sienna. 'Why attack Gran?'

'She loathes everyone,' Lottie said. 'She must've thought Gran was the king pin to take out so she could get the thylacine for herself.'

'So this is the mastermind behind it all, apparently.' Meadow pointed at Sienna, apprising Ava and Juke of what the woman had done. The bad actor playing the roles of redback lady and veiled woman.

'Did she say anything about Gran?' Juke asked.

'Doyle put a tracker in her backpack.' Meadow showed Juke and Ava the map on the laptop. Gran's stationary red tracker still blipped in one spot.

There was a muffled laugh from Sienna.

'Let's bring it over here.' Ava picked up the laptop, placing it on a kitchen benchtop.

'Wait,' Juke leaned closer. 'It's moving.'

They watched as Gran's tracker moved away from her fixed spot near the helicopter. She was moving at a fast pace, a determined pace. It soon became clear that Gran's red dot was moving in a straight line toward the path they'd recently taken themselves.

'I think she's heading toward the tunn…' Ava frowned at herself for almost revealing the existence of the tunnel.

'Has the helicopter moved too?' Meadow wondered.

'The blue one?' Juke said. 'Nope, still stationary.'

Sienna shook her head in frustration, giving another muffled roar.

Juke tapped on the benchtop as he stared at the red dot. 'That's it, I'm heading off to make sure Gran's okay.'

'Thank you,' Meadow said, not sure that her legs would allow her to walk very far at all.

'No worries.' Juke stared out at the night sky. 'If she's on her way back, probably won't be until morning.' Juke glanced at Lottie, his words a softer shade of champagne gold. 'Are you okay?'

'I think so,' Lottie said.

'Can you watch Sienna?' Meadow asked Ava. 'I've got to help Bert.'

'Sure,' Ava looked at Sienna in a condescending manner. 'I'll keep an eye on Gran's tracker too.'

'Make yourself at home,' Lottie shouted from outside, 'snack on anything you want.'

As she exited, Juke gave Lottie a supportive side hug as Lottie looked like she needed propping up.

'Tell Gran everything,' Meadow called to Juke as he jogged toward the river, 'especially about who Sienna is.'

Remembering the earpiece, Meadow gestured for Ava to step outside. Within seconds Ava marched back inside, and there was a yelp as Ava pulled Sienna's earpiece off.

Her friend had saved her twice. Would she ever tell Lottie what she'd suspected, that she was an infiltrator? Meadow had so many questions about Sienna but now was not the time.

As they reached the front gate Meadow said, 'I want to get some first aid supplies.'

Lottie then carried the supplies as Meadow shone the torch up the road.

They located Bert, still struggling along the road at a snail's pace in the dark. Bert's normal hobble now slanted at a precarious angle.

'Bert,' Meadow called as they neared him. 'Wait. We'll help you.'

Lottie retrieved kitchen scissors from her pocket.

'I'm Lottie,' She introduced herself, as she cut the ties and removed the gag.

'That bastard!' Bert said, then cleared his throat. 'Excuse me ladies, but he and that woman put Spencer in the bathroom. She said she'd give it to Spencer if I didn't tell her everything.'

'Is Spencer all right?' Meadow noticed Bert's face was ashen.

'Please help him.' A look of disbelief on his weathered face. 'I still don't know what those two were talking about.'

'It's okay, Bert,' Lottie said. 'We've got her safely detained at the moment.'

She noted Lottie did not state she was Doyle's daughter.

'She's not going anywhere.' Meadow put her arm around Bert to steady him. 'Let's get you home so we can check on Spencer.'

It took some time to get Bert inside as his legs kept giving way on him.

Meadow had never been inside Bert's toilworn home. Only to his front door. Inside she saw tractor parts leaning against the rosebud-print lounge set. Most were covered in hay and she dusted a nest from a worn rosebud chair. Gran had said the lounge had been his wife Mary's pride and joy, and Meadow wondered what his dear departed wife would say. Would Mary be surprised or saddened that Bert was bringing his tractor parts inside. Perhaps she'd smile.

She went to the bathroom and let Spencer out. The old boy was shivering but appeared unharmed.

'Spencer, Spencer,' Bert called, a note of panic in his voice.

Spencer ran and when he saw Bert, the old dog licked his hands furiously.

'Okay, okay old boy,' Bert said, but Spencer would not, or could not stop lavishing relieved licks on Bert.

Meadow pushed aside thoughts of the pups, as Lottie entered the lounge with a cup of coffee and some biscuits. 'Thanks luv,' Bert said. 'But I'm thinking I might need something a bit stronger as well.'

'Not until I see what happened to your chest,' Meadow stared at the blood on his tan trench coat, still seeping into his scarf. 'Screwdriver wounds?'

Bert stared at his blood-soaked scarf. 'Oh that,' he chuckled, nearly choking on his biscuit. 'That's from a bleeding nose.'

He grimaced, 'I headbutted that man when he tried to take Spencer away. Bled all over myself.'

Once again, she saw Bert's words weren't their usual green-grass colour, not at all like freshly cut hay. Instead his mumblings were timeworn and sickly green.

'No worries. Right as rain now,' Bert broke a new biscuit in half and gave it to Spencer. The old dog crunched gratefully, awaiting more. 'Would you bring the biscuit tin here before you go?'

She fetched the biscuit tin and placed it on a small table next to Bert.

Meadow had a sudden thought. 'How long were they questioning you?'

'Couple of days I reckon. Just turned up here in his ute, hightailing it down the road,' Bert said. 'They hid it in my tractor shed.'

That's why Bert's tractor was outside of the shed.

'It was mainly that woman who was violent,' Bert frowned.

'We're you hit on the head?' Meadow said. 'Any other injuries?'

'No, just when I made my own nose bleed,' Bert chuckled again.

There was a sparkle returning to his eyes that gave her hope. She signalled for Lottie to follow her into the kitchen. 'I think we should stay with him for a while. There's no way Bert will go to hospital. And Juke's gone to Gran, so it'll be a few hours until they're back.'

'Ava's capable,' Lottie agreed. 'We can light the fire and try and steer Bert away from having anything stronger. Just in case.'

'I'll get more wood,' Meadow said.

'I'll make sure he's warm enough.' Lottie suddenly grasped Meadow's arm. 'Doyle never used to be like this. It's complicated.'

'Sienna's like Doyle's handler?' Meadow asked.

'I think she has something on Doyle,' Lottie nodded, 'that would have made his backer want revenge. And he was trying to protect me.'

Meadow thought of the lengths she'd already gone to—so as to protect her family and the pups.

Chapter Thirty-four

At dawn they left Bert sleeping by the fire with Spencer at his feet. He was wearing a clean vest, having changed out of his blood-stained clothes during the night. Spencer wagged his tail but didn't want to leave his old friend.

'I'm fine,' Bert woke with a start and waved them on. 'Spencer and I will come down if we need you.'

Nearing the cottage, Meadow said, 'You don't have to go back to your place. I'll go check on Ava.'

Lottie stood near the Drearys' letterbox, her hands shaking as she stared at her house.

'Go into our cottage and make yourself at home,' Meadow urged.

Lottie was torn, her kitten ears were pinned back and she looked damp, like she'd fallen into a puddle.

'I'll be right next door,' Meadow said.

Eventually, Lottie pushed open the front gate, trudging toward the purple door.

As Meadow walked around the back of Doyle's house there was a loud commotion inside.

Gran had returned and she was furious.

'You were behind harming old Bert were you?' Gran thundered. 'And my granddaughter too. And don't even get me started on poor Charlotte, or our tigers.'

'I'm here,' Meadow called as she neared the back door. 'I'm okay. Lottie is okay. Bert is okay and so is Spencer.'

Gran moved to Meadow's side, and whispered, 'all our tigers are okay too.' Her grandmother stared at Sienna. 'Remember when this woman attacked me in town.'

Meadow nodded. She felt concern as her grandmother resumed her tirade. Not for the first time she wondered how her grandmother was still standing. Gran was exhausted and covered in fern fronds and dirt.

'As if the poor tigers didn't have enough to deal with,' Gran said. 'Propaganda, greed, ignorance…'

Meadow knew this particular lecture well and it was long-winded. It could range from Gran's views about the delay in protecting the tigers to her thoughts on the theory that an epizootic disease had caused the decline of the thylacine.

She needed to calm Gran. If Gran started in on rugs made of thylacine skins, or rumours of tiger hats and waistcoats—she could go on for an extended time.

Sienna, now ungagged and sitting on a chair, held her head high. She spat her disdain for Gran.

Meadow noticed Sebastian and John leaning against the kitchen sink, quietly standing with Juke and Ava. John's eyes were narrowed at Sienna, while Sebastian's big-cat gaze observed the captured target, evidently covetous of Gran's interrogative role.

On closer inspection both men had scratches on their faces and blood on their hands. 'What happened?'

'We met with resistance,' Gran held out her bag. 'Ava, take my first aid kit and disinfect those wounds.'

Meadow had a sudden, worrying thought that Doyle might go to the cottage while Lottie was alone.

'Gran, please come back to the cottage,' Meadow urged. 'I need to tell you about Doyle in private. Sienna isn't going anywhere.'

Gran took a deep breath as if readying herself for another outburst, but for once she relented.

'Do you mind staying with Sienna?' Gran asked Juke and Ava. 'I'll bring you something to eat and drink soon.'

Juke and Ava pointed toward some empty packets of corn chips sitting next to empty cans. Ava said, 'We're fine.'

'You ate those quickly,' Gran said to Juke.

'You've been going at her for a while.' Juke glanced at his watch before eyeing Meadow. 'How's Lottie?'

'Couldn't stomach coming over here.' Meadow glanced at Sienna. 'I can't blame her.'

Juke moved toward the sliding door. 'I'll go and see if she's okay.'

'We'll be right behind you,' Gran said. 'Ava?'

'I'm staying right here until everything is sorted,' Ava said with a swan-hiss of protection. Her elegance hid a nesting instinct so strong she would risk anything for the guardians.

'We saw your tracker blinking,' Meadow said as she, John and Sebastian followed Gran toward the cottage. 'And Doyle said you were captured.'

'It's all right. Ava and Juke filled me in,' Gran patted Meadow's arm at their gate, before entering the cottage.

'What happened to the pilot and helicopter? And that Doyle doppelganger with the other men?' Meadow asked as Lottie stoked the fire, while Juke tended to the kettle.

'Oh, we fixed the pilot, didn't we,' Gran gestured for Sebastian and John to sit at the dining table. 'He's not going anywhere in a hurry.'

'Neither are the other hunters,' Sebastian said.

'We used the element of surprise,' John touched his face, 'and waited until the pilot was alone before we jumped him.'

'Element of surprise?' Lottie poured water into the teapot.

'Jumped him?' Meadow set out lemon and sugar.

'Your Gran had a thylacine stashed in the shack,' John said. 'Under the floorboards.'

She could hardly believe her ears.

'I am mortified to say this out loud,' Gran confessed, glancing briefly at Juke. 'But some time ago I came into the possession of a certain taxidermy of a thylacine, and hid him in the shack.'

Meadow shook her head in disbelief.

'It sounds disrespectful,' Gran said, 'but I told myself I'd saved the poor old tiger.'

'Saved him?' Meadow asked.

'He was a trophy in a private collection. My intention was to bury him in the wilderness at some stage.'

An image formed in Meadow's mind. 'You put him in the ferns didn't you!'

'Yes,' Gran shook her head. 'I felt terrible doing it, but desperate times…'

'We waited until the hunters jumped out and went bush, leaving the pilot,' John said. 'Then Mrs Dreary put the old tiger there.'

'And when the pilot saw it, he couldn't resist a closer look,' Sebastian said. 'That's when we jumped him.'

'He scratched like a wildcat but we finally got him under control,' John looked at his hands. 'We contained him all right.'

Meadow looked at them in awe. 'Did he have a gun?'

'Well, it turns out he did, but we didn't know that at the time. Did we John?' Sebastian said.

'It was the ambush factor that got him,' John added.

'And we tied him up with the rope you used for harnesses,' Gran said.

'And I used the pilot's mobile to call for help.' Sebastian, now relaxed, was a confident lion, proud of his pride. 'You could say I know a few people in high places.'

'That he does,' Gran said. 'In a blink of an eye we had a rescue helicopter above us and the police took the pilot into custody.'

'And the hunters who were going after Timba and Tawny.'
John took satisfaction in saying the juveniles' names.

'Turns out,' Sebastian took a sip of tea, 'Doyle's twin
was just someone who looked like him.'

'There was so much going on,' Gran gestured toward
Doyle's house. 'Then it clicked that Doyle must've been
at his place. Can you make a special call about Sienna?'

'You got a phone?' Sebastian patted his pockets. 'I had
to give the pilot's phone to the police.'

'Bert has a landline,' said Meadow.

'Good idea,' Gran said. 'I want to check on Bert anyway.
Sebastian, John, we can talk on the way.'

Gran finished her tea.

Lottie was quiet.

Gran leaned close to Lottie's ear. 'You are one of my
pack now, and you know how I protect my own.'

Lottie's eyes widened as she focused on Gran with
surprise, then relief.

'What about Indigo Bliss?' Meadow said. 'What did
you whisper to her?'

'To get our lot to safety, then leave them with Lee and
Terry and get home.' Gran looked at the men. 'I'm sorry
about all this, I thought we were going out to the shack to
have a productive meeting.'

'Mrs Dreary,' Sebastian said, 'don't apologise. If anything,
after what we've been through in the last couple of days,
it's confirmed how careful we need to be in protecting our
tigers.'

Meadow's heart beat faster at that.

'Let's go,' Gran pushed her cup aside, and stood.

'If you see blood all over his coat and scarf in the
laundry, he had a nosebleed,' Meadow said, 'from
headbutting Doyle.'

'Poor Bert,' Gran grimaced.

'Wait until you see how taken with him Spencer is,' Meadow said.

'Dear old boy.' Gran turned. 'Imagine the hide of that man going into my room a second time.'

Meadow imagined a quoll going into a henhouse.

'That reminds me.' Gran stopped, and rummaged inside her pack until she located a small device.

Meadow stared at the tiny offender, the culprit for the red dot.

'And to think I blamed you two.' Gran glanced at Sebastian and John, before placing the tracker under her shoe and crushing it.

'Wait,' Sebastian said, too late, 'they might need that for evidence.'

'Oh well.' Gran shrugged. 'I'm not taking a chance someone else might track me.'

The hallway was throwing the early morning light into the kitchen as Gran beckoned to the men. 'Let's go.'

The kitchen was quiet, no soft nuzzling of her hands. Meadow took Lottie and Juke out with her to check on Gertie and collect eggs. As Meadow organised a fruit and cheese platter for lunch, Lottie heard a noise out the front and went to investigate with Juke.

After several minutes, Lottie ran inside, puffing. 'Come and see this.'

Placing walnuts on the platter, Meadow followed Lottie to the front door.

'Sienna has been taken and will be facing charges,' Lottie said. 'Ava and Juke have gone back to their tigers. And Sebastian and John are about to leave too.'

Lottie didn't mention Doyle at all.

An official looking black car had arrived at the cottage to collect Sebastian and John. One of the windows rolled down and a rectangular box was held out to Sebastian.

He took the new mobile phone to Gran, who was waiting at the gate.

'Here you are, Mrs Dreary.'

Gran held it out between two fingers, as if it were toxic.

'I'll help you set it up,' Lottie suggested.

'I'd appreciate that,' Gran said to Lottie, before warning Sebastian. 'But I won't be taking it when I go bush.'

'After what we've just been through, I wouldn't expect you to.' Sebastian gave Gran what Meadow could only describe as a wild grin, his dishevelled mane standing up like spiky fur.

'Mrs Dreary,' John wore his brown suit again, 'it was worth it and we owe you a great debt of gratitude.'

Standing with the front door open wide made Meadow nervous and she kept looking back into the empty hallway. She wondered if her own mother had felt such loss, had searched for her daughters in whatever place she'd called home. Had Harmony Belle found herself wandering room to room, looking for those who'd been in her care?

Sebastian, John and Gran were going to be joined at the hip it seemed. Well that was what John said, as he waved goodbye.

Once they'd driven away, Meadow's fake smile faded. 'How are we going to cope, Gran, without the pups. I don't know how I'm going to...'

'Meadow, trust me, I feel what you're going through,' Gran nodded toward Lottie, 'but we are going to be strong for each other.'

Meadow stared intently at her resilient grandmother. Gran's silver words were almost white, pale snowflakes delicate and dissolving. Her grandmother was, in fact, heartbroken. Going public must still feel taboo, forbidden. Bringing in the government went against who the Drearys were.

Meadow hugged Gran and whispered, 'You did the right thing.'

'About Doyle,' Gran patted Meadow's back. 'I've told the authorities everything and it's up to them whether they proceed with charges.'

'Even after everything,' Lottie said, 'I hope he got away.'

Meadow stopped herself from saying she thought it was a weak move, Doyle taking off like that.

They ate amongst the old darlings' gravestones. A small table held the fruit and cheese platter and drinks of apple cider.

Gran told them that each of the Snug and Flowerpot Yarn and Weavers Group had returned to their tigers. Lee and Terry had volunteered to look after the Drearys' thylacines so that Indigo Bliss could return home. The importance of keeping the thylacines safe and hidden meant that Sebastian and John would fast-track the entire process.

Lottie turned on Gran's new phone as the three composed themselves after the mayhem.

'How was Bert?' Meadow asked.

'When I got there, Spencer's head lay across Bert's feet,' Gran said, 'I swear that dog was staring up at Bert like he's the bees' knees.'

'Adorable,' Lottie said, looking up from the phone as it emitted a buzzing noise.

'I told him I was hoping he would keep Spencer on a permanent basis,' Gran said.

Meadow gasped. 'What about Indigo Bliss?'

Gran took Meadow's hand. 'This might be hard for you to hear my girl, but I'm hoping that we can set her free, free to travel.'

Meadow stood, her heart lurched. 'No Gran. I can't lose her too.'

Lottie said, 'Do you want some privacy?'

'Stay,' Meadow and Gran said in unison.

'Okay, but I'm going to remind you of something you once said to me,' Lottie said, her words popping as if unsure whether to continue.

'I'm listening,' Meadow said.

'Remember when you said it was hard for you to let go of things. You know, like in your room.'

Lottie had a point.

'Tell me, Gran.' Meadow took a deep breath.

'It's not like I want to set her free, but I made that mistake once before,' Gran said. 'And maybe in some ways I've done it again.'

Meadow willed Gran to keep going.

Gran was shaking. 'I want you to figure out what you want for your life as well.'

Meadow said, 'I like it here.'

'I thought you'd want to go with your sister.' Gran looked at her with bright brown eyes. 'I wouldn't blame you.'

'I just didn't like all the hiding and having no friends, but now…' Meadow said.

'That's going to change.' Gran marched to the garden shed, retrieving a sturdy saw.

Her grandmother strode to the front of the cottage and began sawing deeply into the wisteria vines. She cut the lowest and thickest vines first, then pulled them from the wall.

'Gran!' Meadow tried to stop her. 'You love those.'

'She didn't,' Gran roared, 'she said they were suffocating. That I was suffocating.'

Meadow and Lottie glanced at each other, not knowing whether to stop Gran or help her. Was this Gran's version of having a good cry? They helped pull the vines away from the cottage, leaving snake-like marks along the sandstone.

Meadow admired her grandmother's honesty, for admitting the sting of her own remorse, but wouldn't point out this went against her grandmother's usually sage advice about guilt.

Panting, Gran sat on a pile of twisted vines. 'What will Charlotte think of us?'

'You're talking to someone who isn't sure if they're a clone or not,' Lottie said. 'I'm leaning towards not, but…'

'That's part of your charm,' Gran caught Meadow's eye. 'What a character our Charlotte is.'

She realised Lottie was quite like her sister, able to be frank, able to make them feel better with her quick wit.

'I keep telling Lottie there's no way she's a clone.'

A plump chicken waddled toward them, curious about the cuttings. Clover pecked at the ground, wondering if worms might be on the menu.

'Is she going to do a golden flamenco dance?' Lottie said. 'Can't wait to do some chook watching with you guys.'

And that was that. Gran stood up straight, setting her shoulders in that determined way of hers. 'We need Old Goldy to see that dance but there'll be time for that. There's a lot to do so let's get started.'

Meadow stood for a moment, her face to the sun.

She wondered if the cottage was surprised by the light on its sandstone face.

Chapter Thirty-five

The young dark-haired woman standing near the stove held up her palms in surrender. 'It's me Meadow, it's only me.'

Expletives echoed in the kitchen, as Meadow's mind processed that the stranger was Lottie. 'Sorry, you look so different.'

And Lottie did look different. No longer was she an amber ragamuffin kitten. Lottie was a svelte brunette cat. It was embarrassing that Meadow kept getting startled by Lottie. Especially as she'd helped Lottie, not liking her two-toned part, to dye her hair back to its natural colour.

Lottie rubbed at one brown pointed ear, as if she were in pain. 'I think you damaged my eardrums.'

'What on earth. Is the air blue in here?' Gran entered the kitchen shaking her head at Meadow. 'Your language is getting even worse.'

It was true that her outbursts at seeing the current Lottie were amongst Meadow's best swearing efforts so far.

Lottie was part of the family. Gran often said she was comfortable being her 'cantankerous self' in front of the girl.

Lottie's presence helped with losing the pups, which was taking some getting used to. Images of Tawny's thoughtful face and Timba's cheeky grin were imprinted everywhere in the cottage. Over time, Meadow hoped the sharp sting of grief would settle into something manageable.

But it was as if loss permeated the cottage. She tried to distract herself by taking long walks and visiting Spencer.

Gran and Lottie managed in their own way. In some ways she felt the loss of her pups even more than that of her sister. Surely that was a violation of their sisterly bond. Or perhaps it was because she could still communicate with Indigo Bliss, who'd been travelling in Europe for months.

After Meadow's last visit to Timba and Tawny, who'd in previous visits rushed to her, leaping and playing with her like old times, something had changed. The last visit was markedly different. The pups had remained with the other thylacines, looking at her with a perplexed curiosity. She had frozen. Eventually Timba had ambled to her side. No puppy-ish behaviour. No leaping. No licking. No gentle nuzzling. Tawny had tentatively followed her brother, her face conflicted, while glancing back at the others. The two young thylacines had stood like ancient statues as she ran her hands over their striped coats. She could feel how tense the pups were under her touch. Meadow sensed a wariness, not in regard to herself, but in being away from the other thylacines.

She knew the pups were staying by her side due to their loyal hearts. They had loved her dearly, but belonged in the wild. They were tigers. No longer ghosts or myth, they were the thylacines of old lore, the wild tigers of Tasmania, who had been protected by her love and needed to be set free by it.

From that day forward she swore she would not cause them such conflict again, preferring to stay away.

This decision had hurt deeply.

'I heard the mailman,' Gran said. 'Go check for postcards would you.'

A postcard from Indigo Bliss was a significant event in the Dreary household. After several months, the postcards from her sister had started to mention a kindred spirit, someone who was also travelling for the first time, someone named Henry Welford. Who Henry might be to Indigo Bliss was widely discussed between Meadow, Gran and Lottie. Especially when her sister used the term 'we' in her travel updates.

'I'll go,' Meadow said, passing by numerous postcards pinned along the hallway. The sunlight through the stained glass door bathed the postcards in an ethereal purplish glow. Perhaps that was why Gran had tacked them there, to remind herself of her sister's violet eyes.

There was an envelope inside the letterbox and Meadow recognised her sister's handwriting. It was addressed to all three of them.

'I'll make us a cuppa,' Gran said. 'Then you can read out what she says.'

She opened the envelope. A postcard from Hawaii fell out, all white sand and tropical trees. It was blank. She held it up, showing Gran and Lottie. 'Is this a clue about her next destination?'

She retrieved another postcard which was like an advertisement for getting married on a beach. The woman, her hair styled into a shoulder-length bob, wore a floral crown of creamy rosebuds and a white sheath dress. Standing next to the bride was a tanned smiling man who was slightly shorter.

Tendrils of wonder swirled around Meadow as she peered closer at the violet eyes.

Indigo Bliss Dreary had become Indigo Bliss Welford.

'So like your sister, to pull a no-fuss stunt like that,' Gran said in astonishment, her silver words flowing like a string-of-hearts plant.

'She looks beautiful,' Lottie's eyes were shining, 'and happy.'

'Wonderful,' Gran gave a wistful smile, 'a new addition to our family.'

'I wonder if there might be another little addition soon,' Lottie's words were now a calm green, 'like a baby.'

Meadow wondered why Lottie's words were now more green than yellow. Then her eyes widened as she looked more closely at the postcard. Realisation struck. 'I'm not seeing a unicorn with a silver horn when I see her. I see her as she is.'

'What?' Gran said. 'Are you feeling all right?'

''Cause it's a photo,' Lottie slowly nodded, 'like videos.'

'In photos, I see people as they are, not animal-esque,' Meadow said to Gran. 'And Lottie's right, in her videos I view them as regular people.'

'Why didn't you tell me?' Gran bemoaned. 'I could've taken photos of you both all these years.'

Meadow rolled her eyes at Lottie, who knew the Drearys had never been a snapshot kind of family.

'But what about the photos I showed the men?' Gran asked.

Meadow thought for a moment about their visit to Parliament House. 'You were wearing your hat, not looking at the camera.'

'Of course. Now, meet me at the willows and get Annabelle on the way,' Gran strode toward Grandfather's study to collect her mobile phone.

'I'm going to change,' Lottie said. 'Meet you there.'

She found the little Jersey heifer, Gertie's calf, in the milking shed getting an affectionate lick from Gertie. The leggy calf was all velvety cream and doe-eyed. Annabelle ran to her expecting a treat or a scratch. Meadow had been halter training the calf for milking down the track.

Meadow, with Annabelle in tow, waited near the willows as the heifer nibbled at tender grass, surrounded by new little stone crosses. Gran, muttering to herself, arrived with Lottie, still grumbling to Lottie that she should've taken photos when the girls were young.

It was a little awkward being photographed so many times. Her cheeks hurt from smiling while trying not to squint in the sun. They swapped places at one point in the photo shoot and Lottie took photos of Meadow with Gran and Annabelle.

'Indigo Bliss is going to love these,' Lottie said.

Afterward, sitting on the stone seats, Gran held her phone up to Meadow. 'Can you see yourself as something mythical?'

'No, just as myself. It's like looking in the mirror,' Meadow said, disappointed. But she was more interested in seeing a photo of Gran. Meadow knew what Lottie looked like from when her gift hadn't worked on her new neighbour. But not her grandmother. Gran had taken off her cloche hat for the photo, so Meadow saw her clearly. Gran was petite, and surprisingly her hair was more red than grey. Meadow had always imagined Gran to have plump, goose-like cheeks, but Gran was fine-boned like Lottie. They were similar in height, weight and if Gran had green eyes and Lottie had kept her copper hair, would have been even more comparable.

'You could be Lottie's grandmother.' Meadow said.

Gran stared intently at the photo. 'I never thought...'

'I did,' Lottie said. 'I've thought about it a lot.'

'What?' Meadow said, 'That you're related to Gran?'

'We look alike...' Lottie's words of emerald-green bubbles began popping.

'Tell us,' Meadow said.

'Say it, Charlotte,' Gran said. 'It can't be any stranger than anything else you have to say.'

'Okay.' Lottie said, 'I've been wondering if...'

'You can tell us anything,' Meadow said.

'Okay. I'm just going to say it,' Lottie took a deep breath.

'C'mon girl,' Gran nodded encouragingly.

'Okay, I think Harmony Belle ran away. Somewhere overseas. Then met Doyle,' Lottie said, 'and you know, they had me.'

Gran gave Meadow a 'softly softly' look.

'It's not the worst theory I've had,' Lottie tried to shrug offhandedly.

'I can see how you'd think that,' Meadow said. 'We don't know much about our mothers.'

She didn't make eye contact with Gran, wondering if her hint had been less than subtle.

'You are family Charlotte, no matter what your DNA is,' Gran said.

'I know, but if I had a choice between being a clone and related to you guys…' Lottie said.

'Let us research for you this time,' Meadow offered.

'I have contacts high up in the government,' Gran said. 'I'll get them onto it.'

'Okay, but if you need help with tech… ' Lottie said.

Her grandmother tapped on the old darlings' gravestones.

Gran sometimes did this when she was grappling with a decision.

'Girls,' Gran stopped tapping. 'I think it's time I show you something.'

After leading the little heifer back to Gertie, Gran took them into her room, retrieving her leather pouch. She pulled out a treasure. Meadow could tell it was delicate by the way Gran held it like a newly hatched chick. It was an instant photo.

'This is Harmony Belle,' Gran said. 'I didn't show you before because I didn't want to upset you girls.'

Meadow had butterflies of anticipation. 'Oh Gran, show me.'

The young woman was sitting near blossoming wisteria wrapped around the cottage. Meadow stared at her mother,

her hair rippling waves of red and gold. Harmony Belle was playing a guitar in the filtered sunlight. Meadow's eyes widened at the yellow crop top and cargo pants her mother was wearing. They didn't look home-made; her mother's clothing was store-bought, as was her velvet choker and chunky boots.

'She said singing and playing the guitar was like a harmony of yellow,' Gran said. 'That her voice and the strings yielded golden threads of yellow and honey notes.'

'She's not my mother,' Lottie gave Meadow and Gran a conflicted look, 'I'm obviously not her clone.'

'Maybe clones don't always look exactly the same.' Meadow stared at her mother with a sudden longing, 'either way, Gran's right, you are still family.'

'Exactly Charlotte, and you always will be,' Gran held up the cream canvas fabric that had nested the photo. 'She painted this not long before she left.'

Meadow viewed the yellow colours and swirls surrounding some musical notes. She realised the painted notes were actually birds, sitting on power lines.

If her mother had stayed, would she have painted for her daughters, written songs for them, sang and played in a harmony of yellow?

She'd thought their household wanting in music and photos, but the image of her mother playing her guitar suggested otherwise. The guitar in Grandfather's old study.

'I'd better get copies of that,' Lottie said, holding out her hand. 'It's priceless.'

It was hard for Meadow to let the photo go.

'Gran, let me take a pic of your daughter with your phone too,' Lottie said, 'so you'll always have Harmony Belle with you.'

She liked the way Lottie called her grandmother Gran.

Gran agreed. 'Then I'm going up to Bert's to take some

photos of the old badger.' Gran winked at Meadow.

'And we'll take Juke's when he comes tomorrow,' Lottie beamed.

Juke was a regular visitor to the cottage. From what Lottie said, he was open to most of her theories; he'd always had his own concerns about who secretly ran the world. When the young couple wandered to the stone seats, their intimacy was captivating.

During these visits, Meadow observed their dark-haired heads bent toward each other, often nose to nose, whispering and sharing secrets. Witnessing these starry-eyed exchanges was riveting but she tried not to linger, not wanting to come across as some sort of busybody.

She often experienced a pang of foreboding at these times. It wasn't that she craved a relationship like that. It was the thought that she might lose Lottie as well, like her sister, and her mother before that. At these times she gave herself a good talking to, and would go for a brisk walk up the road to visit Spencer. Juke was the best boyfriend she could want for Lottie. Her concern that Juke's golden words were similar to Doyle's had been unfounded. Juke's gilded words were courageous, compassionate and full of conviction.

Lottie continued to be concerned about Meadow's relationship status, especially as it was clear John was fond of Meadow. Lottie wondered aloud to Meadow whether her reticence for romance was due to past hurts.

Meadow had pondered that question, concluding that apart from the red crab man, which hadn't had any long-lasting effect on her, she'd never had any romantic attention, and never felt the need for a romantic partner.

'It is what it is and I am happy.'

From the outside looking in, perhaps people thought that it was the Drearys who had given Lottie so much, had rescued the young woman, had given her love and security.

But in reality Lottie's presence in the cottage had produced substantial change. Just as Gran had slashed the wisteria, Lottie had cut away many of the suppressing vines that had stifled the Drearys.

Meadow's friendship with Lottie had been forged under hardship, and Lottie said it was unique but strong, like the Drearys. Meadow imagined that was true. The two shared a kindred spirit of curiosity, enjoying the weird and wonderful. Their conversations ranged from conspiracies to tourist destinations.

Lottie had started her own channel and was currently researching about auroras, sky sprites, and what they signified. But most of her content was about what lay under vast unexplored oceans. According to Lottie, only a small fraction had been investigated because ocean exploration hadn't been considered as sexy as space exploration. Meadow was starting to understand more about timelines, leylines and pyramids throughout the world.

Meadow often thought about Gran's suggestion that she follow in her sister's footsteps, and travel overseas.

At these times she felt small, anticipatory wings burgeoning within. Like that poem about the transformation of a dragonfly. The water nymph had climbed out of water it had lived in for years, into the sunlight. In the light it shook off the old, its wings unfurling. No longer a grey nymph but an iridescent dragon.

Her struggles so far were all a part of her transformation as she metamorphosed into authenticity.

But she wouldn't say that out loud to many people.

She would say it to her friend Lottie, though.

Chapter Thirty-six

'They'll be here soon Gran,' Meadow dried her cup.

Gran strode into the kitchen, a vision in a linen dress with balloon sleeves embellished with embroidery. She picked up a large bowl. 'This is our most important meeting yet.'

'I agree,' Meadow collected her notepad.

Sebastian and John had been meeting with the Drearys and Lottie for several months, and the protected zones and hubs were virtually completed.

One of the most unexpected of good fortunes was a special payment organised for Gran and the other guardians. A hefty sum for all their decades of quiet service. Gran wanted to split her money four ways to include Indigo Bliss, Meadow and Lottie. But Lottie wouldn't hear of it, so the Drearys pooled their money together to purchase Lottie's house and Mrs Hill's other vacant block. It turned out neither Doyle nor his rich benefactor owned the house; it'd belonged to a couple on the mainland. After discovering the unfavourable incidents that had taken place they'd decided to sell quickly.

It was Lottie's task to pick a name for the house next door. She came up with several, 'Grey Ghost', 'The House with One Fork', 'Never Inn' and 'Grey Goose' being her favourites. Gran eventually allowed 'Grey Goose', realising that this title was in honour of herself.

They planted a cherry tree and a pear tree out the front to give it character. Indigo Bliss knitted jumpers for both trees and posted them from overseas.

'I hope Sebastian has some news on Sienna.' Meadow

occasionally still glanced up at the second storey window.

'At least the case is strong, especially with Sebastian and John as witnesses,' Gran said. 'And before you ask, there's no news on Doyle.'

'Figures,' Meadow shook her head. 'Lottie still refuses to talk about him.'

'It's a trauma response so we must give her space and support,' Gran sighed, opening the front door. 'She knows we're here for her.'

Meadow understood, but found it hard to stop thinking about Doyle, the way he'd frightened Bert, not to mention herself. Even now, she often anticipated heavy thudding on the front door.

'Let's stop giving him our energy,' Gran said.

She could see the wisdom in that. She was going to re-imagine Doyle as something ineffective—something nasty and obnoxious—the opposite of a handsome golden horse.

'Gran, we're nearly at the end, so let's try and play nice.'

'You want me to wear my politically correct hat.' Gran adjusted her grey cloche hat.

She knew from experience Gran would be blunt and say what she thought.

Indigo Bliss had phoned with negotiation advice, reminding Gran there were two sides. Her sister pointed out that museums put together vital historical baseline data. And that they were fundamental to scientific classification. Indigo Bliss hoped museums would continue to repatriate items back to communities.

But of late it seemed her grandmother had entirely forgotten about these calls. In the meetings, Gran's views on government and museums often flamed adversarially.

Today would be a particularly delicate meeting. Legalities regarding the study and research of the thylacines would be finalised. Sebastian and John had often been privy to Gran's disagreeable side during the construction of the zones. Gran and Sebastian mirrored each other, but of late Meadow had noted a softening between them, like two weary soldiers after a long battle. Each soldier knew their part, and between the two, at least one could be counted on to be strong and silver-tongued.

John had become a friend to Meadow, and unlike with Doyle's feigned friendship, she believed she could go to him if she needed assistance or advice. At first, convinced of her gullibility, she'd distanced herself. But John's offer to help her learn to drive had facilitated a rapport. He took Meadow in his own car and was a patient instructor.

Before walking to the Grey Goose, Gran picked some cherries. 'I'm going to make us a cherry pie tonight.'

'Let's make an extra one for Bert,' Meadow suggested. 'He's done so many hay bales for us.'

It had been a fertile summer for their garden and their pastures. Bert had finished harvesting and baling hay for the Drearys using his own equipment, Spencer always by his side.

She saw an official looking black car pulling into the driveway next door. 'They're here, Gran.'

'Hello ladies,' Sebastian called out, wearing shorts and a T-shirt, his mane now flecked with grey.

'I had to rush from another meeting,' John said, looking uncomfortable in his brown suit. 'But I wasn't going to miss our final one.'

'You've had a haircut,' Sebastian's silver words stopped in mid-air.

'Looks nice,' John said.

'Thanks,' Meadow smiled. After seeing her sister's fashionable new hairstyle in her wedding photo, Meadow and Lottie had been to the local hairdresser. Both were styled and blow-dried, emerging with shining, shoulder length hair. The next modern twist had been purchasing gym clothes. Meadow, not being one that craved attention was pleasantly surprised at how little scrutiny she received when wearing leisure clothing in town.

Her grandmother ushered Sebastian and John inside. Gran had knocked down the walls adjoining Doyle's office and the specimen room, setting up a conference room. It was a way to change the intention of the space, she'd said.

Lottie had left refreshments. As usual, Gran sat at the head of the table and urged everyone to sit.

'Lottie's not joining us today?' John's earthy-brown words coiled into question marks.

'She's trying to get everything ready for the big screens in the hubs,' Meadow said. 'Went to buy some equipment.' She spent a lot of time in the Grey Goose as she'd become Lottie's assistant in all things live-streaming. She could now edit and upload footage. She couldn't let the world see the livestream of their tigers yet, but she'd practiced with other videos to get her skills up.

As Gran would not allow a television in the cottage, the Grey Goose house was where all the technology for Lottie's ventures were set up. It was also where Meadow and Lottie continued to watch their movies. She had found Gran more than once, while 'dusting', instead sitting in a white recliner watching videos about homesteading.

'The hubs have turned out exactly how we hoped,' Sebastian grinned.

John held up his phone, showing Meadow striking wooden structures with dark stripes cut vertically into the sides. They were furnished in browns and tawny colours. 'We purchased the biggest screens we could for inside.'

The tiger hubs housing enormous screens had been unanimously chosen; the goal being to enlighten and entertain patrons. Not every idea regarding the hubs had gone smoothly. The original design had wide gaping jaws as the entrance. Gran railed that it would give the impression that thylacines were aggressive. It was a firm no. Gran was consoled when facades were placed over the hubs, to ensure privacy until the big reveal.

'Well, it's ribbon cutting ceremony soon,' Sebastian said.

'The final fence is up on all the protected zones,' John said, ticking off his fingers, 'and the cameras are in place.'

The men were exhausted, but still on a mission. Meadow appreciated the strict security protecting her pups and the other tigers.

'Let's get straight to it, shall we?' Gran said. 'The guardians want me to discuss the last part of our agreement.'

Meadow watched her grandmother's fists clenching. If Gran had long nails like Lottie, she'd be pricking herself to the point of bleeding. This was not a good sign.

Even though it had always been her sister's role to calm Gran, Meadow had learned how to mitigate her grandmother's passion and irritation. She found she had a flair for it. During face-to-face meetings she would watch her grandmother's words, the colour and shape, and advocate for Gran, whether to soothe or embolden her. Meadow would turn to Sebastian and John and observe the colour of their words. On his last visit, Sebastian had been so impressed with her negotiation skills that he'd offered her a job. She'd thanked him, and said she would seriously consider his offer.

But there was one particularly dangerous minefield, the tragic death of the last captive thylacine. Meadow had a feeling this was going to come up again during the meeting. As if on cue, Gran began to recite the grievances she had about the government's handling of the tigers. Her

Grandmother kept asking why the protected status for the thylacines had only come through fifty-nine days before tragedy struck the last captive thylacine? Why had the government put bounties on the thylacines? Surely they knew what would happen. 'And some say the poor thing was left out of its enclosure?' Gran said. 'The reason I say "it" is there's been debate about whether the endling was a she. Male and female have pouches you know.' Gran shivered, 'some tigers in zoos were so stressed they chewed on the bars, trying to escape.'

John loosened his tie.

'And that young woman at the zoo. From what I've heard she tried to help,' Gran said.

Meadow could see Gran's silvery words were not sharp, not solid, but like fragile wings. Her grandmother could not fathom what had taken place back then.

She saw both sides: Gran's distrust of governmental bodies, and how Sebastian and John were trying to right that wrong.

'I think Gran needs the government to be sensitive to what the guardians want,' Meadow offered, 'especially when it comes to interactions with our tigers.'

'Exactly,' Gran said. 'We don't want interactions that would harm them.'

'Understandable,' Sebastian said. 'Is there any wiggle room in the guardians' stance on researching the thylacines?'

Gran remained silent.

'Mrs Dreary, we have a…' John swallowed, 'shall we say a delicate situation.'

'Yes.' Sebastian stood for a moment. The big cat padded toward Gran. He placed a hand on her grandmother's embroidered shoulder. 'I want to prepare you regarding something recently found in our museum. Something that hasn't been made public yet.'

Chapter Thirty-seven

Surprisingly, Gran did not shrug Sebastian's hand away, and instead placed her hand over his. 'Right. Out with it.'

Meadow hoped that it wasn't another head in a bucket situation. She'd been keeping that from Gran.

'It has come to our notice that you are correct about the last captive thylacine. The poor animal was indeed female.'

Meadow bit the inside of her lip.

'They miraculously located her.' Sebastian squeezed Gran's shoulder.

Meadow could only imagine the reaction of the person who'd located the endling.

'They found her,' Gran whispered.

'Yes,' John said, 'she'd been transferred to the museum after her death.'

'I always said, didn't I,' Gran turned to Meadow. 'The last captive thylacine was…'

Meadow nodded. After so many decades. She stared into space. 'It's closure Gran, she's been found.'

'Are you okay?' John asked Meadow.

Meadow was picturing a tawny bird flying out of a rusty cage door. 'We need to set her free.'

John held her gaze, 'You have my word.'

'She's special.' Meadow noted her grandmother pinching the top of her nose, as if to ward off tears. 'She needs to be rewilded.'

'Yes,' John said, 'please let me know how to proceed.'

She saw Gran's quivering lip. Her grandmother would be mortified to cry in front of the men.

'We will.' Meadow cleared her throat before changing the topic, hoping John and Sebastian would intuit why. 'Lottie's muffins smell delicious.'

'I agree,' Sebastian took a banana muffin and bit into it hungrily. 'Taste delicious too.'

'Have some fresh cherries,' Meadow said as Sebastian went back to his seat.

John took a handful of cherries.

'I reiterate. No interaction of any kind,' Gran sniffed, reaching for a lemon drizzle muffin.

'That is a firm no to scientists or museums.' John gave Meadow a serious, 'help us' look, as if he understood there was a deep wound that wasn't quite healed.

'This is black and white to the guardians,' Meadow glanced at John. 'There can be no grey.'

'We've come so far and you've done so much to save your tigers,' John said. 'We want the guardians to feel comfortable.'

That hit the mark. She could tell Gran felt heard as she smiled at the men. 'I do have one allowance. After much discussion, the guardians eventually consented to a post-mortem examination of any thylacines that pass.'

'Thank you,' John said. 'I think our research teams will be grateful to hear that.'

'It is to be respectful mind you,' Gran said, 'and under no circumstances are their skins and bodies to be sold or used for experiments, especially overseas.'

'Never!' Sebastian thumped his fist onto the table. 'I mean, I'm with you about that.'

'Afterwards the guardians want the tigers to be buried in their protected zones,' Meadow said.

'Yes, in the Tasmanian wilderness,' Gran said.

'Right you are Mrs Dreary,' Sebastian gave a decisive nod. 'And that includes the endling.'

'Incredibly fitting,' John said.

Gran stared at the bowl of cherries.

'So we can expect the Drearys and Lottie at the grand opening?' Sebastian asked tentatively.

'Yes,' Meadow glanced at Gran, 'we'd love to attend, wouldn't we?'

Gran tried to dodge the question. 'How are your lovely girls, Sebastian. And the toys?'

The toys had been another sticking point. When Sebastian organised stuffed thylacine toys and merchandise, Gran was not sold on the toys. But she was won over after Meadow joined forces with Sebastian and his daughters, convincing them to visit the cottage, both hugging a tawny-striped prototype. One look at the excited little faces of the girls, aged five and six, clutching the Tassie tigers with delight, convinced Gran. That the toys were based on Timba and Tawny helped.

'Wonderful,' Sebastian said. 'I'm taking them on a holiday after the opening.'

Meadow made a mental note to take a photo of the little girls on their next visit so she could see how the little chicks, fluffy and bright eyed, usually looked. She'd pin the photos on the hallway near the clippings and various articles about Sebastian and John. After the men announced the opening of the tiger hubs they virtually had rock-star status.

'So Mrs Dreary,' John cleared his throat, 'we'd be honoured if you'd cut the ribbon.'

'And say a few words too,' Sebastian added.

Gran repeated earlier declarations of wanting no part of being considered a celebrity, but they were persuasive.

Gran mumbled something incoherently before tapping on the table. 'It's been a fruitful meeting but I have things to do at the cottage.'

Within seconds she had left the room.

'You'll make sure she's there, won't you?' Sebastian asked Meadow.

Meadow sighed. 'It'll be hard, but I will.'

Afterwards Meadow wandered into the loungeroom, sitting on her favourite recliner, wondering if she had time to watch something before Lottie returned. She'd discovered television was a great distractor. Lottie had said Meadow should cry everything out about the pups. That's what she did apparently, by viewing sad movies to get herself going. But Meadow didn't cry at the sad movies Lottie showed her. Perhaps she'd built up an immunity of sorts, because her taste ran to sad and sorrowful books.

Meadow had, though, stumbled upon a way to open the floodgate. While searching for videos about colours she'd discovered many uploads about people who had colour vision deficiency. Given glasses to help them observe colours they'd never witnessed before, their reactions to seeing new colours touched her deeply and she'd return to the cottage with puffy eyes.

'I'm back,' Lottie called through the sliding door, 'how did it go?'

'It was mostly a productive meeting.' Meadow said.

'I want to hear all about it, but first...'

Meadow considered the animated look on Lottie's face as she pulled out several paper-clipped printouts from her backpack.

'You have to see this,' Lottie said, handing Meadow one. 'I'm not trying to diagnose you but...'

Then Lottie handed her another printout relating to something called 'synaesthesia'.

'That's quite a mouthful,' Meadow said as she spread the printouts over the table.

'It's kind of a fancy way of saying you have a crossover

between senses,' Lottie said. 'The Greek root means union of the senses, or words to that effect.'

Meadow read the first couple of paragraphs. There were many different types of synaesthesia. Words leapt from the page: voice-colour, aura and voice-shape. Meadow continued to scan the lines, noting more words she didn't recognise. She reached a section where people discussed seeing words or music in various colours. Further down one woman relayed viewing a particular man as a Pegasus. Another saw his mother as a golden pheasant.

'I'm not sure if your animal thing is synaesthesia or something different,' Lottie said. 'But it sounds like the way you see words might be.'

Meadow's eyes widened. 'So there are others like me?'

'You can have more than one type apparently,' Lottie said.

'You're always going on about Nikola Tesla; well this says,' Meadow read out loud, 'that maybe he had synaesthesia or hyperphantasia, like a vivid mind's eye.'

'And he was next-level genius,' Lottie scanned a printout. 'This article says synaesthesia is involuntary while hyperphantasia can be voluntary or involuntary.'

The printout shook in Meadow's hand.

'My sister always thought the animal thing was a creation of my imagination.'

'Could be,' Lottie said. 'It's all new to me but I've heard maybe it's not classified as a medical condition but as a neurological phenomenon. You might want to get checked out by an expert though. But most people say they wouldn't change it.'

'This says it's like a unique variation of perception.' Meadow read from a different printout. 'I need to talk to Gran.'

Chapter Thirty-eight

Sleeping Beauty was covered in icing-sugar snow the day of the ribbon cutting ceremony.

There had been numerous discussions between Meadow and Lottie about what they'd wear. Gran was wearing her usual attire, and Lottie was torn between dressing in one of Gran's outfits or getting something new. Meadow would have worn her comfortable gym gear but both Gran and Lottie said that wouldn't be fitting. In the end, Lottie surprised Meadow by purchasing an outfit for her.

When she opened the shopping bag it revealed a silk shirt in autumn colours of red and gold, and a plain charcoal grey skirt to just below the knee. To finish the look, a pair of black slouch boots, leaving room to show a couple of inches of burgundy stocking between skirt and boot.

Lottie decided she would wear half-in-half, as she described it, an ankle-length skirt of Gran's and a shirt similar to the one she'd purchased for Meadow, except in green and silver.

They'd been advised to meet Sebastian, John and Juke at the tiger hub near the museum but Gran wanted to stroll around the harbour first.

Wandering past glassy water, Meadow wished Indigo Bliss was home. Her sister had been relieved when Meadow was given a clean bill of health. The specialist hadn't had a patient with exactly the same sensory triggers as Meadow, but had heard of similar reports overseas.

Her grandmother had kicked up a terrible stink about the tests, not wanting anyone to mess with Meadow's gift of special sight. This had intensified after Meadow was offered a place in a new study about synaesthesia, which after much thought, she'd declined.

She concluded that while the colours and shapes of her words were probably due to being a synaesthete, an inherited trait from her mother, the animal features she saw in people were likely down to her vivid mind's eye. Her sister had thought as much.

She wondered if her mother would be a mythical creature like Indigo Bliss? She liked to imagine her mother as a brilliantly-plumed phoenix.

'Look at how excited they are.' Gran pointed toward the swelling crowd.

At first the crowd moved in blurry slow-motion. Then a veil lifted. The city felt celebratory and the energy of the people began to thrill Meadow with different hues and tones. Words swirled and shimmered like fireworks, their glimmering beauty mirrored in the harbour. She knew that to everyone else she was a part of the crowd, indistinct, ordinary. And also in harmony, a word that had once symbolised the sorrow of her mother's absence, and now meant so much more—a feeling of togetherness— the exquisite blending and colour of different voices.

Nearing the tiger hub, Gran noted the flags flying outside the museum, flags with thylacines on them. 'Oh look at them,' Gran cried, 'look girls.'

The closest flag had a photo of Gran and Timba and Tawny on it. The same photo Gran had showed Sebastian and John the first day they'd met, with Gran bending toward the pups, taken in that golden hour when the sun threw soft rays and the grass was impossibly green.

Meadow fanned her face, holding back tears, her pups on display for all to see.

Cars displayed the Tasmanian tiger on number plates, a new version with thylacine no longer looking ghost-like but a sandy-and-striped restitution. Tasmania seemed to have stepped into euphoric boldness.

'I've got to show your sister,' Lottie dialled, then held up her phone so that Indigo Bliss could watch the proceedings in real time.

Indigo Bliss popped onto the screen as if from another planet, sitting on a beach, as Meadow stood on a carpet of gold and red leaves.

Gran went so close to Lottie's screen she almost bumped into it. 'Hi Henry,' Gran waved. 'Hi my girl.'

'Please come and visit soon,' Meadow added, walking toward the new tiger hub. 'I miss you.'

Lottie was scanning the crowd. It struck Meadow that her friend might be hoping to see Doyle.

Meadow caught sight of Sebastian and John waving them over. The men wore suits. Sebastian also wore his toothy big-cat grin, while John shook his head at the size of the crowd. Juke stood next to them, his smile wide, stripes in his hair.

An enormous gold ribbon was wrapped around the entrance to the hub. Meadow passed cameras on tripods and the click of flashes capturing the event. People of all ages waved thylacine flags and cuddled stuffed Tassie tiger toys. For a moment the colours were almost too vivid, as crystals and bubbles floated all around her, like a sky filled with brightly coloured stars. There was clapping behind her and Meadow realised she'd stumbled upon a red carpet leading straight to Sebastian, John and Juke. She turned, noting Gran and Lottie close behind, their eyes blinking at the flashes.

Lottie called out to Meadow amidst the noise, 'The livestream of the thylacines has nearly had one billion hits.'

Meadow was close enough to clearly see the big screens in the hub. She was relieved the tigers appeared unaffected, as if they had no concept their every move was being filmed. She momentarily felt a twinge of guilt, but the intrusion was a form of protection. And there would be no filming inside any lairs.

'Come here, come closer,' Sebastian gestured for them to join him at the other end of the red carpet.

Meadow recognised several people from newspaper articles she'd read about the de-extinction of the thylacine. They'd worked tirelessly but wore relieved smiles. She supposed there were so many other extinct animals they could now concentrate on.

John held out an enormous pair of scissors. 'Mrs Dreary, would you like to do the honours after your speech?'

Gran took the scissors, her firm old hands grasping them with an iron grip, but Meadow saw they were shaking slightly.

Juke gave Lottie a peck on the cheek.

Sebastian whispered to Gran, 'Come and say a few words, Mrs Dreary.'

Meadow's dear old goose handed her the scissors, and stepped to the microphone. Gran straightened her back, and the crowd fell silent. Many looked curiously upon the woman dressed like a fuchsia flower wearing a long, bell-shaped skirt.

'There is much I want to say, much I want to share. I wish I could educate you on how violated these animals were, but these…' Gran pointed to the flags, 'were given all the love, care and protection we could muster as guardians. For years my husband and I, and the girls did our best.'

Gran bowed her head, as if giving her departed husband a moment of silence. 'This is a day of celebration. Indigo Bliss, thank you my beauty-with-a-backbone for all your support over the years. I'm so glad you found Henry.'

Lottie held up her phone toward Gran so Indigo Bliss,

could blow her a kiss.

Meadow caught a glimpse of Henry giving Gran a wave.

'And Charlotte,' Gran turned to Lottie, 'you have brought so much sunshine into our lives, and change.'

Juke took Lottie's hand and squeezed it.

'Meadow, you brave girl, I couldn't have done this without you. What a gift.' Gran cleared her throat. 'We wanted to let the thylacines, our tigers, live in the most natural manner we could…'

Meadow knew what her grandmother was going to say next.

'With the exception of Timba and Tawny that is,' Gran said. 'When I wasn't around they became more domesticated than I'd expected.'

She was never going to live that down.

'I would like to read a short poem.' Gran withdrew a piece of paper from her vest. 'I want to dedicate this to my daughter, Harmony Belle.'

That was unexpected. Had Lottie helped Gran? Meadow tried to breathe evenly, as her grandmother's silver words fell like mercury teardrops onto the paper.

Harmony Belle

Lustrous maple of instrument, of tresses
your harmony has magpies in rapture
cherry blossoms shiver, blush and rose aquiver

winsome daughters await your return,
tigers await
I await

The crowd clapped. Perhaps they were wondering why the

older woman hadn't written a poem about the thylacine. But Meadow understood the poignancy of her grandmother's poem; it belonged in one of her collections.

Gran cut the gold ribbon with a ferocious slicing action. A lot of back-slapping ensued as they made their way into the tiger hub. Meadow stood before screens so big that the thylacines were life-sized, appearing to stare right into the viewers' eyes.

She wandered up to one of the screens, searching for her pups. One of the tigers seemed to stare directly at her.

It was Timba.

Meadow held her palm to her chest, feeling their bond, from cottage, to shack, to wilderness.

The expression in his eyes was one of abandon.

Uninhibited, just as he should be.

Tasmanian Glossary

Devil	The Tasmanian Devil is the largest carnivorous marsupial in the world.
Kunanyi	Hobart's mountain, in palawa kani, the language of Tasmanian Aborigines. Also called Mount Wellington. (See tacinc.com.au)
Lutruwita	The island of Tasmania, in palawa kani, the language of Tasmanian Aborigines. (See tacinc.com.au)
Mainland Australia	Tasmanians may also refer to Mainland Australia as 'the big island' or 'the other side'.
Mountain Pepper	*Tasmannia lanceolata* is known as native pepper, mountain pepper or pepperberry. It delivers the heat of pepper with a subtle fruity sweetness.
Nipaluna	Country at and around Hobart, in palawa kani, the language of Tasmanian Aborigines. (See tacinc.com.au)
Tasmanian Pademelon	Short stocky marsupial. Thick brown-grey coat.
Quoll	Eastern Quoll is a marsupial carnivore. Spotted Quoll is a marsupial carnivore.

Sleeping Beauty	Sleeping Beauty mountain range overlooks the Huon Valley, Tasmania and is composed of two mountains: Collins Bonnet and Trestle Mountain.
Swift Parrot	A parrot that migrates from Mainland Australia to breed in Tasmania.
Tasmania	Tasmania is an island state of Australia known for its unique animals, plants, stunning landscapes and a temperate climate. It is a mountainous island, featuring alpine ranges, buttongrass plains, wetlands, coastal heaths, pristine beaches and temperate rainforests. Often referred to as Tassie, the Holiday Isle or the Apple Isle, its shape is reminiscent of an apple or a love-heart. The state has large parcels of protected land and is located south of the Mainland, separated by Bass Strait.
Tasmanian Emu	Flightless bird. Grey-brown feathers. Extinct in Tasmania.
Thylacine	Once the world's largest marsupial carnivore. Commonly known as the Tasmanian tiger or Tasmanian wolf. Considered extinct in Tasmania.

Historical Sources

Thylacine

Branden Holmes & Gareth Linnard (editors), *Thylacine: The History, Ecology and Loss of the Tasmanian Tiger*. Melbourne: CSIRO Publishing, 2023.

David Owen & David Pemberton, *Tasmanian Tiger: The Tragic Story of the Thylacine*. Sydney: Allen & Unwin, 2nd edition, 2023.

Robert Paddle, *The Last Tasmanian Tiger: The History and Extinction of the Thylacine*. Oakleigh, Victoria: Cambridge University Press, 2009.

Notes

In Chapter 15:

1. The Buckland and Spring Bay Tiger and Eagle
Extermination Association
Ch.8 *Tasmanian Tiger: The Tragic Story of the Thylacine*
Ch.6 *The Last Tasmanian Tiger: The History and Extinction of the
Thylacine*

2. Alison Reid, the daughter of the previous curator/the
last captive thylacine
Part 6 *Thylacine: The History, Ecology and Loss of the
Tasmanian Tiger*
Ch.11 *Tasmanian Tiger: The Tragic Story of the Thylacine*
Ch. 8 and 9 *The Last Tasmanian Tiger: The History and
Extinction of the Thylacine*

3. Thylacine vocalisation
Part 8 *Thylacine: The History, Ecology and Loss of the
Tasmanian Tiger*
Ch.4 *Tasmanian Tiger: The Tragic Story of the Thylacine*
Ch.3 *The Last Tasmanian Tiger: The History and Extinction of the
Thylacine*

In Chapter 17

1. De-extinction and cloning
Part 8 *Thylacine: The History, Ecology and Loss of the Tasmanian Tiger*
Ch.15 *Tasmanian Tiger: The Tragic Story of the Thylacine*

2. The Ghost of Huon Valley/Mountain River
Part 7 *Thylacine: The History, Ecology and Loss of the Tasmanian Tiger*
Ch.9 *Tasmanian Tiger: The Tragic Story of the Thylacine*

3. Kindness to Lucy the young female thylacine
Ch.3 *The Last Tasmanian Tiger: The History and Extinction of the Thylacine.*

4. Names bestowed on the thylacine
Ch.1 *Tasmanian Tiger: The Tragic Story of the Thylacine*

In Chapter 19

1. Vampiric/blood-sucking/myths
Ch. 1, 4 and 10 *Tasmanian Tiger: The Tragic Story of the Thylacine*
Ch. 2 and 4 *The Last Tasmanian Tiger: The History and Extinction of the Thylacine*

2. Tendency to follow people in the bush
Ch. 8 *Tasmanian Tiger: The Tragic Story of the Thylacine*
Ch.4 *The Last Tasmanian Tiger: The History and Extinction of the Thylacine*

In Chapter 20

1. Female thylacine shipped to overseas zoo
Part 5 *Thylacine: The History, Ecology and Loss of the Tasmanian Tiger*
Ch.10 *Tasmanian Tiger: The Tragic Story of the Thylacine*

2. The thylacine and sheep predation
Parts 1 and 4 *Thylacine: The History, Ecology and Loss of the Tasmanian Tiger*
Ch. 8 *Tasmanian Tiger: The Tragic Story of the Thylacine*
Ch.5 *The Last Tasmanian Tiger: The History and Extinction of the Thylacine*

3. Thylacine with chicken
Ch.11 *Tasmanian Tiger: The Tragic Story of the Thylacine*
Ch. 4 *The Last Tasmanian Tiger: The History and Extinction of the Thylacine*

4. Purported threat of thylacines
Ch. 8 and 9 *Tasmanian Tiger: The Tragic Story of the Thylacine*
Ch. 4 and 5 *The Last Tasmanian Tiger: The History and Extinction of the Thylacine*

In Chapter 25

1. Suggestion of protective reserves
Ch.15 *Tasmanian Tiger: The Tragic Story of the Thylacine*
Ch.7 *The Last Tasmanian Tiger: The History and Extinction of the Thylacine*

2. Medical treatment referenced
Ch.10 *Tasmanian Tiger: The Tragic Story of the Thylacine*
Ch.9 *The Last Tasmanian Tiger: The History and Extinction of the Thylacine*

3. Police stations report status of thylacine sightings
Ch.7 *The Last Tasmanian Tiger: The History and Extinction of the Thylacine*

In Chapter 27

1. The thylacine were called stupid, dull, unattractive and untameable
Ch. 9 and 10 *Tasmanian Tiger: The Tragic Story of the Thylacine*
Ch. 9 *The Last Tasmanian Tiger: The History and Extinction of the Thylacine*

2. The thylacine graceful with pretty stripes
Ch.10 *Tasmanian Tiger: The Tragic Story of the Thylacine*

3. The thylacine in storage worldwide
Parts 2 and 7 *Thylacine: The History, Ecology and Loss of the Tasmanian Tiger*

In Chapter 30

1. The thylacine ill-defined/native panther
Ch.1 *Tasmanian Tiger: The Tragic Story of the Thylacine*
Ch.5 and 6 *The Last Tasmanian Tiger: The History and Extinction of the Thylacine*

In Chapter 34

1. Disease
Part 6 *Thylacine: The History, Ecology and Loss of the Tasmanian Tiger*
Ch.9 *The Last Tasmanian Tiger: The History and Extinction of the Thylacine*

2. Rug made from the skins of thylacines
Ch.16 *Tasmanian Tiger: The Tragic Story of the Thylacine*

In Chapter 36

1. Chewing on bars
Part 5 *Thylacine: The History, Ecology and Loss of the Tasmanian Tiger*

2. Mystery of the last captive thylacine solved at the Tasmanian Museum and Art Gallery (TMAG)
Ch.11 *Tasmanian Tiger: The Tragic Story of the Thylacine*

Please note: TMAG discovering the last captive thylacine took place in 2022 but poetic licence has been utilised for this one fact in this fiction book, to align with the plot.

Websites

Chapter 17 references a thylacine head found in
a bucket:

abc.net.au/news/2024-10-17/thylacine-genome-nearly-
sequenced/104483150

Chapter 36 references the mystery solved in the TMAG
collections:

https://youtu.be/4y-
5_3bvyYQ?si=IMvpfM1DlXmHFHat

Poems

The following poems were fictionally referenced in the book, and after completion—some sought to be penned—while some sought to be found. Heartfelt gratitude to the poetic brilliance of Merridy Pugh, Debra Johnson Fast and Joyce Edna Appleby for their contributed poems. The latter, my grandmother, left a treasure-trove of poems and thanks to my mother's safe keeping, I was able to read them for the first time. Written decades ago, her poems unexpectedly harmonised.

In order of appearance:

I remember your name
Insomnia
The Swan
end of season
Sea Drift
Mountains
The Water Nymph

I remember your name

I remember your name

in that moment
in the meeting of eyes
I remember your name

in the halting of time
held deeply
in the dignity of your gaze

I can see
you remember me

Merridy Pugh (Page 7)

Insomnia

Tossing, turning on a fevered pillow
Merciless chaos jangling in the brain
Old loves I thought, had long since been laid low
Rise up to haunt, to taunt me yet again

Unfulfilled hopes, deep and silent grievings
And all the musings of what might have been;
Remnants of childhood's long left-over leavings
Like patchwork – coloured pieces are now seen

Thro' time's kaleidoscope of changes wrought
By will or circumstances of our dreams.
The peaks and valleys, highs and lows we sought
Are those the 'Be and End all' of life's schemes?

So what? Another day, the sun is bright.
Come forth, you challenges
Turn off the night.

Joyce Edna Appleby (Page 21)

The Swan

Lakeside at twilight
drowsing in peace
a gentle rustle
and a stir
within the rushes
a swan glides past
all curves and grace
leaving only
a feathered whisper
of violet shadows
in its wake

Joyce Edna Appleby (Page 32)

end of season

all summer the daisies
flowering in pots
flowing from blue urns
spreading purple across the garden
white starscapes under the washing line
yellow bursting from green lawn
faces up to sun

petals closing in synchrony under cloud
a melody of movement following weather and light

friendly crowds
smiling at my comings and goings
waving in sea breezes
an invitation to joy
to sit
to breathe
to stop
to be

now at the turning of the season
the daisies are trimmed pruned
deadheaded
silent as the dunes today
no wind

a single flower
nods
one stem rising

touching a fingertip to this delicacy
I feel the tranquil ache
surrender
its lone-liness as mine

Merridy Pugh (Page 66)

Sea Drift

Bare feet weave
a winding track
on the toe-tickling sands
rollers crash, smash
against the breakwaters
black-shined backs of rocks
huddle together like seals

Ocean – I come to you
sea-winds tangle the hair
the mind finds a sort of peace
amidst your splendid rage

Fantasies take over…
drape me in long strands
of slippery seaweed

Cloak me in fishing nets
and scattered shells
a world within a world
where dolphins leap
like frolicking mermaids
in their play
only to vanish
in the blinking of an eye
drenched in your spray
invigorated as cold
chilled wine

Oh, that I were a
ship's figurehead
on an old sailing-ship
carved in mobile beauty
straining like a Viking
foaming at the prow
cutting onwards thro
the wind and wave
to a foreign shore

Joyce Edna Appleby (Page 90)

Mountains

The mountains huddle
Hunched brooding dark
beasts asleep
in giant shadow shapes

Joyce Edna Appleby (Page 145)

The Water Nymph

The water nymph stands upon the shore,
Her feet dissolve into sand and tide.
Toes curl gently as ripples whisper,
Pippies rise, their shells unfolding wide.

A wave crashes—light shatters and spins, iridescent.
Blues and greens entwine with molten gold.
She lifts her arms, embracing the surge,
Welcoming change as colours take hold.

They wrap her close, a shimmering cocoon,
Until she morphs beneath their gleam.
Emerging bright, reborn in a new elegance—
An iridescent dragon of the water.

Her wings are glass, her body sleek,
She skims the surface, swift and free.
A smile unfurls across her face—
She is the dragonfly she was meant to be.

Debra Johnson Fast (Page 255)

Acknowledgements

I would like to express my heartfelt gratitude to authors Robert Paddle, David Pemberton, David Owen, Branden Holmes and Gareth Linnard for your important work. I was captivated by your rigorous research, vivid description and often poignant stories. I have no doubt that your work will shape future generations, so that the cruelty of extinction will never be forgotten.

Thanks to my brilliant, creative and sensitive editor, Merridy Pugh, who with warmth and insight supported my journey. Your epigraph inspired me and your *end of season* poem resonated with how I envisaged Meadow—feeling faded and lonely. Thank you also for writing *Pig Tails* and *Boars Behaving Badly and The Guinea Pig Test* which are as humorous and delightful as their titles suggest. I can't wait for book three!

Also thanks to the amazing Debra Johnson Fast for your evocative poem *The Water Nymph*, which captured the essence of how I imagined Meadow's transformation. Your new book *Holding the Moment - haiku and photographs*, in collaboration with Judith E.P. Johnson, captivates with visual and poetic depth. I found myself nostalgic for the sparkle, salt and spray of Blackmans Bay Beach.

A very special thanks to Ruth Amos for your meticulous proofreading skills, your optimism and your assistance with formatting. All remaining mistakes are, of course, all mine due to last minute adjustments. Thank you for writing the *Deadly Miss* series which I thoroughly enjoyed. As well as its sleuthing and scientific depth, the setting of Hobart was so wonderfully familiar and Kingston Beach is a hidden gem.

Thank you to my darling grandmother, for writing such poignant and powerful poems and introducing me to so many wonderful books.

Thanks to all the dedicated and passionate content creators out there who expertly guide us down rabbit holes.

Most of all, thank you to my husband, mother, sister and family, for their ongoing support. You are such an endearing and gorgeously quirky bunch who continually model resilience.

To my children, thank you for reigniting my curiosity and for being the best journey companions I could have hoped for.

About the Author

C.Coles lives in Lutruwita/Tasmania and is a happy wanderer. She loves her mountainous island and has resided in the historic cities of Nipaluna/Hobart and Launceston, as well as several towns in the north, east, south and west of Tassie. *The Harmony of Yellow* is her debut adult novel.

www.ingramcontent.com/pod-product-compliance
Lightning Source LLC
Chambersburg PA
CBHW021240060726
47590CB00005B/1830